WHERE LOVE BEGINS

As Mac watched in horror, the boy slipped and fell into the stream. His head struck a rock with a resounding crash. For a split second, Mac waited. Then, as the boy lay motionless, Mac splashed into the water after him. Slipping on hidden, slimy stones, he raised the submerged shoulders. The boy's hat fell off, revealing wavy black hair framing a white face with a finely modeled nose, a fringe of curling dark lashes, and a beautiful mouth with pallid lips above a sturdy, dimpled chin. The boy was a girl, and as Mac held her in his arms, love began.

Books by Emilie Loring

❧ FOR ALL YOUR LIFE
❧ WHAT THEN IS LOVE
❧ I TAKE THIS MAN
❧ MY DEAREST LOVE
❧ LOOK TO THE STARS
❧ THE SHADOW OF SUSPICION
❧ WITH THIS RING
❧ BEYOND THE SOUND OF GUNS
❧ HOW CAN THE HEART FORGET
❧ TO LOVE AND TO HONOR
❧ LOVE CAME LAUGHING BY
❧ I HEAR ADVENTURE CALLING
❧ BEHIND THE CLOUD
❧ BECKONING TRAILS
❧ BRIGHT SKIES
❧ THERE IS ALWAYS LOVE

❧ Published by Bantam Books

EMILIE LORING

WHERE
BEAUTY DWELLS

*This low-priced Bantam Book
has been completely reset in a type face
designed for easy reading, and was printed
from new plates. It contains the complete
text of the original hard-cover edition.*
NOT ONE WORD HAS BEEN OMITTED.

WHERE BEAUTY DWELLS
*A Bantam Book / published by arrangement with
Little, Brown and Company*

PRINTING HISTORY

*Little, Brown edition published March 1941
Grosset & Dunlap edition published March 1943
2nd printing .... March 1943
3rd printing .... December 1943
New Grosset & Dunlap edition published April 1947
Bantam edition published January 1966
2nd printing
3rd printing
4th printing*

*Bantam Books are published by Bantam Books, Inc., a subsidiary
of Grosset & Dunlap, Inc. Its trade-mark, consisting of the words
"Bantam Books" and the portrayal of a bantam, is registered in the
United States Patent Office and in other countries. Marca Registrada.
Bantam Books, Inc., 271 Madison Avenue, New York, N. Y. 10016.*

PRINTED IN THE UNITED STATES OF AMERICA

I

Mac Cameron stopped his black roadster on the rustic bridge to watch the shadow of a hawk flit along the brook which was a patchwork of glistening, moss-covered rocks, clear pools with pebbly bottoms, frills and cascades of white water. It flowed between banks emerald with lush ferns and shrubs. A background of pines and hemlocks reached toward the clear-blue sky.

He jumped from the car, gripped the rail and leaned far over to study the stream. Trout water . . . The answer to a fisherman's prayer. . . . Dollars to dimes there were wily old veterans darting or lying like dusky shadows on the bottom of that dark basin between two jutting brown rocks. But what a trap for fly and line! An uprooted maple leaned across it tipsily. Great, swaying spider webs, among its branches, shone with opalescence in the blaze of the July early-afternoon sun. Its curling leaves scattered the scent of moist, woodsy earth as they fluttered in the light breeze. Their whispers, the tinkle, drip and splash of running water were the only sounds that stirred the cathedral-like silence of the woods.

He drew a deep breath. It was grand to be back in New England. A few weeks of this spicy air should clear his brain of the drabness left by three years of baffling, absorbing engineering problems in South America. He had returned because with Europe in flames the United States needed every one of her citizens. After a month of military training, he had come to Maine, first, to see his stepfather of whom he was fond; second, as an emotional experiment to prove to himself that he was completely out of love with Patty-Lee Deland, the girl who had thrown him over to marry that same stepfather.

Hang it all, someone had just cast into the pool he had picked for his own. He straightened and tore his hands from the pitchy ooze the sun had loosened from the bridge rail and tried to remove the stickiness with a handkerchief as

1

he watched the intruder. Piker! . . . The fisherman wasn't using a fly—even from this distance he could spot a wriggling worm.

Wouldn't you know it was a boy! Serve him right if his line tangled in the maple. He scowled at the slight figure which mounted a wet, moss-covered boulder in midstream, and, back to him, cast again. Blue-denim trousers were tucked into hip-high rubber boots. A shabby pull-over added a dash of crimson to the costume which was topped by a wide-brimmed farmer's hat which drooped to the slim shoulders.

A splash! . . . The reel screamed. A silver fish flapped and flashed in the sun above the tangle of leaves and branches.

"Good for you, stout fella!" Mac shouted, in his enthusiasm forgiving the unsportsmanlike jerk with which the trout had been removed from its tricky lair.

His voice startled the fisherman, who slipped and, with arms describing a grotesque parabola, fell into the stream. His head struck a rock with a resounding crack.

Cameron's broad grin faded. For a split second he waited, then, as the boy lay motionless, he grabbed a flask from a pocket of his car and dashed into a trail beyond the bridge—faint and almost overgrown with ferns. A cloud of brown butterflies rose from clumps of joe-pye weed as he brushed past. Blackberry vines tripped him. He hurdled lichen-covered blow-downs in his path.

It seemed years before he reached a pebbly stretch of shore opposite the figure lying motionless in midstream. Suppose the boy had fallen face down . . . Suppose he were too late. . . . He couldn't be. Such a thing couldn't happen in this woodland paradise.

He splashed into the water. . . . Slipped on hidden, slimy stones. Raised the submerged shoulders. The hat fell off, revealing wavy black hair framing a white face with a finely modeled nose, a fringe of curling dark lashes, a beautiful mouth with pallid lips above a sturdy dimpled chin. A girl!

If his feelings were an indication, his face was as colorless as hers as with her dripping body in his arms he waded and stumbled out of the brook. If only she would open her eyes, just enough to let him know he hadn't frightened her to death. He laid her on the pebbly shore, felt of the back of her head with cautious fingers. A lump as big as a duck's egg. The skin wasn't broken—which was nothing short of a miracle. He listened to her heart. . . . Beating, thank God.

He'd take her home in his roadster—where the dickens was her home?

With his arm under her shoulders, her head against his breast, he forced a bit of brandy from the silver cup of his flask between her lips and waited. No result. A pulse in her tanned throat was beating. She was alive. He gave her more of the stimulant. This time she swallowed, choked, shivered.

Progress! He moistened her lips before he laid her down on the shore and threw his coat over her wet shoulders. Swiftly he gathered driftwood. Lighted a small fire. Even when he drew off the long boots and stout woolen socks she didn't rouse. Her feet were like ice. He held them close in his hands as he looked around for something in which to heat water. This spot was evidently a picnic ground: There were the blackened remnants of a fire; but the picnickers had been brought up with modern manners, there was not so much as the ghost of a can in sight in which to heat water.

Something glistened in a pool. The reel of her rod. Near it lay a wicker creel. There might be a cup in that.

He waded out and retrieved it. Good Lord, but it was cold in the brook. The sun had dodged behind tall trees. He held more brandy to the girl's mouth before he knelt beside her and opened the creel. Three fat, long trout wrapped in wet green leaves. A loose-leaf notebook. A box! He opened it. A bag of tea, two sandwiches, lumps of sugar, half a lemon and a tin cup with a handle which looked as if it had been in a contact with many a fire. Evidently a solo afternoon tea had been on her program.

He filled the cup with water and steadied it with rocks over the fire. He chafed her hands, hands with beautifully cared-for, capable fingers, then gently rubbed her cold feet while he waited for the water to heat.

Behind them the woods were darkening, the rustles, squeaks and hum of unseen life were blending in mysterious harmony. An inquisitive red squirrel scolded from a hemlock and on the surface of a still pool a couple of long-legged bugs skated.

The water in the tin cup hissed. He seized the handle. With heroic control hung on to the hot thing until he could make a holder of his handkerchief. He couldn't afford to waste a drop of it.

He mixed some with brandy in the flask cup, touched his lips to it to make sure it wouldn't scald her before he held it to her mouth. She had taken it. As he waited before giving her more, he wondered how far he was from his stepfather's home where he was expected. If she didn't regain consciousness quickly and tell him where she lived, he might have to take her there. He would hate to put on the return-of-the-Prodigal act with this girl in his arms.

He thought of Patty-Lee's iron determination to get what she wanted from life. He had believed at one time that she wanted him, but when Major Seth Lovel and his wealth had loomed on her horizon, the young engineer with a three-year contract in South America had been wiped from the Southern belle's slate. It had hurt like fury at the time but it had been a blessing in disguise. It had bred in him a distrust of girls and women, especially those hailing from the sunny South, that had kept his brain and his time free for work. . . . And that work had counted, how it had counted. He—

"I—don't know who—you are, but you—are bronze as—as an Indian. You—you look mur—mur—derous." Faint and halting as was the voice it was gracious, sweet and spiced with gaiety.

"Thank God, you can speak." His arm tightened about the girl's shoulders. He pressed the tin cup to her lips. "Drink this." She turned her head away. "Come now. Be good. *Please* or I shall *feel* like a murderer."

The protesting eyes that looked up at him were blue, fringed with sooty lashes as dark as the wet hair spread over his shirt sleeve. Dazed they might be, but they were as deep and mysterious as the pool into which she had cast her bait. She shrugged distaste and pushed away the cup. Winced as she sat up.

"That's—enough of that. I—I'm all right. I don't need—your arm." She frowned at her bare feet with their rosy nails, at the tweed coat over her shoulders, glanced at the brook purling and tinkling its way to the sea. Her eyes came back to him.

"What happened?"

"I hate to tell you. You hooked a trout. Stepped up on a rock. I broadcast congratulations. Startled you. You slipped. I'm on my knees in apology."

Her smile brought a tinge of pink to her colorless face, twin dimples to her cheeks, a surge of passionate relief to him as he knelt beside her.

"Literally on your knees, aren't you? If—I'm such a tenderfoot that I—can't keep my feet in a tame brook like this it isn't your re—responsibility. 'I t'ank I go home.'"

He steadied her as she rose.

"You can't walk without shoes and your boots shipped a lot of water. I'll carry you to my roadster."

"I can walk as—soon as my head—stops cr—crackling like radio sta—static each time I move."

"Like fun you'll walk." He picked her up. "You're not heavy. Must be what the ads call size sixteen. Put your arms round my neck. Close. Hang on. I'll come back for this stuff. Don't talk," he commanded as she opened her lips to protest.

Slowly he followed the narrow trail through the dusky woods. A raspberry bush clutched at her bare foot and clawed an ugly red line along the golden tan. He felt her flinch and stopped. Two great tears rolled from under her lashes. He sat on the lichen-patched trunk of a blow-down and held her in his arms.

"Sorry. Seems as if I never would get through hurting you, doesn't it?"

"You—you didn't. It's only I'm so tired of fight—fighting and your arms are so—so strong—so—rest—restful."

Her voice caught. She hid her face against his breast and sobbed as if her heart were breaking.

Mac held her close and rested his cheek against her hair. What had happened to crack her up like this? Even after her fall she had been debonaire down by the brook. The perky little lift to her eyebrows had been adorable when she said: "Literally on your knees, aren't you?" What was she fighting? She drew a long shuddering breath and raised tear-drenched eyes to his.

"I'm sor—sor—ry. I never did this be—fore, hon—estly. I —I haven't cr—cried for three years. I—"

"Stop talking. Cry. Cry hard. Showers clear the air."

When her sobs had given way to ragged, long-drawn breaths he wiped her eyes with his handkerchief.

"Blow your nose. That's it. Of course you never did this before, because you never before had a crack on the head like that, I'll bet. Come on. I want to get you home." He rose with her in his arms.

"Please put—put—me down. I—I can walk."

"Stop wriggling. You won't walk a step in those bare feet. Listen! What's that? Sounds like a flute."

"A hermit thrush sing—singing his heart out on the top of

one of those high m—maples beside the brook." She turned a convulsive sob into a shaky laugh. "Something tells me you're not a—a native of this part of the country, stranger."

"Nope. Are you?"

"Yes and no. Grafted on, if you get what I mean. My great-great-grandfather settled here. Fi—five years ago, the property was sold, except for fifty acres, half a mile of shore, and an old wh—white house and barn, which came to us. When—when three years ago my sister's health gave out we came here to live thinking she would be better."

"I hope the change helped?"

"N—not much." He felt the sob stifled against his shoulder before he placed her carefully in the deep tan-leather seat of his open roadster. He regarded her anxiously.

"O.K. while I dash back for your boots, rod and creel?"

"Of course, I'm all right. I've cr—crashed in a brook before."

"You won't run away?"

She laughed—a lovely laugh which set her eyes glinting like sapphires in sunlight between their long, wet, black lashes.

"I'm not feeling that energetic. Don't worry. I'll be sitting r—right here when you return and able to talk without c—catching my breath between every few words, I hope."

She was, her head resting against the high back of the seat, her eyes closed. She opened them when he touched her shoulder.

"Was the trout still on the hook? I had just time to see that it was a hardy old-timer before I slipped."

"It was. Thoroughly drowned. It's in the creel." He eased the car into motion. "Where do you live?"

"Keep straight along this road. Our place adjoins the show estate of the county, known as Musgrave Manor. It is the home of Major Seth Lovel who, after having made a colossal fortune, has acquired it as a suitable background for his simmering political ambitions. He was born in the State of Maine. It was just ordinary Turtle Hill when the land was acquired by my ancestors generations ago."

"*Return-of-the-Native* motif?"

"Yes. I'm Diane; my sister is Merry. We're the last of the Vernons. We live at Honeywort House, so named because the original owners found a little clump of that yellow-flowered bee herb of Virgil growing on the land when they arrived. Heaven only, and possibly the birds, knows how the seed came there. Goodness, I'm garrulous. Did my fall upset my mental balance?"

The Vernons! Honeywort House! Mac tried to recall what his stepfather had written. It was something about a faulty deed by which the Vernon property would revert to his estate. He had tried to buy it. He needed it for a private landing field and to extend the golf links. Money had failed. Couldn't do anything with the two sisters who thought they owned it. It wasn't in his line to fight women, but it looked now as if he wouldn't have to, that it would be his by law.

What a mess. When the girl beside him heard his name she would know that he was the Major's stepson and would hate him. Regular Capulet-and-Montague stuff. Already he liked her too much to endure that. Had she noticed the map stuck in the instrument board on which his route was marked? Too late to do anything about it now if she had. If only he could make friends with her before she knew who he was. When she had sobbed that she was tired of fighting, had she meant fighting for her home?

"I was too heavy for you to carry so far. I wouldn't have believed that a bronze face could go so chalky." Her voice seemed to come from a far country. "You'd better tell me who you are, quick. I may have to drive *you* home."

"I chalky! What imagination! I'll bet you are what is technically known as a fictioneer. I spotted a notebook in your creel. You called me 'stranger.' I rather like it. It suggests mystery, adventure. In short, it has a 'Lone Ranger' touch. Suppose you call me that."

"O.K., Stranger. Here we are." She indicated a square, white-clapboarded house with four broad black chimneys. Graduated L's connected it with a long barn. Window boxes were masses of yellow and green and white with a blush of pink. A black-and-white English setter, barking like mad, ears flapping, raced around a corner of the house.

"Don't drive in. It might frighten my sister who knows that I started out on foot."

"You can't walk in those bare feet."

"Watch me." She was out of the roadster before it stopped. "Down, Dopey, Down!" She shut her eyes and caught at the car door to steady herself, then shook her head and smiled at Mac as he stood beside her.

"All right now, for a minute the world whir—whirled like a plane propeller. Give me the boots, rod and creel, please."

His face was grave as he handed them to her.

"You might permit me to carry them to the house."

"Don't need you. Here, Dopey, make yourself useful."

The setter seized the strap of the creel in his teeth and proudly trotted along the drive.

"Why this Here's-your-hat-what's-your-hurry act?"

There was a suspicious glint in the eyes which met his squarely before she answered the question.

"Because Merry might invite you in. We don't want you." She nodded toward the map on which a route was marked in red ink. The words MUSGRAVE MANOR stood out as if printed in letters of fire.

"I was too dazed to notice that at first. Something tells me you belong to the Major and his lady at the Manor who are trying to steal our land. Thanks for the epic rescue. Goodby."

II

DIANE VERNON resisted the temptation to look back at the roadster, which tugged at her head like a magnet as she walked slowly along the graveled drive, bordered with towering spikes of delphinium, Madonna lilies, clumps of pink poppies and shafts of lavender, yellow and rosy columbine. She drew a deep breath of the clean, salt smell of kelp. It helped clear her brain.

Conscience prodded. She had been inexcusably rude to a man who had rescued her from what might have proved a serious predicament. She had known when she saw the words MUSGRAVE MANOR printed on the road map that he was the long-absent stepson of Major Lovel. Probably a grafter like his father. He was an engineer, she had heard. That explained it! Undoubtedly he had come to help locate the missing bounds.

A wave of shame scorched her as she remembered her emotional breakdown. For years she had cheered and comforted Merry. She had had no one to whom she could or would turn for encouragement or help when she could see no hope ahead—except Freda Swenson. Devoted as the Swede woman was she wasn't own-family. The man's arms had been so strong, so tender . . .

Ooch! Why think of it when it burned her up to remember her sobs, her face pressed against his shoulder? Doubtless at this moment he was cynically deciding that she had been putting on an act, that she had known then that he had come to fight for his stepfather against the Vernons.

She hadn't. . . . Not until a second before he had stopped the roadster at her request. She had suspected that he was sidestepping when he refused to tell his name. Suspicion had crystallized to conviction when she had discovered his destination. Apparently a guilty conscience had made him cagey.

She reached that conclusion and the green door with its ancient brass knocker, before which the setter was patiently waiting, at the same time. She heard the roadster start as she slipped into the hall. That was that.

Now, as always when she entered the old house, she had the sense of stepping into a bygone world. A world of crumbling wood fires, candlelight on colonial maple and braided rugs, on portraits of men and women gone many a year, who had helped lay the foundations of a great nation while the secrets of the automobile, glands and hormones, the airplane, radio and the cosmic ray were still tightly locked away in the future.

> "Christian up and smite them!
> Counting gain but loss . . ."

She smiled as she listened to the young voice soaring in a very passion of fervor. Trudy must be doing some chore she hated. She declared that singing helped her carry on.

"That you, Di?"

Her sister's question with its hint of huskiness came from the broad covered terrace that opened from the hall which ran through the center of the house.

"Yes, Merry. I'm a sight. I slipped in the brook. I'll be with you as soon as I change. Give me the creel, Dopey."

The dog released his hold and raced along the hall, his nails going *tick-tack, tick-tack* on the polished oak.

> "Christian! dost thou feel them,
> How they work within?"

To the accompaniment of song Diane padded to the large, square kitchen. Walls and chairs were painted in cool atmosphere-blue. A sleek cat, striped in all the tints and shades of topaz, jumped from the window sill and with plumed tail waving walked back and forth over her bare feet. The round-faced young girl in a pink-gingham frock, with brilliant spots of rouge on her cheeks and a black-velvet ribbon tied around her light hair, seated at a table stringing beans, stopped singing and rose quickly.

"That's right, Trudy," Diane approved.

"I'm glad something's right, Miss Di. Gee, cutting these beans drives me cockeyed. Why do they have to be slivered?"

"They are more delicate and delicious that way. Stop walking over my feet, Scarlet, you tickle."

She pushed the cat aside with one foot and handed the creel to the maid.

"I caught four trout. Big ones. Cook them for supper. Bake large potatoes. Give them a full hour in the oven. It's just three-thirty now. Watch the clock and put them in on time. The last potatoes you baked had marble hearts."

The girl's prominent, china-blue eyes watered. She sniffed.

"Gee, I know they weren't right, Miss Di, but I'd never used an electric oven before and Maw says—"

"That you're 'a right smart girl for sixteen.' Prove it. Be sure that everything Miss Merry will need is on her supper tray before you take it to the terrace. It annoys her when you keep running back into the house for something you've forgotten."

"She never crabs about it."

"Of course she doesn't. Haven't you learned yet that she's a saint?" Diane steadied her voice. "Before you serve supper, rub off those blobs of rouge and wipe that bloody nail polish from your fingers."

"But, Miss Di, it's movie night. Luigi's coming for me an' he gets mad if I'm not all dolled up like the other girls."

"If you sniff once more I shall have a nervous breakdown, Trudy. Stop it. You came to Honeywort House because you wanted to learn to cook and wait on table, didn't you?"

"Yes, Miss Di, but Maw says—"

"You want to be good enough to work in one of the big summer houses here, don't you?"

"Sure, Miss Di. But Maw says Freda Swenson ought to help me more instead of canning everything in sight."

"Never mind what Maw says. When you're working for me what I say goes. You have no heavy work. Freda is here to take care of Miss Merry; that's her job. If she has a passion for spending her off time putting up vegetables and fruit after her home fashion, that's her lookout and our gain. We may be devoutly thankful for our storeroom stocked with food before this year is over. I suspect she helps you more than she should. I know the brand of expert service required in the large summer houses. I—" she caught back "I used to live that way"— "and I'm putting in valuable time teaching you. Do you want to learn or don't you?"

"Gee, Miss Di, *course* I do." Trudy sniffed. "What's eating you? I don't see what I done—did—to be bawled out like this. You sound just like Maw jawin'."

A vision of sloppy, chinless "Maw" in one of her most vituperative moments gave Diane pause. It wasn't what the girl had done, it was what someone else had done and the dull ache in the back of her head that had set her nerves on edge.

"I'm not bawling you out, Trudy, I'm trying to teach you."

"I know, Miss Di, and I do try, honest to God I do. May I choose the china for Miss Merry's tray? I'll be awful careful handlin' it." Her blue eyes were eager, brilliant.

"Yes. Select anything you like. She was pleased with the flowers floating in the finger bowl last night."

"Gee, I'm tickled. I matched 'em to the china. I love the nice dishes and glass here—Maw says there ain't none finer in the big cottages—she cleans an' opens a lot of them—an' I'm screwy about flowers. I'll have everything perfect. You watch an' see. I'm crazy about Miss Merry. Her and—she and I get along just dandy."

Curious combination Trudy, Diane thought, as she shivered under the needle shower. She came from a bare, poverty-stricken home where a scolding mother, a lazy father and four younger boys filled a tumbledown house to overflowing, yet she had a love and appreciation of beauty which amounted to a passion. From what grade-A ancestor had it descended?

She slipped into a yellow-linen frock and sandals, and fastened green beads. As she clasped a matching belt she regarded her reflection in the mirror. The looking-glass girl's eyes were heavy—how could they help being with that dull ache behind them—she was pale under her golden tan, her lips were tense, a betraying redness rimmed her lids.

That last was the result of the attack of crying in an absolute stranger's arms. What had she said? She had sobbed something; she remembered that.

"Imbecile!" She disdainfully wrinkled her nose at the mirror girl whose instantaneous response tipped up the corners of each mouth in a laugh.

"Watch your step, gal. If you let Merry suspect that you've been crying you'll deserve a nice little swish in boiling oil. Get it?"

By a grave nod of the head the looking-glass girl indicated that she "got it."

In the hall she pinched her cheeks till they stung. She clutched the banister rail as she went slowly down the stairs. Curious how the world whirled every few minutes. She stopped before she reached the terrace door to look at her sister. Her heart contracted till it hurt. Only thirty and tied to a wheelchair! Filtered sunlight brought out glints of copper in her chestnut hair; her shirtwaist frock of turquoise-blue cotton was open at the neck. Her throat was as firm and creamy as the lustrous string of pearls about it. On the third finger of her left hand was a ring—a large, square-cut yellow diamond, set in sparkling white ones.

That ring. . . . Pete Holbrook had given it to Merry when they were engaged. She had been on the way to the airport to meet him on his return from a cross-country flight when a taxi had collided with her sedan. She had been unconscious for days—mercifully unconscious, for who would have had the courage to tell her then that Pete's plane had crashed somewhere in the mountains? That he would never come back?

Diane remembered, as if it had happened yesterday, the hour when Merry's questions had been so insistent that the attending specialist had said she must be told what had happened to Pete and at once. She recalled how her own voice had choked on the words and she thought of her sister's tragic eyes as she had whispered brokenly:—

"Pete was such a grand—person. It would have broken his heart, to have seen me like this—We—we couldn't have married."

Later that night she had said:—

"We won't speak of Pete again, Di. I can bear it better that way."

And they hadn't. Gradually Merry had gained strength and had taken up the business of living with gay courage. Before the accident she had been winning praise and a moderate amount of fame as an illustrator of books for children; that had been swept away also—her fingers had been too stiff to hold pencil or brush. The publisher for whom she had worked, Jim Brewster, had begged to see her, but she had passionately refused. She didn't know that he had haunted the hospital during the period of her unconsciousness. Diane remembered her face as she had explained:—

"Jim wanted me to marry him, Di, but I loved Pete. He —he might think he ought to ask me again when—when he sees me—like this. He's the knight-errant type. He won't have the chance. I'll never see him."

A passion of fury swept Diane. Merry was so exquisite, so— so sweet—so helpless. Why—why had it had to happen to her —to Merry, of all people, Merry who was naturally as gay as her name, who had always been so unselfish, so thoughtful of everyone? She wished that her father and mother had not died when she was in college. Perhaps it was better that way. Their hearts would be shredded to ribbons to see their adored daughter as she was now.

"Why are you hiding in the hall, Di? Guilty conscience?"

In answer to her sister's amused question Diane stepped through the doorway with a gay greeting.

She passed up the fine willow chairs, the chaise on wheels, the curved wooden bench with yellow-and-white cushions, to perch on the low granite parapet of the terrace. Back to the sparkling blue of the sea and the rock-bordered shore she related her adventure in the brook, omitting the period of unconsciousness and her weep-jag, as she called it to herself. Dopey, on his haunches beside her, whined as he stared at the gulls, soaring and roosting on the rocks. Scarlet, curled in a chair, watched them through narrowed emerald slits. Little gold sparks of laughter lighted Merry Vernon's brown eyes as they met her sister's.

"Pure fiction stuff. Who is the man?"

"I think he's the stepson returning from South America to Musgrave Manor."

"*Really*, Di? Has he come at last? What did he look like?"

"When I first opened my eyes—I was a bit dazed for a split second after my fall—I have a horrible suspicion that I prattled—I thought I was in the grip of a North American Indian in tweeds. His skin was bronze. He looked murderous and loomed like the Trylon. Expected to see him brandish a tomahawk at any minute. He had four eyes, color uncertain, two clipped bronze mustaches, two Greek-goddish noses, a pair of ears on each side of a head topped with undulating brown hair—and *how* it undulated."

Merry Vernon's laugh was like soft music.

"I don't wonder you sell your articles, Di; you paint with

words. I can see the twin features as plainly as if the man were perched on the rail beside you. How old was he?"

"When the world stopped whirling and had settled into place and the color had returned to his face I decided he was somewhere in the thirties and terribly good-looking in a lean, clean-cut way. His sudden smile, which set sparks of laughter in his eyes and revealed a flash of white teeth, alone would send a picture scout after him with a long-term contract. He's perfect movie material.

"Later, in the roadster, I concluded that he was a man who had or was carrying heavy responsibilities that had tightened the lines of his jaw. Dynamic, to use an overworked word. I presume that engineering in South America isn't playboy life. There was power in that jaw and determination to see things through. I'll bet he knows what self-discipline means." She drew a long breath. "The breeze is coming from the herb garden. Smell the mint?"

"Spicy, isn't it? I love to look across the kaleidoscope of color and think it's our own, that the shore and this lovely old house are ours—that is, if Major Seth Lovel doesn't get them. To return to your adventure with a capital A. Did your rescuer tell you his name?"

"He did not. After I told him mine he said to call him 'Stranger.' Suspicion struck a spark but didn't blaze until I noticed a map marked with the route to Musgrave Manor. I tell you, Merry, he's here to help his stepfather grab this place for an airfield. He won't get it. We'll do something to stop him. The meek no longer inherit the earth. We'll fight."

III

MERRY VERNON rested her head with its short, shining hair against the high back of her chair, as if it were too heavy for her slender throat to hold erect. Her eyes were on the interminable stretch of blue sea.

"How can we fight him? We can't. It's a simple economic problem. No money. In the twinkling of an eye, our assets were turned into liabilities. It takes about all we have just to live. Think of what I will need if I—I never walk a—again."

She shut her lips hard and closed her eyes tight to keep back more tears from following the two that had escaped from under her gold-tipped lashes.

In an instant Diane was on her knees beside the chair, her arms about her sister's slender waist.

"Don't think that, lovely, *don't!* Not even the worst Calamity Jane among those doctors said that. They said we must build you up, keep you from being worried and we have. You will walk. I'll make you. I'll put all the strength in me into making you." Her voice was husky with heartbreak. Dopey whined and tucked his nose under her arm. The cat jumped into Merry's lap and purred content. "Miracles do happen."

"Yes. But they can't yet bring back the dead."

"Merry! Merry! You don't want to get well. You—you want to go to Pete!"

"No. No, dearie! That wail was selfish and cruel. I do want to get well. I do! I do! I *do!* I love life. With the world convulsed with hate and savagery, I want to be useful, I want to help, to count."

"You do count, count tremendously. Don't the girls and women in this town flock here to sob out their problems on your shoulder, figuratively speaking? Doesn't Freda scold that they hardly allow you time to rest?"

"I love it, Di—being able to help a little, I mean."

"You never complain. You never are irritable. I don't see how you can keep from letting off steam occasionally."

"What good would it do? I tell myself that probably as long as I live I will be dependent on others for help. Why make it unendurably difficult for them by being disagreeable?"

"Trudy says you're a saint. She's just one hundred per cent right."

"Your voice is full of tears, Di. It isn't like you. You're the rock to which I cling. One of my greatest troubles is that you are devoting your youth and life to me. You can't do anything with the tips of your fingers. You fling your whole soul into it. You left college in your junior year to take care of me. You had received your certificate after four months in the Civilian Pilots' Training Course and you gave up flying. Three summers ago someone told you of the income-producing possibilities of an herb garden and you studied and worked and prodded Asaph Hicks until you made what had seemed to me a fairy tale come true. Look at it."

She had firmly led the talk away from herself. Diane fell into line.

"It was a fight to get it started but now I'll say it's running on ball-bearings," she agreed.

Still on her knees she turned to follow with her eyes her sister's pointing hand. An acre of land was surrounded on three sides by old stone walls the color of weathered pine, sparkling with mica in the sunlight. Distance merged color into color till the effect was that of a time-toned Oriental rug. The green of balm melted into the red and white of bee balm. The leaves of a patch of purple basil shone and scattered its rich, clovelike fragrance. Above it hummed a cloud of bees. All the better-known herbs were there: marjoram, bergamot, mint, sage, hyssop, lovage and lavender, and others with which she was experimenting. She turned back to her sister.

"I'll have to pick the basil tomorrow for drying. You're right, Merry, I have made that fairy tale come true. . . . That isn't the only miracle I've accomplished," she boasted as she stretched out in the wheel chaise. It was amazing how resting her head against the back steadied it. "Trudy actually got on her feet when I appeared in the kitchen this afternoon."

Her sister laughed. That was the wonderful selflessness of Merry: In spite of the tragedy which had her clutched in its merciless grip, she could attune her spirit to others, could sympathize, thrill with another's mood.

"If you can succeed in teaching that child even the rudiments of courtesy you will be helping her immeasurably. After honor, good manners are the greatest asset a young person can have, young or old for that matter."

"You're right, but, so help me, doesn't the youngster hate me for my efforts? We've got to make her realize that no good can come from her association with that tough Luigi Manchusto who hangs round, but if we don't watch our step we may drive her straight into his arms. Why does a young man who looks as if he belonged in a big city underworld stay around this country village? I'm sure he's at the bottom of every piece of deviltry that happens in this town, but I can't prove it. Who can or will?"

"Curious, how many women and girls fall for the daredevil type."

"Trudy mustn't. She hasn't finished High yet. She really has a lovely voice; she can do something with that if she'll only practise. Now that she's singing in the church choir perhaps she will. Sometimes I ask myself, 'Why in heaven's name do I *care* with whom she goes to movies and dances? Why do I *care* if out of the hundred and fifty young people in this town qualified to vote, only fifty voted at the last Presidential election?'—but I do. If they only can be inspired to fight for their belief with ballots they will realize the evil and futility of fighting with bullets. Trudy accused me of 'jawin'' at her like 'Maw.' Am I getting bossy and disagreeable, Merry?"

Tears again. . . . Darn! . . . She never had been weepy before. Had the fall this afternoon started a leak in the waterworks behind her eyes?

"You are not; but, my dear, you are sticking too close to work. Besides the herb garden, you're carrying on that evening Club you started to make the sub-voters, as well as the young voters, Government-conscious; you play the church organ and rehearse the choir; work at the Red Cross room every moment you can spare; then there's always me. It isn't as if I didn't have Freda Swenson to look after me as if I were a baby. Lady Luck certainly was good to us when she sent that Swede knocking at our door in answer to your ad three years ago. You must go out socially more."

"Don't like to be social."

"Yes, you do, you were the gayest, most popular girl in your class at college, with your music and your dancing. You refuse invitations from the summer people here because you think it will hurt me to see you starting off while I am left behind. Honestly, Di, it hurts infinitely more to see you, who are so brilliant, getting into a rut. You are selling articles. Your writing has a gay touch without the sly maliciousness which seems to pass for wit at present. It's a career for you, permanence, security, not a job which you may lose at the whim of an employer. Your work must grow and nothing enlarges one's outlook more than contact with people."

"You're right, lovely. When I get the herbs picked I'll blaze through the social life here like a major comet lighting the heavens, collecting atmosphere as I go."

"Don't wait to finish picking. Do it now. Nicols came from the Manor this afternoon to bring an English magazine. He gets to be more and more of a mystery. He hasn't always been a valet; sometimes I wonder if he is a remittance man."

"Remittance man or not, he's a gentleman. I'd trust myself anywhere with him. So help me, if there isn't the genesis of a novel! Whence? Why? Whither? Especially whence? He's been grand about the Club. Insists upon helping serve coffee and doughnuts at the meetings here. I can't understand why an Englishman would be interested in my feeble attempt to make good citizens of the village young people."

"Your effort doubtless appeals to his intelligence. You haven't called at the Manor since the house was opened this season. Go this afternoon."

"I can't. I'm all in. No pep. I feel as unmotivated as a crab in a tide pool."

"Di! Were you hurt when you fell in the brook?"

"Now don't get panicky, lovely. Of course I wasn't. Why should I go to the home of that heel, Major Lovel, who's trying to steal this place? Catch me doing it."

"But, Di, the Lovels will think we are afraid of them if we ignore them, perhaps that we know Honeywort House rightfully belongs with their property. Instead of hating the man, from all I hear, we ought to be sorry for him. He is enormously rich, has retired from business to enjoy his hard-won wealth and has acquired a wife thirty years his junior. If that last achievement doesn't spell trouble for our shoulder-thumping neighbor, I'll miss my guess. His Patty-Lee married him for his money—"

"And, my word, is she spending it!"

"If the man who rescued you this afternoon is his stepson—there's an even chance that your fiction imagination has seized the bit in its teeth and he isn't—find out who he is. If he has come here to help the Major seize our property legally let's get a ready on. Go Sherlock Holmes on him. Your frock is perfect. Clap on the big yellow cartwheel hat and knock his eyes out, gal."

"Why Merry Vernon, what language for a perfect lady. I'll say Trudy has been getting in a little training too." Diane rose slowly from among the cushions of the chaise.

"I'll go, but remember, you'll be responsible if Patty-Lee's soft Southern 'honeys' irritate me till I hurl a cup of tea at her. She's such a hypocrite and I suspect she's a liar. I'll bet that all the time she was so sugary to us these last two summers she had that faulty-deed wallop up her sleeve. In these days, when most of us are breathless trying to keep intellectually in step with a world whose plans and problems change over night, you would suppose that her lure-technique would be as obsolete as the infantry tactics of 1914, but how men fall for her. She must be the divinely designed answer to that snappy ad WOMEN MEN WANT. She's surrounded the moment she enters a room by males of all ages. I'd like the secret of her fatal charm."

"I'll shoulder the responsibility of your behavior, Di. Hurry, or tea will be over before you get there. Sorry to report that Asaph has taken the station wagon to the village for its weekly repairs. You'll have to walk or ride your wheel."

"Someday that wagon will lie down on us and never get up. I'll walk—if I go."

"Please go. Pack all the news in your old kit bag and bring it back running over. Freda, as a news collector, is good, but her brand is the everyday, common or garden variety; yours will be de luxe. I'll wait for my tea until you come. Trudy will serve it here and we'll have a talk-fest. I hear that the house has been entirely done over. Bring back all the superglamorous details."

"All right. Keep tuned in on this station for future announcements." Diane paused on the threshold, made a distasteful little moue and sang:—

> "Heigh ho! Heigh ho!
> It's back to work I go."

She mounted the stairs slowly. If she "obeyed that impulse," instead of going to the Manor and trying to be agreeable she would stretch out on the chaise and stay there for hours. Merry really ought to be the executive of an enormous industry. Sitting in her wheelchair she could think of more things to keep a person on the jump. Of course it was because she couldn't use her own energy and it had to have an outlet.

"Still want me to go?" she wheedled ingratiatingly when she returned to the terrace.

"I do. And just to give an extra take-it-on-the-chin tilt to your head, you look like Palm Beach and a *Vogue* model. I've never seen you lovelier."

"That helps. I'll be seeing you. Stay with your best girl, Dopey. I don't want you."

Ears pricked, head tilted, the dog stood motionless. Merry

Vernon listened to the quick, strong *tap-tap* of her sister's
feet along the hall, knew when she stopped to speak to
Freda, heard the swing of the front screen door. She rested
her head against the back of her chair and flexed her
fingers as was her habit when she was alone.

When Di goes it seems as if life went out of the air,
she thought. She's so vital, yet so tender, so gay and yet so
understanding. . . . Understanding! Is she right? Am I caught
in a spell of apathy? Is it true that I am not trying to break
it? That I am letting it weave a net that is strangling all
desire to be active?

She closed her eyes and choked back a sob. Pleaded
under her breath:—

"Oh, God, help me. Before this I have prayed for patience.
Now I pray for strength to fight. *Fight*. Fight to get well.
Fight to the finish if necessary."

"You want something, Mees Merry?"

Merry Vernon looked at the strong, fresh-looking woman
in white standing in the doorway. Her thick hair was the
color of straw in sunlight. Her eyes were as blue and clear
as a mountain lake reflecting the sky.

"Yes, Freda. I want to walk." She brought one closed
fist down on the arm of her chair. "I'm going to w—walk."
Her white throat contracted in a sob.

"So! Now you're talkin'. Sure you are, Mees Merry. Look
how you've limberedt your fingers by keepin' tryin'." Freda
laid a tender hand on the shining hair. "Vhat iss valkin' but
yoost puttin' one foot aheadt of the other? Ya?"

"That's all it is, isn't it? I hadn't thought of it like that
before. One foot ahead and then the other. I'll try. Dear
God, how I'll try. It seems simple enough, doesn't it, Dopey?"
she asked unsteadily.

The setter nuzzled her slim hand before he rested his
black-and-white chin on her knee and looked up at her
with adoring brown eyes. The purr of the cat in her lap
sounded like the whir of a miniature plane. Merry laid a
hand on each silky head.

"You dears. We'll have a secret. Di mustn't know what
I am trying to do, yet. It would break her heart if I failed.
Understand, Freda?"

The woman nodded gravely. The dog drew a long, quivering breath. Scarlet waved her tail gently as if in acquiescence.

IV

MAC CAMERON's eyes followed Diane Vernon as she walked slowly toward the house between flower borders; they lingered on the green door with its heavy brass knocker after she had closed it behind her. What was the girl fighting? Would he ever forget those heartbroken sobs, the shudder of the slim body in his arms?

His brow furrowed in perplexity as he started the roadster. What had she meant by "Something tells me you belong to the Major and his lady at the Manor who are trying to steal our land"?

Had he suspected from something he said that he had come to help the Lovels acquire legally the Vernon holdings? Impossible . . . He hadn't mentioned the Lovels. Bits in the Major's letters began to recur to him; that the present owners were proud, poor and needed money; that it would be an act of charity to make them sell; that they raised pot and medicinal herbs for a living. So convincingly had their desperate need been portrayed that he had pictured them as two tottering old gentlewomen.

And the truth was that one at least was radiantly young and lovely, with an I.Q. that would rate in the higher brackets, or he was no judge of intelligence—which he flattered himself he was. The Major had explained that he wanted to acquire the property not only for a landing field and additional links but because Patty-Lee felt that it was part of the estate. He had written:—

"You know, Mac, that I have a tremendous respect and tenderness for women. I hate this fight, but I deeded the place to my wife. She won't give me a minute's peace till she gets the land that belonged to it originally. That's the old Southern idea, 'Hold all land that borders mine.'"

Why did Patty-Lee want the Vernon estate? Not merely because she felt it would complete her holdings; she was not single-minded enough for that. Hadn't he learned to look for a hidden motive with her?

Musgrave Manor: The name was wrought in one of the two ornate iron-grilled gates opening on a drive which swept between maples. He drove slowly toward the long white house, designed in the Southern manner with an elaborate, lacy ironwork second-story balcony behind the white columns of the broad portico.

Color glowed from every foot of the visible world and changed with each floating cloud. A glittering expanse of sparkling blue water, patched in the distance with green, wooded islands, rippled on and on to hazy purple hills. A launch bobbed at a pier. Halfway between that and a foam-bordered ledge, an impressive fifty-foot power boat swung at anchor. Its deck glittered with chromium steel.

The house was so near the shore that he could hear the scalloped, lacy-frilled tide murmuring deep-sea secrets to the pebbles and sand it dragged oceanward as it retreated. Wood smoke from a great chimney rose and drifted on the soft, salty breeze till it thinned into lavender malines and floated between the clear turquoise of the sky and the sapphire of the sea. White gulls, gray gulls, brown gulls mewed and screamed as they flung themselves into the air, circled, swooped, soared and swooped again.

"Hiar! Mac!"

He shot the roadster forward in response to the hail from the man on the steps. Not until then did he remember that his trousers were wet to the knees, that his coat was damp. What explanation would he make if the Major noticed?

He's handsomer than ever, he thought, as he appraised the tall, erect figure clad in impeccable white slacks and powder-blue pull-over. Snowy hair accentuated the bronze of his face touched with red at the cheekbones. His grin was contagious. His warm handshake, his hearty laugh, his shoulder-thumping enthusiasm, his confidential just-between-us manner were undoubtedly vote getters.

And the best of it is he's sincere and has courage to burn. He learned to fight as an A.E.F. air ace, winning the D.S.M. twice, the Croix de Guerre with palms. On his return from Europe he married Mother, established a business and began to make a fortune. He likes people, believes in them. Take Patty-Lee, for example. He thinks she's an angel. So what? Didn't I think so myself till she threw me over? Who am I to rate his perception of character in the lower brackets?

He reached the steps and that mental conclusion at the same moment. As he jumped from the roadster his stepfather's large white hand with its red intaglio ring landed on his shoulder with a resounding thump. A liveried man materialized from nowhere and drove away the car.

"Well, well, I'm glad you're back from the jungle, Mac. Missed you like the devil these last three years. You're the only child I have, my boy. Been expecting you for the last hour. Great Scott but I'm glad you're here. I've got work for you." The Major's arm was around his shoulders; his hearty voice was booming in the ear on a level with his own. "What happened? Lose your way?"

Now that his face was so near, Mac could see that these last years had taken their toll. The eyes which had been so frank were guarded. Was Patty-Lee responsible for the change? It was his best bet that she was.

"Lose my way after the A-B-C chart you drew for me? I couldn't. Stopped on a bridge to size up a brook. Unless I miss my guess, it's bulging with trout."

"You guessed right, but at present that part of it is closed to me and my guests. It won't be long. It runs through the property I'm fighting to acquire. Wrote you about it, remember? I'm caught between the devil and the deep sea. My wife wants that land. One of the owners has started a club to inspire the youngsters in the town to qualify as intelligent voters. I've come here to lay the foundations of a political career. She claims it's nonpartisan, but even with my World War record to help me can't you see what she could do to my chances if I take her land?"

"But this village is such a small portion of the state."

"Sure it is, but seed has a way of blowing far in a political campaign. However, I have a plan, which for usefulness will match her Young Voters enterprise. I intend to start a Civilian Defense Group here. That's where you'll come in strong: You've had training in modern warfare and you're a pilot. I'll tell you more about it later. Let's forget land and war for the present. There's a gang in the loggia. Patty-Lee likes a crowd around. If you ask me I could do with an occasional day of quiet. Want to wash up before you join them for a drink—or tea? Tea's in again for afternoon, the wife says. Great Scott, how do women keep up with every shift in fashion?"

"They get it out of the air. Their minds are equipped with a special antenna tuned to pick up trends. Where am I to be bedded down? Lead me to it. I'll freshen up and be with you in the drop of a sky-rocketing stock, Major." Apparently the dampness of his clothes had escaped notice.

After three years in an engineering, and a month in a military, camp this sensational house seemed fantastically unreal. More like an opera-bouffe setting than a home, he thought, as he followed the maid in amethyst silk up the curving ivory-white staircase carpeted in the same rich shade as her uniform. As he passed along the corridor he glimpsed through open doors tints and shades of the same color accented by soft pinks and blues and greens.

A valet was unpacking his bags when he entered the room assigned him. A slim man of medium height with a face which reminded him of the Dukes of Great Britain's reigning family.

"Will you change, sir? The gentlemen are still in slacks." A perfectly cadenced Oxonian voice was as British as the man's face. Before Mac could answer he added, "I'm Nicols, Mr. Cameron."

"With an h?"

"No, sir. N-i-c-o-l-s, sir. English spelling." Color rose slowly to his brown hair. "I was gassed in War '14, sir. They didn't want me in War '39."

Had the man read his thoughts, known that he was wondering what an able-bodied Englishman was doing in the United States when his country was struggling in that boiling caldron of tragedy overseas? Was it keen perception or a guilty conscience?

"Sorry about the gassing, Nicols. We men who were kids at the time can have no conception of what you went through. I've heard Major Lovel tell of air fights that made my hair rise."

"Our experiences doubtless would seem tame to the men fighting this war, sir. This coat is wet. Did you meet with an accident?"

As Mac looked at the tweed garment in the valet's hand he felt the pressure of a head against his breast, the weight of a slim, warm body in his arms, heard again those convulsive sobs.

"I look pretty soggy, don't I? In my enthusiasm to discover trout I got too familiar with a brook. Have the suit pressed, will you, Nicols? I'll wear whites."

The sense of moving in an opera-bouffe setting persisted as he passed through the enormous white living room with its complete American flavor of luxury to the loggia, with its violet-cushioned chairs and benches, its yapping Pekingese, its tea table with massive silver, pink sweet peas and paper-thin china. Palms waved, clematis and English ivy climbed, goldfish flashed in the pool of the patio beyond. He was aware of a group of men and girls talking and laughing. His hostess behind the purring kettle greeted him with a little shriek of welcome. Her white pull-over which matched her slacks was belted with a string of amethysts.

"Honey boy! We'd given you up for lost. Stop barking, Precious, don't you know Mac's my friend? Handsome fella! How long have you been here?"

When a woman, a small, exquisitely dainty woman, flings her arms around your neck, shakes back her short yellow curls, gazes adoringly up at you from violet eyes with startlingly dark irises, and lifts pouting, vivid lips to yours, there's only one thing to be done even if she is your stepfather's wife, Mac decided, and he did it. He kissed her.

"That-a-boy!" The Major's hand fell on his shoulder with an approving thump. "Glad to see you two friends. Now that he's back in civilization we'll have to find a wife for him, eh, Patty-Lee?"

His jocular voice set little flares in his wife's eyes which reminded Mac of the crimson light he had seen in the heart of an amethyst. He recognized danger signals he had cause to remember and laughed.

"That's the trouble with you happily-marrieds. You can't rest till you get your friends paired off. If it's all the same to you, Major, I'll stay as I am, single, white and thirty. Cecily Cole! What luck to find you here. Still topping the world in tennis?"

The small girl in white slacks and thin-silk shirt cocked her head with its sleek Titian hair like a bright-eyed bird and put her hand in his.

"This part of the world only. I'm glad you're back, Mac. This is the time for every American who believes that 'government of the people, by the people and for the people shall not perish from the earth' to be in his own country."

"I had the same idea, Cis. I—"

"What'll you have, honey boy?" Patty-Lee had edged between them. "Still on the wagon?"

"Sure. I want tea. None of your afternoon brew, either. I like it to stand alone."

"As if I had forgotten, forgotten that you like smoky Lapsang Souchong. I'll prepare it myself and then we'll take it to the pool and you'll tell me every little bitsy thing you've been doing in the centuries you've been away." She flung the last words over her shoulder.

"I'm not sure, but I think if she calls you honey boy once

more, Mac, I'll hit her even if she is my hostess for the afternoon. Honey boy for a super he-man like you," Cecily Cole flared.

"Thanks for thinking the name a misnomer, Cis. I loathe it, myself, but I long ago discovered that short of beating up Patty-Lee there was no way of stopping her when she has made up her mind to pursue a certain course. Apparently the holy estate of matrimony hasn't changed her."

"What's the present course? To make her husband jealous? This wouldn't be the first time. You haven't been here long enough to realize that the Major lacks his usual *joie de vivre*. You're putting on a good act about her now, Mac Cameron, but time was when your pals dubbed you the Man with the Broken Heart."

"Was I as bad as that?" he inquired, even as he wondered why the relief he had felt, the knowledge that he had had a miraculous escape from tragic unhappiness hadn't tempered his furious anger that his fiancée had deceived him. "That was three years ago. Ancient history. You couldn't find even the scar tissue of the wound now. Tell me who these people are."

"They're a queer mixture. Reading from the left, the man with the brick-red hair and the nose, in blue slacks and green cardigan with sleeves a couple of inches short, is Doctor John Reynolds. Poor as a war refugee but a crack-a-jack at his job. He's been working his head off in hospitals. Getting a rest here before he settles into regular practice. The Major picked him up somewhere. He's a wow at contract. You know our host and hostess like their little game. Reynolds wants to be that *rara avis* a G.P.—general practitioner to you— thinks he can be of more help to humanity that way, though I've been told he's a wizard at surgery. All he needs is a chance to show the world what he can do and he believes that patients will wear a trail to his door."

"I hope he gets his chance—but not on me. Who's the marcelled blond with the dimples in the opulent white outfit?"

"Larry Crane. Has a lawyer's degree. Could have made a big reputation practising if he weren't filthy rich. He's a petty officer in the Naval Reserve. Lives on the big power boat anchored offshore. He could be made to amount to something if the right woman took him in hand but at present he's just another playboy. He's off his head about a girl in this village."

"What girl?" Mac had a curious hunch that he knew.

"Don't snap. I haven't heard her name."

"Then how do you know he is in love?"

"Patty-Lee spread the glad tidings this afternoon, Professor Quiz. She was pretty nasty about it, too. Life is a stage to her, with herself the lead and all the rest of us supernumeraries to feed her fat part. I presume she had counted on Larry for her own tame cat. Up to this minute—" she treated Mac to a gamine grin—"he's been her latest heartthrob. He's the season's prize for a beau, has the orchid habit. The white-haired men in my stag line say it with gardenias. Speaking of cats, it's pretty disgusting of me to slam my hostess."

"We'll forget it. Who's the girl in sky-blue linen skirt and thin white sweater? I like the snug way it's belted. She has a fine, plain face and superb figure."

"Sally Arnold, from a whistle-stop town in Texas whose streets suddenly ran with 'black gold'—oil to you, suh. She's a graduate nurse. Money to burn now, but she's a dear. Wealth won't spoil her. I'm trying to pull off a match, she and the Doc. With her money and his skill they could go places. She's at the hotel, also. I introduced her to Mrs. Lovel."

"Tea for two, honey boy." Patty-Lee smiled alluringly up into Mac's eyes and offered a tray. "Take this and I'll carry the plate. It's loaded with sandwiches. Anchovy. Mushroom. Slivers of hot marmalade toast. I haven't forgotten what you like. There's a seat by the pool in the patio—"

"Miss Diane Vernon," the purple-liveried butler announced.

Not for three years had Mac's heart performed the acrobatic feat of shooting to his throat and plunging back into place as it did when he looked at the girl in yellow who stepped into the loggia. A lovely color spread to her dark hair as she smiled at his stepfather, who grasped her hand as a drowning man might clutch at a floating spar. His expression was fatuous with relief.

"This is a great pleasure, Miss Diane."

"I'm sorry we've been so unneighborly, Major, but, you know how it is with us farmers—the days are filled with just one thing after another."

"I understand. Glad you came. I am sure that all our little disagreements can be ironed out, once we have a heart-to-heart talk. Also, you've arrived in time to help us welcome my stepson, Mac Cameron, just back from engineering in the jungle."

V

THERE was an instant of palpitating silence in the loggia before Patty-Lee purred:—

"How sweet of you to come, Diane. Doc Reynolds, see that our charming neighbor has tea, or maybe you need a cocktail, *chérie*? You're looking utterly done up. Don't tell me you walked in this heat. Had we known you were coming we would have sent the car for you, wouldn't we, Sethy?"

Patty-Lee's drawl was sugared to stickiness. She hadn't extended her hand when the girl had offered hers, Mac noticed. The soft color which had tinted Diane Vernon's face had receded, leaving her so pale that her eyes looked as if they had been set in with smoochy fingers.

She shouldn't be here after that crash in the brook. Hadn't any member of her family had the sense to realize that she should be in bed? Would she leave if he offered to take her home where she belonged? Fat chance . . . She had practically called him a robber. Doc Reynolds' piercing eyes, under scowling brows, were regarding her. Did he suspect that she was steadying herself by gripping the back of a chair? He had taken a step forward as if to carry out the order of his hostess when Larry Crane forestalled him.

"I'll get Di her tea, Doc."

His expression was that of a man whose dearest wish was gratified as he slipped his hand under her arm.

"Come over to the table under the spread of yon waving palm," he proposed theatrically. "I know how you like your tea to the last slice of lemon, Di."

"Why waste your life on the social stuff, Larry, when with a memory like yours for faces and people's weaknesses you'd make your fortune as a Cruise Director?" Diane's eyes, almost black now, smiled up at Crane as she passed Mac, still holding the tray, and his hostess standing close beside him.

Patty-Lee shrugged. Her heavily-fringed lids narrowed.

"Apparently I am not needed here, honey boy." She tucked the yapping Peke under one arm. "Larry seems to have taken over my hostess duties. Come on to the pool before our tea is stone cold and tell me all about South America."

"Who's the new gal, Patty-Lee?" he inquired in a voice pitched for Diane to hear as they passed the table at which she sat. The glance she threw him in return dismissed him coolly, indifferently, completely.

Putting on an act, pretending she'd never seen him before, was she? Crane had gone for tea and the Major was bending over her with that deep, tender, if-only-I-had-met-you-before look which, with his head-back laugh, would be one of his big assets with the female of the species who voted. In this case the female not only voted but was training the young to be voters. The change in the Major had not been his imagination. Cecily had commented on it.

"She's just a little country girl. Raises herbs for a living." Patty-Lee's answer to his question switched him from troubled consideration of his stepfather to his companion. As they seated themselves on the broad curb which framed the cerulean-lined pool, she curled up with the dog in her lap in the catlike way he remembered.

"She's Larry Crane's present heartthrob, honey boy. She thinks she's made a rich catch; he has even more money than your stepfather and that's saying something. How do you No'therners get so rich? He has an LL.B. with honors, I understand, though he isn't doing much at law at present. She's in for the surprise of her life. Someday he'll flit to another flower. You know Larry."

He didn't, he told her; never had heard of the man, much less seen him, before this afternoon; while he wondered how he could have thought himself in love with this woman with the cruel voice and malicious eyes. He had been. He couldn't fool himself. An acute attack of brainstorm must be the answer. . . . But had she been like this then? Perhaps living three years with a man she didn't love had turned tendencies to traits.

With the tray between them he drew her on to tell what she knew of her neighbors. She dismissed the elder sister with "Poor thing, she's an invalid. I call on her once a season and let it go at that." Touched on the herb garden, on their limited income, became voluble on the subject of Diane and the Young Voters' Club. "I hear she's been engaged *four* times."

"Four! Ye gods, even for a girl as lovely as she I'd say that was a pretty high batting average. How do you happen to know so much about her love life?"

"The Budge woman who opens the house for us told me. She hates her, claims that she is turning her youngest daughter, who works as a general maid for the Vernons, against the family. The Dominie's wife accuses the sisters of enticing the Reverend to their home for tea when he should be making pastoral calls. You know what a hotbed of gossip a country town like this can be."

"I wouldn't say that gossip is confined entirely to country towns. Didn't the Major meet these girls when he first bought this place four years ago?"

"No. They hadn't settled here then. He has tried to have business conferences with them, to which they reply only, 'We won't sell.' He doesn't like them. Thinks them terribly provincial and just between you and me, honey boy, even with his distinguished war record, he's afraid of Diane and her Club. They're getting on his nerves. Didn't you notice that he went absolutely gaga with relief when he welcomed her?"

Patty-Lee laid her small white hand with its gleaming nails on his sleeve. The dog growled.

"I'm telling you this—" her voice was soft and sweet—"not because I hold anything against Di Vernon, though the sisters are putting us to tremendous expense to prove that we really own the land they claim is theirs, but as a warning to you. It would break my heart to have her tricks succeed with you, now that Larry with his fortune is eating out of her hand."

"And I have no fortune you are delicately reminding me." He was glad that a curious sense of caution had kept him from telling her that he had inherited a fair living income from his mother. In the last few years it had been doubled by the Major's investments for him.

"Honey boy, don't be mean to me."

At that very moment Crane was saying:—

"What changed your mind about coming to Musgrave Manor, Di? I've heard you swear time and time again that you wouldn't set foot in the house this summer."

"I'm not in the house, I'm in the loggia." Diane took a huge swallow of the scalding tea. Much as she hated to accept anything from the Lovels she needed it if she were to keep her balance. Every few minutes chairs, tables, pillars appeared to swim into different positions. She should have had sense enough to stay at home after her fall, but she had wanted to please Merry and she never had believed in coddling herself.

"Don't quibble. I want to know why you came. Did you know this Mac Cameron before he arrived today? He's had his eyes on you ever since you appeared."

"Know him! Do you mean the man by the pool with our hostess? Is he the stepson I arrived in time to welcome? In her surprise at my appearance Mrs. Seth Lovel forgot to make me known to the assembled multitude. As to the stranger's interest in me, why not? I thought before I left home I was something rather worth looking at. My mistake?"

"Skip it, Di. I haven't been seeing you every day for a month—"

"Only three weeks and four days, to be accurate."

He laid his hand over hers, which she slid away quickly.

"I'm glad you've counted the days; I've checked up on the hours." He cleared his voice of huskiness. "You know that I think you're the loveliest girl I've ever seen. That I want to—"

"Please, Larry, not *here*."

"That's what you always say when I start to ask you to marry me! 'Not here! Not now!' When?"

"Never. I have too many problems to face to think of love or marriage." Those darn tears were rising again. She shut her eyes tight in an effort to crowd them back.

"But, Di, I'd be so glad to help with them. I could do so much for you. We'd comb the world until we found a man who could put Merry on her feet, we'd—"

"Merry isn't the only problem. The Lovels claim that our house and land belong to them. They do *not*. We've got that fight on."

"I've been thinking of that, Di. I'm a lawyer—though I haven't been doing much at it lately. I'll take your case."

"Really, Larry? Can you practise in this state?"

"By courtesy. I—"

"Look here, young woman," Doc Reynolds' gruff voice interrupted. He shook his out-size head, crowned by flaming red hair, and pulled at a bushy eyebrow. "I've been watching you. Every few minutes the world swims, doesn't it? Unless you want to make a spectacle of yourself by crashing— and from my observation since you arrived, you don't—go home and go quick."

Hand on his arm, Diane steadied herself to her feet. The loggia wavered grotesquely.

"Something tells me you're right, Doctor. Will—will you take me? I haven't a car outside. I walked here."

"Diane!"

She shrugged her shoulder free from Crane's hand.

"I'd rather go with Doctor Reynolds, really I would, Larry." She smiled vaguely. "He seems to know just how I feel."

"Come on, quick. My car is in the drive, if you can call it a car; anyway it goes. Stay out of this, Crane."

It seemed years to Diane before she was in a shabby jalopy headed toward home. She drew in great gulps of the salty air.

"Better now?" Reynolds asked gruffly.

"A whole lot better. How did you know?"

His laugh was surprisingly musical.

"I've seen plenty of tipsy women. As you passed up the cocktails and didn't look like a drinker, I concluded that you'd had some sort of a shock, possibly mental, probably physical. What happened?"

She told him of the crash in the brook; that she suspected she had passed out for a while.

"How long?"

"I don't know."

"Anyone else there?"

"Yes. A man pulled me out."

"What man?"

"He—he didn't tell me his name."

"Will you tell me why you hadn't sense enough to stay at home after a knockout like that? Haven't you even ordinary intelligence? I see red when women, the mothers of the nation, show so little sense and the youngsters know as little about the care of their bodies as they do about atom smashing."

"Thanks for the orchid handed my sex. Thanks also for giving me an idea. Won't you come to a meeting of my Young Voters and forcibly feed a little knowledge of the care of their bodies into their minds? You would be doing a work of charity. There isn't a physician within twenty-five miles to help them with advice. Here we are. Don't frighten my sister about me."

"Why? Has she even less sense than you have?"

"She has heaps more. Will you come and meet Merry? She will be having tea on the terrace."

"Sure. I shan't leave till I see you settled down in a chair."

He stopped the car at the front door and jumped out.

"Take it easy. Then your head won't spin."

As they entered the long hall, Merry, in her wheelchair on the terrace, saw them and beckoned. A man in clerical black, standing beside her, waved his hand. Reynolds' bushy brows drew together in a sharp frown.

"I see," he muttered.

Diane drew him into the living room.

"Then if you see, don't refer to my crash," she warned in a low voice.

"I won't. Who's the white-haired cleric, with the fine intellectual face, with her? Stands like a soldier and an officer. Your father?"

"No. Dominie Richards. He's the clergyman of the village. He was a chaplain in the first World War. Came back and built up a large city parish."

"Why in heaven's name did a man like that settle in this backwash town?"

"It isn't a backwash town. You couldn't find more up-to-the-minute, finer people anywhere than many of the so-called natives here. Now that that point is nicely settled I'll tell you about the Dominie.

"He took to himself a wife before he went overseas. It was one of those get-married-quick affairs indigenous to wartime. He accepted the ministry of the small parish here two years ago, thinking it would be better for her health. Quote, she can't breathe in a city, unquote. For the last ten years she's had a heart, if you know what that means, afraid to go anywhere. If they are invited out, at the last minute her heart acts up and she keeps him at home. She's afraid to do housework; I suspect that in the early years of their marriage she was afraid to have children. She's afraid to open her mouth. She talks like this." She mumbled something between lips pressed close together. "She's a dead weight."

"Does he think so?"

"If he does, only he and his Maker know it. He waits on her by inches. His parishioners, the whole village, adore him but they loathe her. I'll bet there isn't a thing the matter with her heart. There's a chance for you to make a reputation:

Convince her there isn't. She's a grafter. Merry and I try to spoil the old dear, encourage him to drop in for tea."

"Don't spoil him too much."

"What do you mean by that 'Beware the Jabberwock, my son' warning?"

"I mean that vitriol can escape from between lips as tightly pursed as Mrs. Richards'."

"She! Harm us? Don't be foolish. Merry will wonder why we are lingering here. Don't say that you're a doctor. She doesn't like them."

"I see. I'm John Reynolds. If she's curious, you might say, well, that I'm—I'm legal adviser to the Lovels."

"That's not so good either. Evidently you haven't been at Musgrave Manor long. Come and meet my sister."

VI

"Di, you've beaten your own record for short calls. I didn't expect you back for an hour at least." Merry Vernon greeted her sister as she appeared in the doorway.

"There was a crowd at the Manor. I was invited to ride home. I suggested to the driver that we have our tea with you. That's the story. Merry, Dominie, this is John Reynolds."

A curious sense of uneasiness flitted through Diane's mind as she noticed the startled flash in her sister's eyes as Reynolds' fingers closed strongly over the delicate hand she extended in welcome.

"We'll need more cups. I'll speak to Trudy," she proposed hurriedly. "She has turned on her radio. She won't hear the bell above that dance music."

"Sit down." Reynolds camouflaged the sharp command with a laugh. "Let me do my Boy Scout deed for the day. I'll speak to Trudy. Where will I find her?"

Diane flung a look of warning at him before she sank gratefully into the orange-cushioned chair he drew forward. Every few minutes her head spun like a top. Merry glanced quickly from his face to her sister's.

"Have you two conspired to keep something from me? You look guilty. Neither of you need go for Trudy. Even with the radio on she keeps one ear open for my bell. Two jingles mean two more cups. We have a system."

She was gay, debonaire. "What a sport she is," Diane thought and blinked back a surge of tears.

The Dominie rose.

"I really ought to be on my way."

"But you've just arrived. You haven't had your tea," Merry reminded. "When Trudy saw you coming along the drive she fairly rushed out your favorite fruitcake."

"It's quite a way to the village even on my two-wheeled steed Pegasus. Violet may have a heart attack if she becomes anxious because I am late."

Even as he protested there was a boyish gleam in his black eyes as they strayed to the silver plate of fruity cake on a stand beside the table. Dopey, squatted on his haunches near, slightly moist about the lower jaw, was regarding it with equal wistfulness.

"We won't let you go without your tea, Dominie," Diane declared. "I'll wager you've been making parish calls since your noon dinner. You must be tired. Pedaling a bicycle isn't my idea of a joy ride, to say nothing of the fatigue of having the trials and tribulations of your flock poured into your long-suffering ears."

The clergyman laughed and resumed his seat.

"The fleshpots of Egypt tempt me. I stay." His eyes twinkled. "It is rare that such delightful company and delectable cake fall to the lot of a man at the same time."

He reached for a plummy slice.

"We never have it at home—I'm referring to the cake, not the company—it's bad for Violet's digestion. Trudy, my child, how goes it with you?"

He smiled at the pink-frocked girl with the tray, who beamed in response.

"Swell, Dominie. You told me I'd like this job and I sure am crazy about it. Anything else, Miss Merry?"

"That will be all, thank you, Trudy."

"Mind if I speak to the minister a minute? Dominie, can't you stop Maw whinin' at me because I don't come home oftener? 'Tain't, 'tisn't that I don't love my family any more, like she's always crabbin', it's just that it's so quiet and neat and peaceful here. At home everyone does just what they want to and let the others go hang. Here there are—gee, I don't know how to say it—perhaps it's laws that keep you from doing or saying things to hurt or bother other people. Maw lets the brats go the limit. If they get too high Paw licks 'em an' Maw jaws at him. I know now that isn't the way to bring up younguns. They've got to be made to obey the little laws, then when they get older they won't break the big ones and land in the hoosegow."

"When did you learn all this, Trudy?" The Dominie's voice was very tender.

"Since I came here to live. Miss Merry and Miss Di are so— so, well, I guess what I mean is polite to each other and to Freda and me. Sorry I said brats, Miss Merry, I know you think it's kind of a cheap word to call kids. Will you try to make Maw let me alone, Dominie?"

"I will, Trudy. I'll talk to your mother, my child."

"Thanks, Dominie. Clean up the cake, folks. Don't leave any for me. I don't like it."

"That girl will have a keener appreciation of her job if she diets. She's overweight. I'll bet the bulk of her intake is chocolates." John Reynolds' matter-of-fact statement broke the silence which followed the maid's departure.

Diane glared at him. Merry might suspect from that observation that he was a dyed-in-the-bone physician.

"Here we are philosophizing while the tea cools," she observed gaily. "Merry, I am loaded with news. Flash one! The Major's façade is more impressive than ever. Flash two! The Manor, with its Old Charleston front, has gone Bermudian in its rear. Loggia, patio and what-have-you. It has been done over inside, all green and orchid and violet running into purple like a garden of iris. Flash three! Larry Crane has taken our case. He'll fight the Lovels for us. Flash four! The stepson has arrived from South America. I'll pour," she offered as her sister reached for the silver kettle.

"Don't let her do it, Miss Merry. You look as if you would be adept at the job. After you serve the Dominie, I'll have mine as it comes."

What was John Reynolds' idea in stopping her from saving her sister's strength, Diane wondered? Whatever it was it pleased Merry for she smiled as she lifted the kettle.

"You see, Di, Doctor Reynolds doesn't believe in spoiling me as you do." Her eyes looked straight into his. "It is Doctor, isn't it? Your profession fairly oozes from your voice. That remark about overweight clinched my suspicion. Now I know the secret between you. Diane told you that I sidestep physicians, didn't she?"

"You're not going to sidestep me though; I won't stand for it."

"A doctor!" The Dominie's voice was vibrant with excitement. "Have you come to practise here? I hope so. I *hope* so. This county has no resident physician. The need of one is tragic. There isn't one within twenty-five miles and the nearest hospital is one hundred. There's not even a clinic."

John Reynolds shook his head.

"Sorry. I intend to settle in New York. I want to be in constant touch with the big hospitals. I'm thirty-five, late in starting practice because I have had to work my way. I've no time to waste in the country."

The Dominie thoughtfully stirred his tea.

"I wonder if it would be wasted. Of course, of course you know your business, Doctor Reynolds. Miss Merry, may I have one more lump of sugar?"

"You wouldn't notice me at the Manor, so I came to see if you reached home safely," announced a voice.

Diane's heart leaped up, turned around and sank back into its accustomed place. The man who had rescued her from the brook was standing in the doorway. In his white clothes he appeared taller, was even better-looking than he had seemed then, which was quite unnecessary. Her sister was looking at her expectantly; so was the Dominie.

"Merry, Dominie Richards, this is the mysterious stranger who rescued me from the brook," she announced theatrically.

"If I had rescued you from a brook and you spoke of me in that voice, *I* would wish I had let you stay there," Merry remarked spiritedly. She smiled at the man in the doorway. The name is . . . ?"

"Cameron. Mackenzie Cameron—Mac to you—*very* much at your service, Miss Vernon. Doc, your hostess was about to send a crier after you, so I volunteered. A little matter of contract."

John Reynolds rose with a groan. "I'll have to go. I'm a paying guest at the Manor, paying with my contract game." He grinned companionably at Merry. "Which if I say it who shouldn't is a corker." He scowled at Diane.

"Will you go directly to bed after your supper?"

"I promise."

"I've never met you before today so I don't know what that promise is worth. I'll drop in this evening to see if you've kept it. If I find you up I'll put you to bed myself."

Diane's face was no longer white. It was crimson.

"And who appointed you my guardian?"

"I was appointed by the Lord to look after girls who

haven't sense enough to look after themselves. Does that answer your question?"

He laughed when Diane turned her back on him. He held out his hand to Merry Vernon.

"Have I made such a bad break that I can't come again?"

"You may come—but, but what happened to Di? I knew she fell in the brook but she laughed it off and I didn't think about it again."

"She didn't want you to know, thought it would frighten you, but I knew the minute I saw you that you aren't easily scared. Apparently she had a slight concussion. How long was she unconscious, Cameron?"

"Actually about five minutes. If you judge by my feelings— I was responsible for the crash—an eon or two."

"You see, Miss Vernon, it wasn't very serious, but she should keep quiet."

For a few moments after Reynolds' departure the tinkle of silver and the faint swish and swash of the tide were the only sounds audible on the terrace. Then Mac Cameron exclaimed:

"It's good to be in New England again! I was born in Massachusetts and lived there until I was ten. What a corking view! A limitless blue sky and a sea all blue-green ripples. Those white gulls look like out-size snowflakes, falling. What a superb summer estate that long wooded island would make."

The Dominie shook his head.

"There would be wigs on the green if it were sold to one person. It looms so large in the life of the village we spell it with a capital I. It is the favorite picnic ground and berrying place of our young people. Also, there's a hut which the fishermen and hunters use spring and fall, so don't set your heart on buying it, Mr. Mac."

"I won't, Dominie. I have reached neither the summer-estate age nor fortune yet. That's a wicked ledge looming like a shark's fin halfway between us and the Island. The solitary tall pine on it makes me think of the spar of a sunken ship in a cove near our South American camp."

"That ledge is the pride of the village. It carries about the only legend we have here. It is said—" the Dominie's eyes twinkled as he lowered his voice to a hoarse whisper— "that on foggy nights a sea captain in sou'wester and yellow slicker, whose ship foundered there with all on board, creeps along the shore road, swinging a lantern, moaning."

"The macabre touch. Your voice, sir, set me almost as

much a-shiver as Miss Diane's when she welcomed me—if you can call what she looked a welcome—a few moments ago."

As he spoke Cameron's direct eyes met Diane's and sent prickly chills merry-pranking through her veins. He rose.

"Having heard your sister promise to take care of herself, I'm not needed here, Miss Vernon. Doc Reynolds can't go back on that eagle nose of his; he'll see that his orders are obeyed. May I give you a lift, Dominie? I am going to the village."

"Thank you, thank you, Mr. Mac. I'd be delighted if there is room for my wheel in the rumble."

"Sure, there's room."

His bow to Diane had nothing on hers for frigidity. He turned up the collar of his white sports jacket and shivered. His teeth flashed in a smile. Sparks of laughter pricked through the gray of his eyes.

"Cloudy with increasing cold. Good afternoon, Miss Vernon."

For the space of five minutes after the roadster started there was silence. Then Mac Cameron exclaimed to the man beside him:—

"Isn't there any hope for Merry Vernon? Is she doomed to spend her life in that chair, Dominie?"

"Who can tell? 'More things are wrought by prayer than this world dreams of.' Tennyson said that, you may remember. We are all praying for her recovery and for a minute when I looked at that rugged Reynolds I thought, 'Here's the answer. He'll put her on her feet.' But I was wrong; he won't settle here."

"Science is striding along in ten-league boots. Something is sure to be discovered that will help. Think of the miracles medicine has worked already. No one should give up hope in this age. If a tough physical condition isn't conquered today it's bound to be tomorrow."

"You're right, my boy. Those are remarkable young women. Whenever I am in Honeywort House I am reminded of the line of an English poet's 'I came to a land where beauty dwells.' Beauty dwells there. Merry has beauty of spirit, it shines through her eyes. So has Diane. She has such gay courage. She is fighting. Fighting back utter helplessness, perhaps death, for her sister and smiling as she fights. She's a soldier. She loves the bright lights of the city. So do I. Occasionally we have a nostalgic heart-to-heart as to its lure."

"Where did the Vernons live before they settled here?"

"New York City. Their father was an eminent lawyer. There was money and social position. The parents died. So did the fortune. Merry met with an accident. They came here. Diane is trying to make our young people realize the privileges and responsibilities of citizenship. She has great influence. The girls here take her for their model. They say she's a 'snappy dresser,' if you know what that means. Since she came they no longer go through the village streets in those immodest—'shorts' I believe they're called. I love those two Vernons as if they were the daughters I've longed for and never had."

The Dominie cleared his throat and tugged at his clerical collar as if suddenly it had grown tight.

"We are passing the oldest church in the village. It is considered one of the finest examples of eighteenth-century architecture extant," he explained proudly.

Mac slowed the car the better to look at the rosy-brick building with its white spire and colonnade. Time had touched it gently as if loving its grace and beauty too much to permit it to be dimmed and crumbled by destruction's disintegrating breath.

"It's perfect outside. I wonder how many prayers have consecrated it inside during the centuries. Is this your home next door?"

"Yes. The Manse, we call it. Will you come in?" The Dominie stepped out as the roadster stopped.

"Thanks, no. I . . ."

A short, plump gray-haired woman, with a small Paisley shawl drawn tight over the shoulders of her white polka-dotted black dress, appeared around the corner of the house. She walked slowly as if afraid the next step might be her last. Her breath came as if pumped from her lungs, but the eyes which met Mac's were as brilliant, as hard and cold as blue zircons.

The Dominie hurried to meet her and drew her forward with his arm about her.

"Take it easy, don't overexert yourself, Violet, my dear."

"How can I help it?" Mac wondered that even her faint voice could squeeze between her tightly closed lips. "You are most inconsiderate, David, to make me worry on top of my other trouble. Calling on the charming sisters again, I presume."

Mac didn't hear the Dominie's apologetic answer. He was

thinking: "Of course she means the Vernons. Don't they realize that they have a sly enemy in this woman?"

VII

THE COOL night air, impregnated with the tang of the sea and vagrant little waves of spicy scent from the herb garden, stirred the gay yellow-chintz hangings at the windows of Diane's bedroom. She smiled as she heard the imperative *rat-tat* of the brass knocker on the front door. Would that be Doc Reynolds checking on her promise?

She listened. Heard Freda Swenson clump through the hall, heard her voice in answer to a question.

"The young ladies, they are both gone to bedt, Mister. They can't see no vun this evening. Vat's that you vants I should tell her? So! You coom to see if she kept her promise. You might have savedt yourself the trouble. Miss Di, she alvays does yoost vat she say she vill. Goodt-by."

The door closed with a bang. Footsteps on the stairs. A voice at her door:—

" 'Tvas a fella asking for you, Mees Diane."

"I know. I heard, Freda. It was Doctor Reynolds. Come in."

The erect, perfectly proportioned figure in white linen loomed over the bed—no bulges on Freda.

"Miss Merry all right and comfy tonight?"

"Sure, she iss all right, Mees Diane. I ben vith you three years an' you ask me that qvestion each night an' mornin'. Yoost trust me to tell you if she bain't, can't you?"

"I can and do to the limit. But why can't I help her more, why *can't* I? Don't you realize, Freda, what it means to love a person with all your heart and soul and be powerless to help her?"

"Sure I do, Mees Diane. I tank maybe, if you not try to help her so much, maybe she help herself more, maybe. Yoost because I ain't got husbandt or family you think I don't know lof? My fella in Sveden, he run off vith a dancin' girl. I tank I die. My heart break. I coom to this country. It got whole again. I lof Mees Merry. I lof you, else vy I stay in this small town v'ere only vun picture a veek? You two all I lof in the vorldt. Your eyes are big as dem glass doorknobs downstairs. So! On the chair you shouldt sit up an' I give your hair a goodt brushin'. Then you go to sleep an' stop vorryin' about Mees Merry, ya?"

"Freda, you're a dear."

Diane slipped into a daffodil-yellow lounge coat and sank into the low chair the woman pushed forward.

"I fell in the brook today. There's a lump big as an able-bodied ostrich egg on the back of my head. Go easy on that, will you?"

"Sure, I go easy." With slow, smooth strokes the woman brushed the girl's dusky hair up from her head. "I tank that feel goodt, ya?"

"Heavenly." She would have to call in a master plumber to stop the leak behind her eyes if this tendency to weep every few minutes didn't stop soon. "Has Trudy gone out, Freda?"

"She go yoost as soon as the dishes vere done. She didn't slam them, though, she vas real careful. She sang pooty all the time. I vas ironing an' I vatchedt her. She vants to be a goodt girl, Mees Di. She say she vant to be lak you."

"Me! Like *me!* You're wrong, Freda, she adores Merry."

"Ya, she tank she sveet an' all that, but she say you 'got vat it takes.' That Manchusto vas vaitin' for her. A girl so young like her has no business to be runnin' out nights in a no-goodt car vith a no-goodt fella like him; he taks her to dance place after the pictures. He talks mooch that there should be no rich peoples in the village. So. If they didn't coom here, his fader sell little of his fruit, ya? I tank he, an' Asaph Hicks's stepson, Danny Stark, belong to that gang that bustedt into the city folks' houses last vinter."

"I suspect them too. But Danny and the other boys are weak and easily led, not treacherous and bad like Luigi. I want to stop his coming to the house but, if I do, Trudy may meet him secretly, though she promised me she wouldn't."

"So! Don't you vorry about that girl, Mees Di. You got plenty on your mindt. She ain't your business."

"I feel as if the security and happiness of everyone who works for me is my business. I can't do much to help in the world outside my home but I can try inside."

"Sure, you can try. Bain't you helpin' havin' all them boys an' girls in the big barn one night each veek? But how far vill you get vith that fool mudder of Trudy's pullin' the odder vay? She iss crazy to get the girl marriedt. I tank she got empty room up here."

Freda slapped her broad brow with a large, capable hand.

"Fool mudders likely make fool children. I tank that. The folks in the village say . . ."

The smooth, even voice, serene as the woman's personality, flowed on and on. During the years Freda had lived at Honeywort House she had acquired the habit of collecting news, facts, gossip, to retail to Merry while she massaged her. The soothing, rhythmic monologue rarely was spiced with unkindness or malice.

"To stay right in the house he's coom, the man Mrs. Lovel broke off vith to marry on his stepfather, her husbandt. I tank it not so goodt."

It took a few seconds for the meaning of the words to penetrate the Nirvana of peace in which Diane had been drifting. Her eyes flew open. Was Freda talking about Larry Crane? Had he been engaged to Patty-Lee Deland before she became Patty-Lee Lovel?

"Who did you say was staying at the Manor, Freda?"

"Now vy you sit up straight like that ven I tank I talk you to sleep? I yoost say that Mrs. Lovel's old fella come to visit her an' you yoomp like I set off a bomb."

"What is his name?"

"I guess you vas asleep. I toldt you. He stepson of her husbandt. That Asaph Hicks he toldt me ven he brought the milk tonight. He said the fella coom today in a svell black auto an' Mr. Barnes, the butler at the big house, toldt him that Mrs. Lovel threw her arms roundt the fella an' he heardt them kiss vay back in the hall."

"Faulty technique."

"Ya!" The sound deep in Freda's throat registered her disapproval. "Such goin's on an' she marriedt. I tank it badt. That Asaph Hicks, he wiggledt his donkey ears and sniggledt.

" 'Perhaps now the Major iss startin' in politics his missus thinks she can play roundt with this—this Camera fella.' There, I tank I remember the name right."

So that was why Mackenzie Cameron had come. To see his old love. He had kissed her. Sickening.

"Don't brush any more, Freda. I'm practically in a state of coma now."

"I tank I talk you to sleep. I'm pooty goodt at that, ya? On the bedt you should go, quick."

"You're an expert. I can't wait to tumble in and keep my date with the Land of Nod."

Freda drew the covers over her.

"You sleep goodt now, I tank. Don't you vorry 'bout Mees Merry. I tak care of her like she iss a baby." She put out the bedside light and stole softly from the room.

The sea boomed against the ledge and set the buoy moaning. The wind was rising. It chattered in the blinds and set the old house creaking in all its joints. The Land of Nod must have been a mirage, Diane concluded. Wide-eyed she watched a golden rain of stars while on the screen of her mind memory projected scenes in the brook, in the loggia, at the Manor, the doorway to the terrace, with Mac Cameron occupying stage center in each.

She thought of the heavenly restfulness of his arms about her, forcibly ejected that memory and recalled the laughter in his eyes, the vibrant clearness of his voice as he had said, "Cloudy with increasing cold." There would be no pussyfooting in his life. He knew what he wanted and intended to get it. Dislike him as she did—how could one trust a man whom one suspected was here to help steal one's property —he hadn't seemed like a two-timing homebreaker. Apparently he was. He would get plenty of encouragement from his hostess.

Major Lovel had changed since last summer. He had been as urbane as ever, but she had felt that he was making an effort. Freda's yarn about "this Camera fella" explained it. He didn't trust his wife.

If Larry Crane took the case for Merry and herself, was there a chance that he would win it? He would be smooth, suave with judge and jury if it reached court. He was brilliant, but he had had no experience; yet beggars couldn't be choosers. As Merry had reminded, they had no money with which to fight and he would not want money. Would he expect her to marry him if he won?

She couldn't marry. . . . Ever. Merry needed her. She could have no divided interest. That was that. She would have to think up some other way of paying the debt. Perhaps he would accept a piece of their shore for his fee— there was none finer on the coast. Suppose the Lovels proved that it did not belong to the Vernons?

Why worry? Larry hadn't heard even the facts of the

case; perhaps he wouldn't take it when he did. Perhaps there was a chance that Patty-Lee would run away with her ex-fiancé, Mac Cameron, turn her back on the Manor and the Vernon acres forever. With that heartening conclusion why couldn't she park her problems and go to sleep? She could. Surprisingly enough she did.

She woke with a start. Had someone touched her shoulder? Had Merry called? How long had she been asleep? Wide-awake now, she swung her feet to the floor and reached for her green sandals.

No sound inside the house. It couldn't have been the swish of the tide, or the faint moan of the buoy, that had roused her; she had heard them for the last three years. Had a car stopped?

She belted her yellow lounge coat over matching pajamas and stole to the window of the book-lined room, at the front of the house, which was her study. A dark shape was silhouetted against a field of stars—Luigi's car in the road. Two figures. One had a hat pushed back on his head; the other, a girl, was twisting in his grip. Trudy!

She tiptoed down the stairs, gently opened the front door. Merry's rooms were on the first floor. If she wakened she wouldn't close her eyes again. She ran along the drive, into the road, to the car.

"Trudy," she said breathlessly. "Trudy, I waited up for you."

For an instant the world was as weirdly still as a shore road in a fog: then with a curse the man dropped the girl's wrists. She clutched Diane's arm. A firefly, caught in her hair, frantically flashed its tail light.

"Say, what ya go buttin' into other folks' business for?" the man snarled through one pulled-down corner of heavy lips. His voice was guttural but his speech was surprisingly free of foreign accent. The green stone in the cheap ring on his pudgy hand, which held a cigarette, glinted in the headlight like a sinister eye.

"I guess Trudy don't need no nursemaid to tell her can she go to a dance."

His face was rather handsome from the hair down until the mouth spoiled it. His eyes under their hooded lids were surface eyes. Diane wondered what thoughts went on behind them. She said as coolly as if her heart were not thumping like a tom-tom:

"Do you want to go to a dance, Trudy?"

The girl clutched harder.

"No, Miss Di, honest to God, I don't. I told him I didn't. I'm tired."

"Then come into the house, quick, before Miss Merry hears us. Good night, Luigi." The hint of triumph in her voice had not only been silly but dangerous, Diane realized as with a blasphemous mutter the man sprang into his battered car. He ground the gears with vicious force.

"Gee, I hope the noise don't wake up Miss Merry," Trudy whispered as they stole along the grass border of the drive. "He's awful mad. He frightens me stiff sometimes. He and Danny Stark are always talkin' about 'Soak the rich!' I guess if 'twarn't for the rich there wouldn't be much money in this village; just think of the jobs they hand out in cottage building. They've both got it in for Major Lovel at the Manor. They say he's come down here and is settin' out to tell the village folks how to run the town, brags he'll have the guys arrested who had high jinks in his cottage and some of the others which were closed last winter." She stopped, for lack of breath to continue.

"Don't you think they should be, Trudy? They not only destroyed property. They stole it." Diane wanted to ask the girl if she had a suspicion as to who were the ringleaders, but she was afraid to antagonize her.

"Well, perhaps, but they didn't start out with the idea of doing any harm. I guess it just grew from fun to wrong-doin', Miss Di."

"Lots of trouble begins that way when property rights aren't respected. We'll forget Luigi and his wild talk, Trudy. Let's get something to eat; I'm starving. We'll have a party."

With the remains of a roasted chicken on the kitchen table between them, crisp-lettuce leaves, a jar of mayonnaise and a loaf of bread they perched on stools.

"This sure tastes swell, Miss Di. Luigi didn't come across with a chocolate sundae after the movie as usual. Said we'd go somewhere after the dance and get one. I'm hungry."

"Curious how much better things taste when you raid the icebox. I could do with another second joint."

Trudy stopped nibbling a drumstick.

"I'll bet you were a lot of fun when you were young, Miss Di."

When she was young! Diane choked. A piece of bread had gone down the wrong way. At twenty-three did she seem so old to this girl? How could she appear youthful when most of the time her heart ached like an exposed nerve?

"Oh, I had a good time before I lost my hair and teeth, Trudy."

The little maid giggled.

"I didn't mean you were old like the Dominie's wife, Miss Di; gee, she must be 'bout a hundred. Don't you bother puttin' things away, I'll clean up." Her china-blue eyes sparkled. "I've had an awful good time at your party."

"I've loved it. Anytime you come home from a movie, Trudy, and don't want to go to a dance we'll do it again. I'll help you now."

Side by side they worked in silence. As Diane reached for the button to snap out the light, Trudy whispered:

"Don't you worry 'bout me an' Luigi, Miss Di. I don't like him special, but he's the only fella in town who has a car and a boat and plenty of bucks. I like to go places. I wasn't born yesterday; I can take care of myself. Just watch out for yourself. He's terrible mad at you, like he is at Major Lovel, and when he's mad, well, he won't stop at nothing to get even."

VIII

EXCEPT for the awareness of a tender lump on the back of her head Diane awoke the next morning refreshed and ready for the day's work. In worn brown-denim slacks and checked tan-and-white linen shirt she stopped at her sister's door. The redecorating had been worth the money, she told herself for the nth time. The spacious room was a soft shade of French blue from ceiling to floor. Sheer curtains of fine white dotted net stirred in the soft breeze. Over-draperies and two chairs were of chintz splashed with pink and crimson roses against the same blue ground. There was a slipper chair and chaise longue done in the plain pink. The few choice old pieces of mahogany added a note of dignity and serenity.

Merry was braced up in bed by pillows. A fluffy white swansdown jacket accented the delicate flush in her cheeks;

her brown eyes were clear and brilliant. Were they alight with excitement? Silly idea. . . . What was there for her to be excited about at this time of day?

"Have a good night, lovely?"

"Perfect, Di. How was yours? Freda said she 'tank you vere jittery so she talk you sleepy.' How's the head this morning?"

"Wouldn't know I had one."

"I expect your self-appointed physician will appear to check up on his patient."

"Did Freda tell you he came last night? Yesterday afternoon when that man beetled his brows, drilled his steel-point eyes into mine, cocked his brick-top head at me, all I could think of was a hawk preparing to swoop on a silly hen. He had me hypnotized. This is my busy day. If he comes you'll have to entertain him. I could tell that you liked him."

"I did. When his hand closed over mine my blood tingled. Was it magnetism or just my jumpy nerves? What are you planning to do this morning?"

"Asaph and I are scheduled to pick basil. Did Trudy waken you when she came in last night?"

"No. Did you hear her?"

"Yes, Luigi's brake groaned like a banshee. When I saw that he was getting rough I made my entrance. That lad's a bad actor."

"What do you mean, 'getting rough'?"

When Diane had finished telling what she meant Merry shook her head.

"It's dangerous for you to interfere with Manchusto, Di."

"Dangerous! Don't be foolish, lovely. What could he do to me? I'll admit though that I'm getting fed up having that girl on my mind. Her coming has changed me from a safe and sane person to one all suspicion with a dash of jitters. It's not the girl herself, she's harmless enough, but what she brought with her—'Maw' and Luigi. I have the feeling that I'm walking through a mined sector. It's curious how a person who works for you can become woven into the very fabric of your life. As if that wasn't enough I've picked up the good-citizen bug and am trying to teach the young— when I could do with considerable teaching myself."

Merry laughed at her rueful face and voice.

"Don't be low about *that*. Life will look after you. I notice that the lady, if Life is the female gender, never gets fed up with her disciplining job. You'll feel more hopeful after you've had your breakfast, dearie."

It wasn't only breakfast, which had been excellent—as an omelet and bacon chef Trudy certainly was improving —that sent her spirit soaring like a trial balloon. It was the air which shimmered and cast an illusion of unreality over the familiar world, and the gorgeousness of coloring which made anything seem possible. The smooth sea stretched and stretched like an enormous blue-velvet rug patterned with green islands, from bouldered shore to purple, hills. The buoy was silent. In a rock-spotted field a safe distance from the beehives a black-and-white dog was digging frantically, sending up a shower of dirt as he pawed. On the top of a near-by boulder a bunch of tawny fur crouched in watchful waiting.

"Morning, Di. War news turrible this mornin', ain't it?"

The small, loose-knit man in work-stained overalls and torn striped shirt, with deeply lined face, weasel eyes set near together like black shoe buttons in tanned leather, and enormous hairy ears, leaned an elbow on the top of the terrace parapet and peered at her from beneath the flapping brim of a big hat. With a knobby hand he shifted his pipe from one corner of his platter mouth to the other.

She had discovered three years ago that Mr. Asaph Hicks scorned prefixes. At their first meeting he had called her "Di." It had startled her at first; now she took it in her stride.

"It is, Asaph. I turned on my radio while I dressed. It makes one heartsick. No matter what I am doing, all the time in the back of my mind I hear the beat of drums of war. One can't ignore it in the life of today any more than one can a minor motif in a symphony."

"Well, I guess ther' ain't nothin' you an' I can do 'bout it yet. What in heck makes you so lazy this mornin'? Looks as if you was listening to sperits."

She had been listening, but not to spirits. It had been Freda's voice: "One! T'other!" like a chant. What was she counting?

"I'm still on earth, Asaph, and ready for work." She pulled on a pair of gloves which had done veteran service.

"Then if you be ready let's git at the basil. If 'tain't picked today somethin' may happen to delay us, then we can't git it in proper condition to dry."

His words whistled through his teeth. Whether the hiss was congenital or should be charged to a faulty dental restoration Diane never had been able to decide.

As on their knees they worked side by side she inquired for his wife.

"Martha's upset. She's always upset 'bout Danny, that long-legged kid of hers. When she ain't worryin' fer fear he'll be drafted into the army—I tell her he's too young, don't do no good—she's worryin' because he won't study. He ought to be at work; stid of that she's bound to keep him on at school. School's all right enough if you've got a head for learnin'; he ain't. She gives him all the money she makes from cookin' an' balsam pillers. He's always off shootin' with thet camera of his an' then workin' in a dark closet developin' films when he ain't trailin' at the heels of Luigi Manchusto. He ought to help her more. He don't set out to be bad, but he's gettin' into bad company."

"Have you ever known Luigi to have a steady job, Asaph? He dresses well and apparently has plenty of money to spend."

"He picks up a livin' with his string of lobster pots, an' clammin' an' fishin'. Good one too, looks like. He's got a log shack on the bluff above the cove where he keeps his boat. The Dominie's wife hires him to drive her in that old car of his an' M's Lovel has him for odd jobs. That fella's cut out to be one of them slick small-town gangsters you see in the movies. He's smart as a steel trap. He talks American almost like a native but he's like a rotten apple in a barrel that spoils all the others if 'tain't yanked out quick. He's leading the younguns in this village into bad ways, but no one's been able to prove anything against him. Danny was all set to join your Young Voters, then all of a sudden he says it's 'kid stuff.'"

"Do you think Luigi was behind that?"

"Sure he was. I wish you'd talk to Martha, Di. Tell her the boy ought to git a job. If I say anything, she cries an' says I'm a miser, that I count every cent's worth he eats. I don't. Cripes, I wus gettin' along all right by myself. Why in heck did I hev to go an' marry a woman with a kid?"

Why did she marry you, you old grouch, Diane wondered before she championed.

"Martha is a grand person, Asaph. She's a wonderful housekeeper and her cooking can't be matched by anyone in this town. I don't believe in giving advice but I'll drop in on her as soon as possible. Perhaps she will bring up the subject of Danny herself. I agree with you that he would be a whole lot safer at work and she would be happier about him."

"She thinks a powerful lot of you, Di. She'll listen to you when she wouldn't to me. If we could only hang somethin' on that Luigi Manchusto so's we could railroad him out of town then the whole village would breathe easier. Well, this conscription law they're goin' to put through ought to mop him up. Heck! Here comes Major Lovel. They tell me he's fit to tie 'bout the things that was done to his cottage last winter. Swears he won't pay a cent of taxes till the parties who stole and messed the house up is landed in jail. Can't say's I blame him.

"But of course, he may be doin' the youngsters injustice. It might have been some tough guys off the boats that put in for pulpwood durin' the winter that done the mischief. Several folks said they saw fellas in yellow oilskins sneakin' round one of the nights things was stole. What's Major Lovel got on his mind to bring him here this time of day?"

Diane glanced from under the brim of her hat at the man in slacks and cardigan no whiter than his hair. A half smile indicated that he was occupied with his usual smooth, successful thoughts. He was handsome enough to qualify as a musical-comedy father. She had no one but herself to blame for this visitation. Her call at the Manor yesterday had opened the door for it.

She disciplined an urge to hide, instead walked between rows of herbs, through the gap in the stone wall.

"Were you looking for me, Major Lovel?"

His face beamed like the rosy orb of day about to disseminate benign sunspots on a troubled world, all but his eyes—they were remote and tired.

"Oh, there you are, Miss Diane. The very person I want to see."

"Then come up on the terrace." She pulled off her work gloves. She had raised her voice hoping that Merry might hear and be wheeled into the room with its open window. A witness to the forthcoming conversation was greatly to be desired.

With an air the Major waved her to a chair before he seated himself.

"Charming, charming home you have. How jolly all this looks." He indicated his surroundings by an all-embracing movement of his hand. "Such a pleasant spot in which to spend the warm hours of the summer. Tremendously good of you to welcome me here. Mind if I smoke?"

She didn't, she told him, and tried to curb her impatience as she waited for him to light his cigarette. He settled back in the chair and crossed his knees.

"I've come to lay all my cards on the table, Miss Diane, to appeal to your well-known belief in fair play. My wife wants this place; we really need it to complete Musgrave Manor. There are two planes in my hangar. An estate the size of ours without a landing field is a back number these days. We are planning also to extend the links. Naturally I want to give her what she wants—I am sure you are romantic enough to understand a man's great love for a woman. Now, as neighbor to neighbor what's your price for your holdings?"

He spoke with all a rich man's assurance that his money could buy whatever he wanted, with a suavity tinged with patronage.

Diane matched his smile.

"As neighbor to neighbor, Major Lovel, we have no price. We will not sell." Her voice was quiet, incisive.

"Have you and your sister so much money that you can afford to refuse my offer, Miss Diane?"

"That's another question, Major, and you'll forgive me, I hope, if I remind you that the answer does not concern you. We will not sell."

There was a "They shall not pass" quality to the reply that set a smile twitching at the corners of her lips. . . . Good theater.

He rose and tossed his cigarette over the rail, his urbanity gone.

"You understand, I hope, that I have offered you money for that which is Mrs. Lovel's by law?" His voice was sharp, taut. "I have discovered deeds to prove her claim."

"Of course, when you prove it the estate will be yours. Meanwhile . . ." Diane glanced expressively toward Asaph on his knees in the herb garden.

To her amazement the Major's laugh boomed.

"Meanwhile I am holding up your work; I get you. Work! Great Scott I know what that means. I began as a boy of sixteen and kept it up until two years ago when I retired from active business with the intention of devoting my time and strength to giving this state good government at low cost; old-age social security; extended vocational education; better roads; industrial surveys; a fairer deal for farmers, a decent deal for the fishermen and adequate defense."

He paused and Diane wondered if he were unconsciously waiting for applause for what was undoubtedly a choice morsel from a future campaign speech.

"It's a grand platform, Major. I hope that also you will devote a little time and attention to the protection of property. It's a scandal that houses can be entered and abused as some of them were in this town last winter, that the vandals are still at large."

"I shan't wait to be elected Governor to take the leaders into custody, Miss Diane. Already I have them here ready to squeeze when the right moment comes."

He opened his smooth white hand and closed it slowly, then smiled his large, assured smile.

"That's enough about that at present. To get back to my errand this morning. There must be no hard feeling between neighbors, my dear. Right is right, you know. When we prove that this estate belongs with Musgrave Manor—there is a boundary rock marked V at the southeast corner of the land you consider yours which will clinch our claim—we must still be friends."

" 'If,' not 'when,' Major," Diane corrected gaily. "Now that the matter is nicely settled—that we are to remain friends, I mean—will you excuse me if I get to work? Asaph is such a tyrant. Good morning."

She knew that his full, crimson mouth hung slightly open as she ran down the ramp.

IX

AGAINST the dark-pine walls of the living room at Honeywort House the orange and yellow marigolds, in a gleaming copper bowl on the grand piano, glowed like flames. Larry Crane forked smooth fingers through his fair hair and looked up from the blueprint spread on the flat desk.

He frowned at the girl in lime-yellow slacks-and-jacket outfit perched on the broad sill at an open window.

"Read the last sentence in the description of the southeastern boundary of the land sold to the Lovels, Di."

She smoothed out the sheet of foolscap with its red seals.

" 'From thence to a rock with a V cut in it at the southeast corner.'

"There isn't such a rock, Larry. I've spent the greater
portion of my waking life hunting for it and most of my
sleeping life dreaming of it, since the Major assured me
when he called to negotiate a peace pact a week ago that
it marked the boundary of the land his wife could legally
claim. If it is there, and his deed is genuine, we're wiped
out. If he gets that, the next thing we know he will claim
that the emeralds Grandmother willed to me and the pearls
she left Merry belong with the part of the estate he bought."

"The Major wouldn't cheat. Under that supersuave manner of his he's a grand person with grand ideas. His latest
is to train a Civilian Defense Group here. He honestly believes the land he's fighting for belongs with Musgrave Man-
or. Even were he tempted, he wouldn't dare be dishonest;
he has settled in this village to lay the foundation of a
political future, hasn't he?"

"Yes, Larry, but politicians aren't always strictly pure,
are they?"

"If they have brains they are likely to appear to be until
after election." Crane referred to a letter he had picked up
from the desk.

"He writes that in the interest of fair play, he has engaged an engineer to excavate for the buried bounds and—"

"Mac Cameron, that precious stepson of his, I presume.
Why didn't he stay in South America? So what! The letter
changes nothing. Our old deed still holds. As our attorney,
you may reply to said Major that if his wife's representative
steps foot on our land to excavate without our permission,
I'll take measures to see that it doesn't happen again and I
mean it. I'll stand guard with my trusty gun." She laughed
and nodded toward a rack at the end of the room.

"Good Lord, Di, your temper is ninety per cent com-
bustible, isn't it? But I like it," he approved fondly. "What's
the idea of the rifle?"

"To protect my property from marauders. You may not
know, not being a horny-handed son of the soil, that skunks

have a weakness for hens, that hawks kidnap young chicks, that foxes hypnotize geese. I'm good with a gun."

At a sound outside the window she turned.

"Why are you prowling round here, Luigi? You know that Trudy has no time in the afternoon to see you."

The swarthy-skinned youth regarded her with a hint of slyness in the surface eyes beneath hooded lids. As she looked at him Asaph's words clanged through her memory:—

"If only we could hang somethin' on that Luigi Manchusto we could railroad him out o' town."

"Ya got me wrong," he pointed out smoothly. "I didn't come to see her, Miss Diane. I brought these for Miss Merry. Trudy said she liked 'em. They're the first pickin'. Got 'em on the Island." His words, which were intended to denote friendliness, soured as they squeezed past the cigarette dangling from a corner of his mouth.

He thrust forward a shiny-tin quart pail full to the brim with large, luscious high-bush blackberries.

"They are perfect, Luigi. What are you asking for them?"

"I ain't selling. They're a present for Miss Merry. I picked 'em for her."

He held up the pail. Diane hesitated before she leaned from the window and lifted it by the handle.

"Thank you, Luigi. She will love them."

He touched his hand to his rough black hair and swaggered away. Her eyes followed him as he stepped into his decrepit car, lingered on it until with a snort and grinding of gears it twitched and hopped out of sight.

She looked up at Larry Crane standing beside her, then down at the pail.

"Luigi is a caveman if ever I saw one. Something tells me I shouldn't have accepted these for Merry."

"'I fear the Greeks even when bearing gifts.' Why? What's the matter with the chap?" Crane popped an over-size berry into his mouth. "Golly, nothing the matter with his berries." He picked up another.

Diane slid from the windowseat, held the pail behind her and laughed.

"Grafter! These are for Merry. Luigi will pick some for you, if you make an offer financially alluring."

She explained her distrust, added:—

"He doesn't come to the meetings of the Young Voters' Club and I'm ashamed to admit that it's all right with me."

"How many do attend?"

"An average of thirty, which is not so good as it might be, but a whole lot better than when it started. The high-school quarterback is President. He's a born leader. That fact has brought a number of his satellites into the fold. I'm after the to-be voters as well as the indifferent registered voters. Since the summer people have come I've managed to have an interesting speaker at each meeting. Doc Reynolds is slated for next week. He's bringing lantern slides to illustrate his talk on the importance of the care of their bodies and a knowledge of first aid."

"That sounds like sense to me. Now you'll have to invite the Dominie to orate to them on the care of their souls."

"He has done that. I'm trying to decide to ask Major Lovel to speak. He's a spellbinder, I understand."

"Fair enough. It is a club for voters, isn't it? You've given them medicine, religion, why not politics?"

"I'm in a spot. I don't want them to admire the Major. I am afraid they may vote for him. He'll be a colorful candidate. He is planning to start high; the Governor bee is buzzing merrily in his bonnet."

"Just like a woman. You boast that your club is nonpartisan and you are letting a prejudice make it partisan."

"It is nonpartisan, Larry, honestly it is. I never say a word to influence their vote—but, well, it's not a prejudice but a fact that the Major's so darn glamorous they will be apt to forget that when they are voting for a governor, they not only are voting for the highest executive in the state, but also for the man who will appoint judges over life and property. Since he has tried to grab our land I wouldn't trust to his sense of justice."

"Say, where did you learn so much about politics?"

She dimpled adorably.

"The dominant male. Surprising as it may be to you, though only a woman, I read the papers, tune in on the radio to follow this country's problems, and the most terrific fight for freedom this old world has ever staged, and, on occasion, think, just when I can't help it, mind you."

"You're ribbing me!" He caught her hand and drew her close. "Di, I love—"

"Look out, Larry, or I'll upset this pail." She extricated her hand. "The berries remind me—I wonder how long Luigi Manchusto had been behind me at that open window, how much of our conversation he overheard."

"Suppose he heard it all. It wouldn't mean anything to him."

"I'm not so sure. Wasn't I bragging that if the Major or his representative set foot on our land without permission I would do direful things to him? Stand guard with my trusty gun? I wouldn't be surprised if he repeated everything he heard—if he heard anything—to 'Maw' Budge, who is thrusting Trudy at him, while I'm trying to save her from him. She would be glad to hear anything she could use against me.

"The woman argues that married he'll settle down and in time take over his father's fruit business which is a going concern. Thereby the Budges will come in for a rake-off. That's enough about the town's bad boy. If I don't watch out he will get to be an obsession. I'll take the berries to Merry. Put away the papers—we shan't use them again today—and then come to the porch for tea or a cold drink."

"Make it a cold drink. Cameron's the tea hound. Probably picked up the habit among the English in South America. Just to keep the record straight don't forget I love you, that I've put the Indian sign on you. I hear that Doc Reynolds has been dropping in here every day. I don't like it."

"He doesn't call on me. I hardly ever see him. Too busy. I'm a working woman. Freda tells me that he and Merry have grand talk fests."

"That makes me feel better. I've had a snappy launch sent down for you. It's at the Manor but the man in charge of the boathouse there understands that you are to use it whenever you feel the urge. I'll join you in a few minutes. I want to make notes from the blueprint and copy of the deed."

"You're a prince to provide a launch for me to use. Thanks a million."

She wished he hadn't imported the boat, she thought as she left the room. If Patty-Lee knew why he had sent for it she would be poisonous about it. She stopped in the hall. Voices . . . Someone must have come by boat. That purr could belong to no one but Mrs. Seth Lovel. Who was with her? How many?

She carried the berries to the kitchen. There would be none of the luscious things left for Merry if the callers saw them. She would insist on sharing.

"Serve some of these for Miss Merry's supper, Trudy. Are the tall glasses frosting in the icebox?"

"Sure, Miss Di, with swell sprigs of mint as you told me. I put 'em in every day. Miss Merry's sure to have callers. Gee but she's popular."

"That's because she makes people realize that she is interested in them. Get some lemons, quick. I'll mix a drink. When Miss Merry rings, bring out the filled glasses and a plate of thin cookies on the silver tray. We won't serve tea."

"Yes, Miss Di." Trudy beamed. "That's what I like about my job, something always going on in this house."

She would say there was something going on at the present moment, Diane agreed, as she stepped to the terrace. Patty-Lee Lovel in an amethyst-linen frock, an orchid kerchief tied over her fair hair, was lounging in a deep, low chair. The Peke, tucked under her arm except for its black mask the color of red amber, was growling at Dopey, who squatted on his haunches beside Merry. The English setter's reaction to the visitor's haughty superiority was a bored yawn. Scarlet, on a window ledge, thrashed her plumed tail as she regarded the visitor through wary green slits.

Mac Cameron, in tan slacks and matching golf jacket of gabardine, perched on the terrace, slipped to his feet. Merry's cheeks were as delicately pink as her crepe frock. Diane heard her soft sigh of relief.

"Oh, here you are, Di! I sent Trudy to find you. She said you weren't in the house." Her head dropped back against the cushion.

A hand of steel squeezed Diane's heart. How easily Merry tired.

"That Trudy girl couldn't find an elephant in a hayfield, if elephants park in hayfields," she evaded lightly. "Ring for her, Merry, she's preparing a cold drink for us."

"Before I forget it, Di, my memory for *trifles* is about an inch long," Patty-Lee confessed indifferently. "I'll deliver my husband's message. The Newcombs, he's that sensational best-selling author who is summering here, and their guests are coming for dinner, next week, Friday. Twenty at table. Cards to follow. The Major wants you to come. He says, 'Why act like enemies because we differ about a boundary?' Formal dress—I hope that won't embarrass you. I presume that life in the country doesn't require much of a wardrobe. If you haven't anything suitable, we'll excuse—"

"Thanks for counting me in. I will be charmed to come," Diane accepted with a promptness that cut Patty-Lee's sentence in midstream. She had been about to decline but at the crack at her wardrobe the intention had veered like a weathervane in a gust of wind. What a chance, what a divinely provided chance to wear Grandmother's spectacular emeralds and cause her hostess' eyes to pop with amazement and envy!

"The Major is right," she conceded. "Why act like enemies? I haven't an enemy in the world," she proclaimed theatrically.

"No? That's a break." Mac Cameron sighed with exaggerated relief. "Then I won't have to apologize for my intrusion, Miss Diane. I didn't want to come, but as there was no one else to play skipper for my hostess here I am. Patty-Lee's afraid of the water even in a trim little number like that."

Diane's eyes followed his to the slender, gleaming launch swaying lazily at the Honeywort House pier. Was that the boat Larry had sent down for her use? If it were he had shown his usual lavish disregard of cost in selection.

"Trim is the word for it. This year's model, isn't it?"

Patty-Lee shrugged indifference.

"I really wouldn't know." She dropped a kiss on top of the head of the Pekingese. "Stop growling, Precious. Mummy doesn't like it. Larry imported the launch for me. He insists that I get sea-minded before we go to Bermuda. He's taking a party of us there in his cruiser in September."

Diane wondered what would happen if she announced that the launch had been imported for *her* use. Unless Patty-Lee was lying he had handed her the same line. At that instant he loomed in the doorway.

"Why Larry, where did you come from?" Merry Vernon exclaimed.

"Come from! Didn't you know that my client and I have been in consultation in the living room since luncheon? Howdy, Patty-Lee. Greetings, Cameron."

Mrs. Lovel sprang to her feet. Precious, held tight under one arm, yapped at the arrival.

"*Your* client! What do you mean, Larry?"

He shrugged and ran his fingers through his light hair.

"I mean that I am the defendant counsel in the Lovel *versus* Vernon case, though there won't be any case. I'm sure that the matter can be settled out of court. It's dumb in these days to fight over fifty acres of land when nations are fighting to grab nations."

"So what? All that rigmarole adds up to the fact that you've bought her, I presume?"

"What do you mean, Patty-Lee? Bought *who?*"

"Don't put on the dumb act, Larry. I mean Diane, of course. It's a trade, isn't it? You help her fight for the land she claims is hers, and she marries you."

"Marries me! Say, where did you get that beautiful idea? Did you tell her, Di?"

"Don't go haywire with joy, Crane," Mac Cameron cut in coolly. "Of course she wouldn't tell us before she told you. Don't you know Patty-Lee well enough to know that she has to have her little joke?"

"It isn't a joke, you'll see. I'm going at once to tell the Major that you have betrayed his hospitality, Larry," Mrs. Seth Lovel announced furiously. "Honey boy, come."

"If you mean me, no," Mac refused lightly. "I can see from Crane's furrowed brow that he is fairly bursting with eagerness to explain to you why he is appearing as counsel for the defendant. I should be in the way. Let him run the launch. I'll walk." He laid his hand lightly on Merry's shoulder. "You're not to worry about anything, remember." He grinned at Diane. "A good time was enjoyed by all," he chaffed and entered the hall.

"Cameron is right, Di," Larry Crane admitted. "I'd better go along. I do owe Patty-Lee an explanation; she and the Major have been mighty nice to me. I'll be seeing you."

He pressed his lips fervently to her hand, before he followed the woman who was hurrying toward the boat landing along the path bordered with Orange King and Lemon Queen calendulas, which glowed like two rows of footlights against a background of dusky purple petunias.

The frenzied barking of the Pekingese drifted back. Planted firmly on all fours, nose quivering, Dopey followed the departing figures with his eyes.

Merry watched the launch as it slid away from the boat landing; her trapped, tortured eyes came back to Diane.

"I can't bear it, Di, I can't! To see you all so alive and I—I all my life to be like th—is!" Her voice broke in a harsh sob.

Diane pressed the shining head tenderly against her breast.

"Don't you mind, lovely, don't you mind," she comforted brokenly as she smoothed the soft hair. She blinked furiously to keep back tears. "You won't be always like this, you *won't*."

She held her sister close as if by the very strength of her love she could make those words come true. In her heart she pleaded:—

Why can't I do something to help? Why can't I, God?

Merry's convulsive sobbing quieted. She freed herself from Diane's arm and dabbed at her eyes with a wisp of pink chiffon.

"I'm all r—right now, Di. Sorry, I went to p—pieces. J—jitters. Just plain j—jitters. Happens in the best-regulated families at times, you know."

Her breath caught in a strangled sob but her eyes, between long wet lashes, glinted with laughter.

"Run up the clear-weather signal, dearie. S—storm's moved out to sea. L—let's have a game of rummy."

A few minutes later she looked at Diane, seated across the small table.

"I'm glad Mac Cameron wasn't present when my nerves crashed."

"Why? Who gives a rap for what he thinks? Your deal, lovely."

Merry Vernon held a card suspended. "Di, have you ever heard the expression 'More flies are caught with molasses than with vinegar'?"

"Meaning *what?*"

"Meaning that if we treat Mac Cameron as if we liked him,—to be honest I wouldn't have to try; I like him already *very* much—his smile warms my heart through and through —we *might* win him over to our side."

"So help me, you've got something on the ball." Diane's eyes shadowed; she shook her head. "Not interested. You may like him; I don't. I don't trust a man who plays tame cat to another man's wife. That's what he's doing. I can't be a hypocrite. I won't. It isn't in my line."

"Of course, if you'd rather lose this place, that settles it. We'll leave him to his Patty-Lee. Listen. Trudy's singing."

> "Work for the night is coming.
> Work through the morning hours—*ooch!*"

"She must have cut her finger. She sings that song—or 'Christian, up and smite them'—when she's paring potatoes or doing any other chore she hates.

"'Work through the morning hours.' Work. *Work!* That's the answer, Di. Work is the only remedy that can immunize me against despair." Merry flexed her fingers. "Notice how much more limber they are? I keep exercising them. Why shouldn't I try to draw? Why *shouldn't* I?"

"You should, lovely, you should. Write to Jim Brewster

and ask him to let you try some illustrations." Diane's voice was shaky with eagerness.

"I—might do that, now. He—he wrote me that he is engaged." She drew a letter from under a cushion. "I've been holding out on you, Di. Read it."

"Well, of all the gay deceivers, you're the ace, Merry Vernon." Diane ran her eyes down the page.

"Hm, short if not particularly sweet. Doesn't even tell you the happy girl's name. Write to him, will you, Merry?"

"Yes. Now that he is engaged, he won't want to see me, so I won't have to fight his coming."

Diane glanced at the letter she had dropped to the table.

"I—wonder—" she breathed softly.

"What did you say, Di?"

"Just wondering whose play it is. Yours. Attagirl!"

X

$\mathcal{P}$ERCHED on the low granite wall of the terrace Diane thoughtfully watched the shadows move along the herb garden as fluffs of cloud drifted across the slanting sun.

The scene reminded her of the morning she and Asaph had picked basil and she remembered that he had asked her to talk with Martha about Danny and she had said she would; that had been, also, the morning that Major Lovel had called to lay all his cards on the table.

The days that followed had been so filled with work and social affairs, which Merry had insisted upon her attending, that she hadn't been to the Hicks's cottage, which was on the upper side of the highway halfway between Honeywort House and the Manor. She would go this afternoon. . . . Now. She had planned to slip away to her favorite cove on the shore with a book she had been eager to read. That could wait. She dreaded the talk with Martha. All the more reason to get it behind her.

"Why that prodigious sigh?" Merry closed the book she had been reading. "What's on your mind? Anything I can help about?"

You are on my mind for one thing, Diane thought. You are getting thin and there's a look of strain about your eyes and mouth. Even that pink-linen frock doesn't give you color. Freda says you're "doin' fine." Why can't I believe her?

"You are troubled, Di. You can't fool me. It's not like you to sigh."

"Did I sigh? Must have been because I'm getting lazy and hated the idea of trudging upstairs to change this playsuit to an honest-to-goodness frock."

"Why change? That full green-and-white striped skirt covers the shorts under it and the socks and shoes don't leave quite the expanse of bare leg affected by most of the girls who come here. Going somewhere?"

"Yes. To call on Martha Hicks. Ostensibly to order doughnuts for the Young Voters' meeting tomorrow night—Doc Reynolds is to speak—really to talk with her about Danny taking a job. Asaph asked me to. As a rule I don't take much notice of his crabbing—it's a chronic condition—but this time I think he's got something. The boy is palling with Luigi Manchusto."

She resisted the urge to repeat Asaph's "If we could only hang something on that Luigi Manchusto we could railroad him out of town." The words were becoming an obsession; they flashed through her mind at the most absurd times. She had even repeated them to the Major's valet, Nicols, one day when he had brought a magazine to Merry.

"Why go? You have enough on your mind without taking on the Hicks's family problems. You're too young, dearie, to have so much care. You put in a lot of time at the piano teaching Trudy, but do you realize that you never sing yourself now? At home you were always trilling arias, singing ballads or gay popular songs. I miss it."

Don't you know that when you were struck down my singing went with you? Diane only thought that. She said:—

"A little canary in the home. Sounds rather boring to me." The smile in her eyes and on her lips vanished.

"How can I trill and sing, lovely, when night and day I listen on the radio or read of the tragedy taking place overseas? When the security of our own country is threatened and even in this village citizens are breaking the laws made for their protection and are so darned indifferent to their privileges as voters? What chance will we have of riding the gale of internal trouble, or external for that matter, if the people don't wake up to their responsibility?"

"It is terrifying."

Why had she brought up the memory of tragedy to one

who was living in a little private inferno of her own? Her attempt at a laugh was not too good but it brought a responsive tilt to Merry's mouth.

"How'm I doing as a campaign loud-speaker? Perhaps the Major will hire me to hop on his bandwagon. I may have lost the inner urge to sing, lovely, but I can still dance. I practise each day against the time Hollywood will hand me a glittering gilt-edged contract on a gem-set silver platter. Like a preview?"

"I'd love it."

There was no doubt of Merry's sincerity. It was in her voice, her smile.

Diane set a record in the phonograph. To rhythmic swing and beat of brass and strings and horns, she tapped with amazing grace and finished her dance with a kick which set the vines in a hanging basket she touched with her toes shaking as if with a nervous chill.

"Bravo! That's a honey!" From the doorway Doc Reynolds shouted and applauded approval.

Hand on her heart Diane took a bow.

"A Di Vernon Production," she announced grandiloquently. It was a second before she dared look at Merry. Had the dance emphasized her helplessness? No—she was laughing and clapping her hands.

"Isn't she wonderful, John?" she asked.

"Wonderful. My favorite dancer and telegenic, too, I'll bet. How's tricks, Merry?"

So he calls her "Merry" and she calls him "John," Diane thought as in her room she slipped into a yellow-linen frock. Why not? He sees her every day, doesn't he? Be pretty silly to stick to "Doctor" and "Miss Vernon," wouldn't it?

The memory of the two greetings pricked like a splinter in her mind as she walked along the road toward the village. Suppose Merry fell in love with him? He had nothing to marry on. . . . She wouldn't, of course she wouldn't. Pete still had all her heart.

She forced her attention to the gardens she passed. The pinks and blues and violets of early summer were changing to the yellows, russets and reds of August. A cicada shrilled. Apples showed a faint touch of crimson. Their fruity scent was considerably denatured by the fumes of gasoline trailed by automobiles as they whizzed by.

"Hi, Di."

The hail came from a black roadster. She had only time to recognize Cecily Cole's titian hair and Mac Cameron beside her before they were out of sight. Giving the Cole girl a rush now, was he? How did his Patty-Lee like that? He certainly had a way with women. Hadn't Merry confessed that she liked him *very* much? It was that gay smile of his which did the trick. Just why was she getting hot about it? It didn't matter to her whom he took out, did it?

After her walk along the sunny road Asaph's white, vine-covered cottage with its window boxes rosy with petunias seemed drenched in coolness. She could hear the trickle of water through a labyrinth of lush green ferns as she waited for an answer to her knock, could see gnarled old apple trees, heavy with fruit. In front, fields loped to the ocher-tinted boulders along the shore and beyond them the sea sparkled as if the contents of sapphire and emerald mines had been scattered over its surface.

Martha Hicks opened the door in answer to her knock. A faint light wavered over her thin face, with its twitching left eyelid, and went out. She was gray from the top of her head to her feet. . . . A depressing person.

Diane stepped into the sitting room where the spicy scent of balsam, from a pile of gay pillows on a table, fought with the lingering smell of baking and won. A crayon portrait of a bewhiskered man on the wall was flanked on each side by a black-framed, waxed funeral wreath which encircled the silver plate from a coffin. Green-checked gingham draped the windows. The furniture consisted of poor-relation pieces from many periods, but all was immaculately clean and polished to the grain. A tan-and-white dog on an old bed puff in the corner thumped out a welcome with his tail.

It was a second before Diane discovered chinless Maw Budge, with face as full of ridges as an English-walnut shell, rocking by the fireless fireplace. This helps, she thought as she returned the woman's sullen nod. Where do I go from here?

"Sit down, Miss Diane; I'll put the kettle on and we'll have a cup of tea."

"Thanks, Martha. I'd love it. No one can match your tea and cinnamon toast."

Mrs. Hicks drifted into the kitchen like a gray wraith. Di heard her lift the lid of a stove, stuff in a stick of wood and drop the lid back. Maw Budge stopped rocking. Her faded, closely set eyes sharpened. She leaned forward.

"If you don't quit turning Trudy against Luigi Manchusto, I won't let her work for you no more," she threatened.

Diane shrugged. She watched a ruby-throated hummingbird fanning its wings like the propeller of a plane above a pink petunia outside the window as she answered:—

"All right with me. I don't really need her. A number of girls from High have applied for her job."

The woman's bluster oozed like the air from a punctured gasbag. Maw Budge knew that Trudy was being paid wages which, inexperienced as the girl was, she couldn't earn anywhere else at present, and that she was taking home the bulk of the money.

"Don't get me wrong, Miss Diane," she whined. "I wouldn't take Trudy away, what with your poor sick sister needin' her—"

"My sister isn't poor and she isn't sick and you can take Trudy—"

The door burst open. A frowsy-haired small boy, dirty as only an uncared-for dirty small boy can be, charged into the room.

"Maw! Maw, come quick. Joey's fell off the leanto roof and busted his head wide open."

"Land sakes, what'll that brat do next?" Mrs. Budge jerked the ends of the small shawl about her bent, round shoulders into a knot. "Anyone had the sense to patch him up, Cal?"

"No, Maw. Paw, well, Paw's—" he glanced slyly at Diane —"he's asleep, I guess. Betta hurry. Joey's bleedin' something terrible. Someone said there was a doctor stayin' at the Lovels'. I phoned from the drugstore but he ain't there. What'll we do, Maw?" He jumped up and down in his terror. "Why don't you come? Joey's awful bloody. What'll we do?"

Diane laid a comforting hand on his shoulder.

"Stop crying, Cal. I think I can reach the doctor. You and your mother hurry home and keep Joey quiet."

She waited till the door had banged behind them before she dialed. Doctor Reynolds was still at Honeywort House, Freda answered. She would tell him about the Budge child.

"That's that," Diane reflected as she hung up the receiver. Doc might not thank her for wishing the improvident family on him, but it seemed the only thing to do.

"What's become of Maw Budge?" Martha asked as she dirfted into the room with a tray. "She never goes before she has her tea. She sets and sets till she gets it."

Diane explained. Perhaps this was the psychological moment to approach the ticklish subject of Danny and his job.

"Those small Budge boys will grow up to be town pests, if something isn't done about them."

"Grow up to be! Them kids are pests now. How's Trudy

gettin' on?" Mrs. Hicks filled a cup with tea which looked strong enough to curl her lashes up tight. She picked up a half-finished dark-blue sock and commenced to knit.

"Very well. She's a bright girl. Having a job and earning money has done a lot for her. But then, it does a lot for anyone. It gives a person a sense of responsibility and a sort of *What-a-big-boy—or girl—am-I* satisfaction."

"Asaph thinks Danny ought to go to work, but I don't know's I—"

"I ain't goin' to work, Ma, no matter what the old skin-flint says."

The dog on a pile of rugs in the corner languidly thumped a welcoming tail. A seventeen-year-old youth was standing in the kitchen doorway. His hair, light as flax, waved over his long, narrow head, except for one lock which dangled above his right eye. His eyes were brown; there were laughter lines at the corners. . . . Nose inconsequential. The lips of his large mouth were full and red. Not a bad face.

"Now don't get mad, Danny," his mother placated. "No one's goin' to make you work, if you don't want to, dear. Come in and speak to Miss Diane."

His tread was as light as a panther's as he crossed the room.

"How are you, Danny?"

A smile dispelled his sullen frown. It was a likable smile. He shook the lock of hair away from his eye.

"Fine. How's yourself, Miss Diane?"

"Simply grand. If you'll sit down and be good I'll let you have a slice of cinnamon toast." She passed a plate and laughed. "Only one, mind you. I can't spare more. Oh, Martha, I almost forgot what I came for. Send up eight dozen doughnuts tomorrow. It's Young Voters' night."

"Eight dozen! Gosh, you're expecting a crowd, ain't you?"

"Almost all the village young people have joined, Danny. Often they bring friends and you know your mother's dough-nuts. Nobody stops at one. Doctor Reynolds is to talk to them this week and will show slides."

"Pictures? *Camera* pictures?"

"Yes. He thinks you all ought to know how to take care of your bodies and what to do in case of accident. First aid has saved many, many lives."

"Do you suppose he'd know how to mend Skip's leg? Come here, fella."

The dog rose, hopped forward on three feet, laid his head on the boy's knee and looked up with melting eyes.

"Hurts, don't it? He got it broke chasin' a fox that got one of our geese. If I had a gun, I'd blast that critter to kingdom come."

"Why Danny, you can take that pistol of your own pa's that's in a trunk in the attic. The cartridges are there an' it's got something he called a silencer. It's yours, dear. He was real proud of it and kept it clean as a whistle."

"Martha! Martha. Danny mustn't have a pistol. He isn't old enough. It isn't allowed by law."

Mrs. Hicks set her lips in the obstinate line which only a weak-willed woman can achieve. Her eyelid twitched as if electrified.

"I guess Danny can have his own father's pistol, if he wants it, without you interfering, Miss Diane."

"Ma, keep your shirt on. Miss Di ain't interferin', she's just tellin' you. I know the law, what I can do an' what I can't 'less I want to land in the hoosegow. Luigi's got it down fine. D'you think the doctor would look at Skip's leg if I come to the Club meetin' tomorrow?"

"I'm sure he would." Diane rose and crushed on her hat . . . No use in staying now to talk about a job for Danny. "Come and bring him."

"O.K. I'll come—if I'm let."

"What do you mean by 'let'?"

"I guess he means me. I'm his boss. What I say goes."

It was Luigi Manchusto's thick voice—Luigi himself leaning negligently against the frame of the kitchen door. A cigarette hung from a corner of his mouth.

"You mind your own business an' let my Danny alone, you—you devil! Or I'll—"

Martha Hicks's tall, angular body twitched with fury; so did her eyelid. Diane regarded her in amazement. Could this be the drab, spineless woman whom she had known for three years?

"Now Ma! Now Ma!" Danny's eyes appealed to the scowling face in the kitchen doorway and came back to his mother. "Don't you take on. 'Course he'll let me go to the meetin' if I want to. Won't you, Luigi?"

"Sure, dope, sure. P'raps I'll be there myself." His laugh had menace in it. "Come along out. I wanta talk to you."

Martha Hicks was shaking as with a chill as she watched them leave the room. Her teeth were bared. A tigress defending her young. Diane laid a tender hand on her shoulder.

"Sit down, Martha. Luigi wouldn't dare hurt Danny."

The woman's fists were clenched till the knuckles showed white.

"Let him try it, that's all. Let anyone try to hurt my Danny an' they'll be sorry."

The fight went out of her. She dropped into a chair. With elbows on her knees she pressed her hands to her head.

"I hadn't ought to get wrought up like that, I hadn't ought to." She drew a long, sobbing breath.

Diane refilled her cup.

"Drink this hot tea, Martha. It will pick you up. You don't want Asaph to find you upset, do you? Almost time for him to come home."

"Land sakes, is it?"

The mention of her husband's name worked a minor miracle. Mrs. Hicks sat up, seized the cup and drained it. She smoothed her hair with shaky hands before the old mirror.

"Do I look's if I'd been cryin', Miss Diane? Asaph will say sharp things if he thinks I have. He's so upset 'bout the way the Lovels are carryin' on 'bout your land that he's ready to snap at me 'bout anything. Some husbands are like that."

"Dab your eyes with hot water and then cold, Martha, and you'll be all right. I'm going. Eight dozen doughnuts tomorrow, remember."

Diane was considering the household she had left as she walked along the road and wondering if there were any way in which she could help Danny Stark break away from Luigi. She must. If only she could discover something to hang on Luigi—

"Cab, lady?"

She jumped as the voice derailed her troubled thoughts. Beside her, Mac Cameron was holding open the door of the black roadster. Could he help? In an engineers' camp he must have had experience in managing even tougher characters than Luigi Manchusto. She met his eyes, which always held a quizzical light when they met hers. She didn't like him. Why be a hypocrite and pretend that she did for the sole purpose of getting his help? She shook her head.

"Not interested. Thanks," she said and walked on.

She heard the slam of the door; from the corner of her eye saw the black roadster shoot ahead.

XI

Oᴜᴛsɪᴅᴇ the long barn, which in its prime had housed forty cows, the tide crooned in a low B-minor to accompany the
muted moan of the buoy. Stars winked knowingly. A cloud
fluff floated across the face of the one-eyed moon. Amber-
green waves foamed over the ledge. A salty breeze set the
twisted pine swaying like the ghostly periscope of a submerged submarine.

Inside was the dusk of lowered lights, the scent of hay
fringing the laden lofts; the fragrance of drying herbs; the
hum of a projector, the voice of a man; the squeak and groan
of collapsible chairs as the Young Voters and to-be Voters
craned their necks and twisted their bodies to see the picture on the screen.

The Stars and Stripes and the State Flag with its solitary
pine tree flanked the table at which Diane sat, beside the
presiding officer, the president of the Club. She could see
the pale blurs which were faces. Who was in their midst
handling the films? It couldn't be! It *was* Mac Cameron. Doc
Reynolds had told her that he had brought an assistant to
run off the pictures. She had been too busy before to question whom it might be. His face was ghostly as he bent his
head within the radius of the lantern light. Was there merit
in Merry's suggestion that they try to win him to their side?
Would it be inexcusably hypocritical if she pretended
friendliness? Merry wouldn't have to pretend. She had declared that she liked him. Why consider it? That approach
had been blocked when she had so snootily refused to ride
with him yesterday.

She forced her attention to the speaker's strong, resonant
voice; it helped thrust the memory of Mac Cameron into the
background.

"If when you reach home tonight you find a shining new
car that is to be yours, all yours, will you shove it into the
barn or garage and leave it there, to use when you feel like
it, boys and girls? I bet you won't. Every moment you can
spare, and a lot you can't, will be spent learning the strength,
the possibilities of that machine, polishing it, caring for it,

keeping it in perfect condition that it may give back to you the maximum of efficiency.

"That's the way you should regard your body, only more so. Know it. Care for it. Keep it in perfect condition. Money won't buy new parts. It's an invaluable machine which, with you at the controls to steer from the tower room we call the brain, can do anything, get you anywhere. That's all."

The lights went up. The soft sough of released attention swept through the barn. Chairs were pushed back and folded. The youthful audience surged toward the speaker.

Diane wove through the crowd, returning affectionate greetings, noting the interested faces, the awakened eyes. She gave the lantern stand where the operator was checking up on films a wide berth, stopped to speak to her sister, who, with Freda Swenson like a white sentinel behind her chair, and Dopey, stiff with responsibility, squatted beside it, was near the door.

"Smash hit I'd call it, Merry. I've never seen the Young Voters so intensely interested."

"How could they help being? Doc Reynolds has strength, force, also a wealth of sympathetic understanding, I've discovered in our many talks. I had the absurd feeling that his eyes were reaching mine through the dusk. While listening to him it was easy to believe that I could spring from this chair and walk to him." A wave of color as delicately pink as her frock spread to her hair, as if she only that instant realized what she had said.

"Miracles do happen, if not always those for which we long," Diane answered gruffly to hide the emotion which swept through her as she remembered her sister's reply once before to those same words: "But they can't yet bring back the dead." Diane cleared her voice and reminded lightly:—

"Time for refreshments. Smell the coffee! Dee—licious! I'll tell Nicols we are ready to eat. What would we do without that man? He's priceless."

Mysterious sort of person Nicols, she thought, in an effort to push her sister's breathless exclamation and the memory of her lovely flushed face into the background. She and Merry hadn't had the heart to refuse the valet's offer to help at the Club meetings on his free evenings. He had been so pathetically eager to be of use, so respectful without being in the least humble, and apparently so very lonely.

"Is everything ready, Nicols?" she asked as she entered the large box stall which had been converted into a serving room.

Bugs beat and buzzed against the screen at the open window. The smell of kelp blew in. A huge electric coffee urn sent forth an appetizing aroma. Long pine tables held trays of plates with cups set on paper doilies, flanked with spoons and cubes of sugar. There were wicker baskets heaped with plump, crisply brown doughnuts and wooden boards with a half-dozen different cheeses.

"All set, Miss Diane." Nicols removed the huge white apron which had enveloped him. Pulled down the sleeves of his blue shirt and linked the cuffs. "The doughnuts look especially good tonight," he approved as he slipped into a brown-tweed coat.

"Good! They are poems in bronze. Makes me ravenous just to look at them. Martha Hicks has bettered her best tonight. Are you sure we have enough? Many of the members took advantage of their privilege to bring guests."

A smile, like a sudden flash of sunlight in a dark room, illumined his thin, grave face.

"Eight dozen! Enough? Not having plenty to eat is a sort of fixation with you, isn't it, Miss Diane? We always have a lot left over as in the Miracle of the Loaves and Fishes."

She looked at him quickly. "Who are you really, Nicols?" was on the tip of her tongue. She caught back the words. What right had she to be curious?

"I haven't forgotten how hungry I was when I was the age of these boys and girls. My appetite now isn't on the anaemic side. You know, don't you, Nicols, that we couldn't serve refreshments at such large meetings if we didn't have you, that I appreciate your help more than I can say?"

His face flushed.

"Thank you, Miss Diane. It is I who should be grateful. I can help you more. Ever since you told me of your distrust of Luigi Manchusto I've been on the watch. He's a clever cad. I suspect there is more going on than fishing in that log—"

"Well, well, here you are, Miss Di. I was told to look for a red frock and I would find you. And it's a corking frock and mighty becoming if you ask me."

Major Lovel, in white dinner clothes, loomed in the opening of the box stall. His snowy hair shone like silver; the pine walls sent back his booming voice. His smile was as debonair, his certainty of welcome as assured as if his clash with her on the porch two weeks ago never had taken place. His eyes flashed to his valet, then back to her.

"Don't look so startled, my dear. You and Nicols have every right to whisper together, if you want to. A little bird told me that the Young Voters were meeting here and I dropped in to pay my respects. I'll say a few words of encouragement to them if I may. Also, I would like to explain my plan for a Civilian Defense Group. The young, my dear, the young are a vital force in this country. Glad that my valet has the time to help you."

If the Major had thought to embarrass the man by the hint of sarcasm in his voice he had missed his guess. Diane watched the lean, highbred face as Nicols replied:—

"Thank you, sir. I knew you would be glad to have me help the young ladies, your neighbors. Shall I sound the gong, Miss Diane?"

"Yes. Major, the Young Voters will be thrilled to meet you and hear you—*after* refreshments. You'd better join the speaker and my sister at the other end of the barn pronto, or you stand a chance of being trodden under the hoofs of a hungry horde as the boys rush here for trays. Hurry! Here they come!"

"I'll follow . . ." He dodged the brawny quarterback of the high-school eleven, who was making a flying tackle for a tray, and vanished.

"I'm crazy to know what you've found out, Nicols. It won't be safe to tell me here. I'll plan to see you," Diane whispered. "I hope that helping us won't make trouble for you with the Major," she added as she placed the cups he had filled with steaming coffee on the doily-covered plates.

"Why should it?" The man's voice was honestly surprised. "My time is my own after my work is done. It is far more likely that what I have discovered may be dangerous for you, Miss Diane."

Had he really added that low warning or had she imagined it, Diane wondered later as she adjusted records in the phonograph. The boys had made such a racket getting the trays to pass that his voice had been almost drowned. Now the Young Voters, having satisfied the pangs of hunger, were dancing to the rhythm of "Beautiful Lady."

"Let me do that. I had a lot of practice in camp. Listening to music was our number-one diversion," Mac Cameron offered as he stopped beside her.

"Thanks. I don't need help."

"*My* help you mean. Look here, Diane . . ." He answered the flash of her eyes. "Oh, all right, *Miss* Vernon. Sorry. You see I've come from three years in a place where we thought a prefix unnecessary. Rather silly for you to insist on formality when we are likely to be neighbors for weeks."

"*Weeks!* I understand that Mrs. Lovel has engaged you to probe for the missing bound. Don't tell me that you expect it will take weeks to find it."

"Taking up sarcasm in a big way, aren't you? I hate it in a woman."

"You prefer the purring type?" Diane snapped back and immediately wished she had held her tongue. She was handing out vinegar, not molasses.

"That's what you think." With hands thrust into the pockets of his white dinner jacket he faced her. "You've been hearing things about me. Not half so much as I've heard about you. You write for magazines. Raise herbs. Run the Young Voters' Club and the Red Cross. Play the church organ, train the choir and have been engaged *four* times. A four-ring love story. Gone modern like the circus, haven't you? You're three down on me there."

"Engaged! *Four* times! Why I've never . . ." She caught back a word. "Good heavens, give me full credit for my mass love affairs. Make it five. With fifteen million men in the United States neither married, widowed nor divorced and only eleven million in a corresponding group of women I just have to encourage some of the poor dears, don't I? I just have to love them."

She flashed him her best smile and knew by the quick contraction of his brows that her flippancy had scored, that her change of mood puzzled him. She had stalled on her furious denial of having been engaged even once in the nick of time.

"You're wasting your talents in the State of Maine. Hollywood should be your home."

"Who is being sarcastic now? I am trying to be friendly and you won't—Oh, John Reynolds," she hailed the doctor as he approached, "I can't thank you enough for your talk tonight. You have put something into the minds of these boys and girls they will never forget. You made me think, too. You made me feel that anything is possible of achievement."

"I hope I made someone else think. I wasn't talking entirely to the Young Voters. As I looked at your—the audience—I decided something. I shall settle in this village. Start my practice here."

"Really! Do you *mean* it? It sounds too wonderful to be true. We need, the whole county needs, a resident physician, terribly." Diane's eyes darkened with sudden doubt; her enthusiasm trailed away.

"But you've said that a man could get a better start to be near the big hospitals."

"That's right. I've thought that by so doing I would acquire the fame which every intern believes to be his inevitable destiny. But I've come bang up against an assignment—call it duty, if you're old-fashioned—and I can't dodge it. That Budge family you wished on me makes me sick. The physical condition of those four kids is a disgrace to the town, the state, the country. There must be more like them. I've got to stay here."

Diane drew a startled breath.

"It's rather terrifying when one thinks how quickly and entirely a plan may be ditched by a chance happening, isn't it, Doc? I drop in to see Martha Hicks; Maw Budge is there; her boy Joey 'busts his head wide open'; I phone you. Presto! The design of your life is changed. It isn't only the physical condition of those boys that is alarming, they are *les enfants terribles* of the present and are on the toboggan to be the problem boys of the future."

"I gathered as much." Reynolds pulled at a bushy eyebrow and lowered his strident voice. "Here I am blaming others for not doing what I swore I wouldn't do myself—settle in a small town. I've promised the Major to head the medical-service unit in his Civilian Defense Group. I see work here that needs doing and I'm going to lick it to a finish—unless I'm needed in the army." Dogged purpose was in his narrowed eyes, in the rigidity of his jaw.

"'Christian up and smite them,'" Diane chanted dramatically. "I'll stand on the ramparts and cheer."

A laugh eased the tension of his face.

"And that means," he interpreted, "that you will have to give me your help and an unqualified recommendation. You're a witness, Mac," he reminded the man who apparently had been absorbed in examination of the record discs. "I'll deputize you to check up on her and see that she keeps her agreement."

As Cameron did not answer he focused his steel-point eyes, cocked his brick-top head, at Diane.

"Have you thanked Mac, prettily, for his part in the program? He passed up a gilt-edged dinner and cards to help me."

Cameron regarded her quizzically.

"She has. Overwhelmed me with gratitude. She—"

"Say, Doc, I liked your pictures a lot. Gosh, I'm crazy to be a real photographer." It was Danny Stark's voice which interrupted. He shook the lock of flax-colored hair away from his eyes. "Will you think I'm awful fresh if I ask you to take a look at my dog's leg?"

"What's the matter with it?"

"Busted I think. I'm awful sorry to trouble you, but Miss Diane said she thought you'd look at it. You know—I—I—well, I guess perhaps I'm screwy about Skip." He brushed his sleeve across his eyes.

"I was screwy about a pup myself once. I'll take a look at him. Where is he?"

"In the fliv. Outside. Gosh, I'm obliged, Doc."

Reynolds grinned at Diane.

"Looks to me as if my offices will be crowded if you have anything to do with it. Come on, fella."

They walked off together. Mac Cameron laughed.

"I can see where the Doc will get plenty of work. Who's the good-looking chap who is crazy to be a photographer?"

"Danny Stark, our handyman Asaph's stepson. He and I are worried about the boy. He's in dangerous company. I'm sure he isn't bad. If only we could get him interested in some sort of work. There's nothing more steadying than a job, but he refuses to take one. He's too young to be called for military training. If only I could find something to hang on Luigi Manchusto which would railroad him out of town." She laughed ruefully. "Those words of Asaph's are getting to be a refrain in my mind."

"Is Manchusto a native?"

"No. His father, honest, public-spirited, was here when we came but Luigi appeared for the first time about two years ago."

"Two years! Only two years?" He smiled as he met her troubled eyes. "Don't take life so hard, soldier. Together we ought to be able to beat a small-town bad boy. I've just had a hunch that we can. I may be able to help with Stark, also. I—"

"O Mr. Cameron! Mr. Cameron!" It was the quarterback with a rosy-faced, scarlet-lipped, eager-eyed girl clinging to each arm. "Doctor Reynolds told us that you had some corking colored movies of your work and location in South America. Will you show them to us at the next meeting? I'm slated for M.I.T. when I get through High. Nuts about engineering. Will you do it? Ask him to, Miss Di? You're the Honorary President. He'll do it for you."

Why didn't Mac Cameron say something, instead of standing there regarding her with aloof detachment? Having practically told him that he was not wanted at Honeywort House the first time they met, she was now forced to go on her knees to him, figuratively speaking.

" 'Now is the time for all good men to come to the aid of their party,' " she reminded jauntily. "Please show the pictures, Mr. Cameron."

"What's the date of the next meeting?" he asked the quarterback and wrote the answer in a notebook. "I'll be with you."

"Hiar! That's great. Come on, I'll make the announcement; after that we'll have to listen to a pep talk from his nibs the Major. Can you bear it?"

As the boy dragged the two girls after him, Mac Cameron grinned.

"Almost choked you, didn't it, *Miss* Diane?"

"What do you mean? *What* almost choked me?"

"That hunk of humble pie you had to swallow. Watch your step, soldier. 'Pride goeth before a fall.' . . . That applause is for the Major. Let's move nearer. Handsome fella, isn't he?"

Much as it irked her Diane had to acknowledge that he was. He stood on the platform against a background of the Stars and Stripes. An overhead light turned his white hair to silver. He outlined his plan for a Civilian Defense Group, named the eight departments that would be taken care of by subcommittees and closed with a short peroration on the need to defend the country against all aggressors. It wasn't altogether what he said, it was the sheer power of his personality that brought the audience to its feet applauding till the rafters shook.

Diane turned from the speaker to glance over the eager faces. Suddenly her blood chilled, her heart stood still. Near her, Luigi Manchusto leaned against the big door. His face was chalky. His eyes, fixed on the white figure on the platform, were narrowed with hate; a cigarette hung from a corner of his saturnine mouth. She caught Mac Cameron's arm.

"Look! Look at Luigi," she whispered.

He laid his hand over hers.

"I've been looking. In fact I've watched him since the Major began to speak. Is it the Major himself or the Major's plan that's burning him up? Guess which."

XII

DIANE VERNON dropped her white-marabou jacket on a chair in her sister's sitting room, and turned slowly for inspection, before the old-fashioned, gilt-framed pier mirror between the windows.

"Think I'll be able to hold up my head among the other evening frocks at Mrs. Seth Lovel's dinner, lovely? Will I do?"

"Do!" Merry Vernon drew a long, unsteady breath. "Do, in that enchanting costume of embroidered white organdie? Your neck and bare arms look like pale gold in contrast. You've done a beautiful job of tanning, Di. To add the final touch of perfection, Grandmother Vernon's jewels. With every move of your head the diamond leaves above the pear-shaped emeralds in those sensational earrings gleam like locomotive headlights. Why didn't you wear the necklace?"

"Too much glitter." Diane held out her right arm. "The enormous ring and two bracelets are enough. Of course, anything so sumptuous is out of place with an organdie frock, but I couldn't resist the temptation to dazzle my hostess. I'm just a little show-off at heart."

"Appropriate or not, I'm glad you have a chance to wear them; it doesn't happen often. The pearls Grandmother left me, valuable as they are, can be worn every minute. I love them." She touched the lustrous string about her neck with her left hand.

"Lovely! Where's your yellow diamond? You haven't lost your ring?"

"No." Merry Vernon thoughtfully regarded her white fingers. "No, it isn't lost, Di. I decided that it was holding me in the past when I *must, must* be looking forward, setting sail on uncharted seas with banners flying, instead of back over my shoulder like Lot's wife. The metaphor is slightly mixed, but you get what I mean. The girl who loved Pete was killed when the truck struck her sedan; a woman was born at that minute, born into a world already smoldering with hate and savagery. She must go forward. That's why I asked Freda to put the ring in the safe." She cleared her husky voice and smiled. "That's the story. Title, *The Rebirth of Merry Vernon*. . . . The glamorous Patty-Lee will be consumed with envy when she sees those emeralds, dearie." Her tone indicated that the subject of the yellow diamond was closed.

"I hope so. That's the underlying idea—that and forcibly feeding her with the fact that living in the country on a small income doesn't automatically bar one from owning swank frocks, even if they are more swank than expensive."

"You have a flair for clothes, Di. They are not only swank, they're always in good taste and dramatic. I hope you will meet interesting people tonight."

"That goes double for me. I accepted because Patty-Lee Lovel made me see red, shot through with green rockets, when she so indifferently delivered the invitation; now I'm glad I'm going. Getting into evening clothes has proved a pick-me-up. I'm fed-up with slacks, ballerina swimsuits, tweeds, linen frocks with an occasional burst into prints. Won't it be a joke if, after my snooty attempt to dazzle my hostess, she thinks my jewels are costume? If she doesn't think so, I'll bet she intimates as much."

"Never mind what *she* thinks. If she tries to snub you, just remember that *I* think you're too beautiful to be true. Isn't she, Freda?" Merry asked as the woman entered the room.

"Ya! She sure iss very pooty. Your coat, I holdt it for you, Mees Di. So."

"Thanks, Freda. Here goes Cinderella," Diane announced gaily, to ease the hurt consciousness that she was off for an evening of gaiety leaving Merry behind. How would it feel to fare forth really lighthearted, with no regrets?

"This frock may look like dream stuff, but the magic spell will be broken when I rattle up to the Manor in the dingy station wagon, with that asthmatic engine breathing like a grampus. I don't know what a grampus is, but it sounds as if it would puff. No fairy godmother touch to that."

"You can't go in the station wagon. When Asaph was coming from the post office it laid down in the road and refused to budge."

"Why didn't you tell me? I can't walk in this frock. Too late to phone the village for a car. I would have sent last-minute regrets if I had known."

"I knew you would so I got busy. You're not the only executive in the family, dearie. I telephoned Nicols. He is coming for you in his car."

"The Major needed Nicols," announced a voice from the doorway. "So I came. Hope you don't mind, Miss Diane."

It was Mac Cameron speaking, Mac Cameron standing on the threshold. He wore a light topcoat over his white dinner clothes.

For one hectic second Diane was tempted to pull off the fluffy marabou jacket and declare she wouldn't go. She had had several attacks of repentance for her coldness to him that evening in the barn when he had given up his own plans to assist Doc Reynolds, when later he had offered to help break Luigi's hold on Danny Stark. It was after that they had stood close together watching Luigi Manchusto, as with burning eyes on the Major his face had registered hatred and rage. . . . Did that twitch of Mac Cameron's lips mean that he realized she was tempted to put on the spoiled-child act? She'd fool him.

"Not only ready but willing," she announced with a smile and could have bitten her tongue through for that "willing" as a wave of dark color swept to his hair.

To hide her answering flush she bent quickly over her sister and laid her cheek against the top of her head.

"Good night, lovely. I'll tuck a cake from the party into my bag for you. Don't lie awake listening for me, promise."

"I promise. Ooch! Di! Your earring! It's caught in my hair. Don't pull, dearie. Mac, can't you free it? You have a gift for straightening out spiritual tangles. I'm sure you can do this."

He was beside them in an instant.

"Don't move, Diane. I'll unscrew the earring; then it will be easy to get it out of her hair."

She was barely aware of his fingers at her ear. Merry's words "You have a gift for straightening out spiritual tangles" were going round and round in her mind. There had been something in her voice—an unsteady warmth. Through her memory echoed Mac Cameron's tender reminder that afternoon on the terrace, the very afternoon Merry's endurance had crashed:—

"You're not to worry about anything, remember."

She saw again his hand on Merry's shoulder. She had put away Pete's engagement ring. Was she falling in love with the man? "O God, don't let that happen! Don't," she prayed.

"It's a tough snarl, Merry. I can do it better alone, Freda." His voice broke into the turmoil of her thoughts.

"A hair appears to be caught in every one of these diamond leaves. Don't move your head. It's almost—there it is!" He held up the dangle of glitter in triumph. "Here you are, Miss Diane."

As she fastened the earring before the long mirror, he added:—

"Hope I didn't pull too much, Merry."

"You didn't hurt at all. If I squirmed, it was because I was afraid you would."

The old clock in the hall wheezed and began to strike the hour.

"Good heavens, run along. You'll be late for dinner, Mac," she urged anxiously.

"No hurry. Dinner is announced for eight but there will be at least an hour of cocktails, more likely two, before it is served. It means nothing in my life, but perhaps Miss Diane—"

"I don't drink," she cut in curtly. The tragic idea that her sister might care for Mac Cameron, a man who, from all indications, was still in love with his stepfather's wife, had her in its vicious grip. She remembered now how often Merry had said casually, "Mac Cameron dropped in today with a book [or fruit or a game]. I like him. He's so companionable."

"I think we should be on time even if the dinner isn't," she reminded quickly. "Good night, lovely. Don't lie awake, remember."

"I won't, but if you should see a light in this room you'll know I couldn't sleep, so come in and tell me about the party. What everyone wore, what you had to eat, etc., etc., etc. Thank you, Mac, for rescuing the family jewels. Good night. Happy landings!"

"Happy landings"— The words she had so often called to Pete. Diane was tense with heartache as she sat rigidly in the black roadster. Had this man at the wheel come into her sister's life to change the pattern? Had he brought back a dream which Merry thought now might come true? It couldn't be that she was in love with him; life wouldn't be so cruel. Yet she had put away Pete's ring.

"Relax, lady, relax. You're not going to your execution; you're going to a party." Mac Cameron's voice held the note of amusement which always tinged it when he spoke to her.

What would he think if she tried to make him understand that Merry, because of the narrowness of her world, could be easily hurt? Did she dare try it, or might she make matters worse by betraying her sister?

She looked up at him. There was light enough for her to see every feature. His eyes met hers. Their quizzical expression changed to concern.

"What's wrong, soldier? It isn't just going to dinner with a man you dislike. It's something more serious. Is it Merry?"

She nodded.

"Your sister isn't *worse?*"

She gathered her courage, clenched her hands together and plunged.

"No. Physically she's better, but—but you probably don't know that the man she was to marry was killed, on the very day she met with the accident that crippled her. That her heart broke, that she's just beginning to be a little happy. I—I can't bear it if she's hurt again. She—she just mustn't fall in love, that's all. Don't you understand? Won't you *please* keep away from her?"

She saw his eyes change from troubled interest to surprise, to incredulous amazement; saw the quick blood color his tanned face.

"You don't mean, you *can't* mean that she—I—oh, it's too ridiculous. Why me? Why not Doc Reynolds? He sees her every day. Don't you understand that Merry is friendly to make up for the fact that you treat me like the dirt under your feet? Where'd you get the idea of playing God?"

She had made herself ridiculous and him contemptuously angry. Why should she care if only Merry were spared? Her emotional strain culminated in a long, unsteady breath.

"I'm not playing God. I'm—I'm just trying to protect my sister."

"Ever thought that she might not want your protection? That she would prefer to work out life for herself? What have you ever achieved to make you so cocksure you can run it for her?"

She didn't try to answer. What had she achieved that would qualify her to manage another's life? She had made a mess of this attempt to shield Merry.

"Also, while we're on the subject, where did you pick up the idea of presuming to qualify as my Jiminy Cricket?"

"I wouldn't take the responsibility of acting as your conscience for a million dollars."

His laugh was edged.

"We agree temporarily but we agree, and—in closing—I'll remind you that I shall continue to call upon your sister when and as often as I please. What are you going to do about *that?*"

She didn't answer. What could she do about it? She couldn't think it out now. She would drop the question into her subconscious mind. It was bound, sooner or later, to shoot an idea to the surface. That technique had produced satisfactory results many times before.

The roadster shot ahead smoothly. Headlights silvered the black ribbon of road, flashed on stone walls, picked out looming pines and turned them to gold, touched shrubbery and flower borders, rested on the white columns and lacy balcony of the Manor.

"Here we are. Just a minute before we go in." His hand closed hard on her arm. "If you were to treat me as if I were a human being I'll bet your anxiety about your sister would be at an end. Want to try it?"

"Being friendly, you mean? Not interested."

"You're wrecking my life." The amused derision in his voice made hers seem the attempt of a rank amateur. "Curtain!" he said and threw open the roadster door.

Mac Cameron had been right about the lateness of dinner. A clock struck the half-hour as they entered the living room. The butler and a waitress were passing trays of glasses and hors d'oeuvres—judging from the laughter and high-pitched voices, not the first round.

The room seemed full of strangers as she made her way, uncomfortably aware of Mac Cameron beside her, to the fireplace before which her hostess stood in a sequin frock which turned from pale violet to amethyst with each movement of her lithe body.

"I began to believe you'd lost your courage, Diane." Patty-Lee's eyes, almost as purple as her frock, flashed to her guest's right hand and arm, swept her from head to foot, came back and lingered as if hypnotized on her ears. Her lower lip hung slightly open. She colored as she met Diane's amused eyes.

"Where did you get those—?"

"Glad you've come, Miss Diane." The Major's booming voice cut in on his wife's tense question. "We've been looking for you. Here's a chap who says he used to know you before you became a farmer." He thumped the shoulder of the man beside him.

Diane looked up. Her heart glowed as if a huge incandescent lamp had been snapped on. She held out both hands. "*Jim!* Jim Brewster! Jim, you *dear!* How did you happen to come here?"

His hair has whitened at the temples, his eyes are blacker

than ever, his smile is still adorable, he remains slim as a movie lead and one of the best-looking men I've ever seen, she thought in the instant of silence before he answered:—

"Newcomb, the current best-selling guy, has a house here. He's on our list. Remember him? I dropped in to see how his new novel is getting along. We publishers have to keep after these writer fellas, you know, to be sure they're not sojering on the job."

"Honey boy, where have you been? I needed—"

Laughter from a group at the other end of the room cut off Patty-Lee's petulant voice. Brewster slipped his hand under Diane's arm.

"Come out where we can talk. No use to try above this chatter. Lord, how I hate cocktail voices."

They crossed the loggia, stopped at the step that led to the patio.

"This will do. We can hear each other now. How's Merry?" The question was harsh, abrupt. "Is—is she forgetting Pete a little? Don't get me wrong; I don't mean forgetting, exactly: Is she bearing it better?"

"Yes. She said only tonight that she must look forward instead of back. She wants to attempt illustrating again. Said she would write and ask if you would let her try a book."

"I know. She wrote." He drew a letter from his pocket. "Look at it. She gets a job, all right."

Diane moved into the light which came through an open window and glanced over the page, at the pen-and-ink sketches in the margin.

"I'm so glad. So glad, Jim. These drawings, the fact that she's eager to get to work, means that she is improving, doesn't it?"

"Sure. Why shouldn't she improve? She's young. She was in superb health before the—the accident. Been through hell with her every step of the way, haven't you, kid? It's all there in your eyes and in your voice. Why did you bury yourselves in the country, leave New York and the friends who could have helped you through this tough time?"

"I didn't know what else to do, Jim. There wasn't much left after Father's estate was settled. We had the house here. Merry refused to see anyone; she was abnormally sensitive about her condition; she wanted to get away from it all. Each friend confidentially told me what I ought to do; each suggestion was different. I had no one to really advise me—"

"You had me."

"But I didn't have you. You were taboo. Merry made me

promise not to go to you. She—she can't bear to be pitied. Sometimes I wonder if we had remained in New York if she wouldn't have gained more in courage if not in health. Why wonder? I did what seemed best for her at the time. What more can a person do than what she thinks is best?"

"Nothing. I should have broken in on Merry long before this—but I was afraid I might turn her against me forever. Fear! My God, how it cripples. . . . I've *got* to see her to explain just what I want for illustrations."

"She won't see you, Jim."

"Why not? In this letter she congratulated me on my engagement. She must know that my love for her has—has blown over, though of course I'm still tremendously interested in her. Make her see me, Di. Make her, will you?" His voice was strained.

Eyes on his, she nodded.

"I'll do my level best, Jim. But wait, wait until I phone you to come or you may spoil everything."

I'll wait, but not long. You always were a sweet kid. Thanks." He laid his arm about her shoulders and kissed her lightly on the cheek.

"Sorry to intrude, but I'm slated to take you out to dinner, Miss Vernon, and dinner is served." Mac Cameron spoke from the dusk behind them.

"Good lord, I'll be in the hostess' black book. I'm to take in somebody, I've forgotten who. Don't forget, Di," Brewster reminded before he dashed across the loggia.

"You really shouldn't stand in the spotlight when a man kisses you. Poor technique. Which fiancé was that?" Mac Cameron demanded. "When you looked up and saw him your face was as radiant as if you'd caught a glimpse of heaven. Is he One, Two, Three or Four?"

"Why stop at four?" Diane's spirit had spread wings. Merry could again use her fingers. She would have work to keep her from despair. THE IDEA shot to the surface. She knew now how to break Mac Cameron's hold on Merry's interest. Exuberance spilled over into her voice.

"I'm no piker to stop at *four*. He was Number Five. Shall we go in to dinner?"

XIII

A MASSIVE red-brown boulder shaded Merry Vernon's chair in the sheltered cove. With a long sigh the English setter sprawled at her feet, rolled over and over out of the shadow until he lay on his back, in the full glare of the early afternoon sunshine, forepaws folded as if in prayer.

Ordinarily the shore near the path which led up to the house was quiet, but today the white-capped waves swept in, driven by a misty breeze. Roller upon green roller broke against the ledge with a shower of foam and spray, which glittered and shifted with rainbow colors like the iridescent rays of the aurora, and gemmed the purple heather among the rocks with diamonds.

A gull perched on the top of the pine on the ledge, swayed with every motion of the tree. Its lemon-colored bill shone like pale gold in the sun—the same gold which gilded the tips of the pine needles. The diving raft plunged and cavorted like a live thing tethered. Just above the tide line three slim-legged sandpipers daintily pecked and picked their way.

Merry Vernon dropped the book she had been reading into her crisp Wedgwood-blue chambray lap and looked at her sister who, in chalk-white slacks and shirt, was stretched flat on her back on a brown-and-tan–plaid steamer rug on the pebbly shore. A red, broad-brimmed, crownless straw hat was tilted down over her eyes, protected by white-rimmed dimmers. The tip of her nose, the determined line of her mouth and her dimpled chin were all that was visible of her face.

"Heavenly here, isn't it? Reminds me of that old hymn Grandmother used to sing—'Where every prospect pleases and only man is vile.'"

Diane rolled over, pulled off her hat and the sun glasses, shook back her wavy dark hair, rested her elbows on the rug, her chin in her hands and laughed up at her sister.

"Meaning?"

"The Major, of course. Why should he spoil this paradise by trying to get our land?"

"Page the glamorous Patty-Lee."

"But why should she want an estate with whose traditional history she can have no sympathy? It has come down the generations to us."

In silence they watched amber-and-green waves hiss and foam, send showers of spray high over the ledge, cream to dainty white frills on the shore. Merry's eyes came back to the girl on the rug and lingered thoughtfully.

"What's on your mind, lovely? I can feel you staring at me. 'Time to stump the experts.' Shoot!" Diane encouraged at the same time that she wondered if Merry could have heard that Jim Brewster had brought her home from the Manor last evening and was about to accuse her of deception.

"Was I staring? I was reflecting that you hadn't told me about the party last night. I must have been asleep when you came in. Was it a frost? Did you hate it?"

"No, I didn't hate it. It was perfect. Snappy frocks. Most of them very covered-up. Wonderful things to eat. Brilliant conversation. To crab from the reviewers' stock phrases, Writer Newcomb was 'at his superb best.' He fairly scintillated."

"Unusual for an author, isn't it? I've never met one who wasn't rather hard sledding conversationally."

Diane laughed, sat up, hugged her knees and looked out to sea. Her move startled the dog who, after a reflective second, frisked from sight in pursuit of a challenging gull.

"That's because when they think of clever repartee they immediately think that it can be used in something they're writing and save it. I've done it myself."

"Was your hostess impressed by the emeralds?"

"To speechlessness. I wish you could have seen her strapless sequin frock. It shimmered into every tint and shade of purple. It was gorgeous. She shook out her whole bag of tricks to charm Newcomb on one side of her and Larry Crane on the other. The Major boomed as usual at the opposite end of the table, but his eyes were savage when he looked at his wife. I have a feeling that all is not sweetness and light in that partnership. But then, is marriage ever?"

Merry Vernon leaned her head against the back of her

chair and watched a cloud swan and cygnets sail across
the blue sky. Her throat contracted. Her eyes came back
to her sister, who was throwing pebbles into the water.

"I can't bear to have you so cynical about marriage, Di.
There's nothing the matter with the institution. It's the parties to the contract who fail. It shows up those who can't
take it. It is high adventure. Heaven if you love—"

"And hell if you don't."

"Why marry if you don't love?"

"Expediency, perhaps. I can think of a dozen other reasons."

"Expediency isn't a reason. It's an excuse. Never marry,
Di, until the touch of a man's shoulder against your cheek
catches at your breath, the look in his eyes sets you afire
to feel his lips on yours, turns you weak with desire to be
in his arms."

"Why, Merry. *Merry!* You were always so cool, so—so
poised. Did Pete mean that to you?" Was she beginning to
feel like that about Mac Cameron? It could mean only unhappiness. Was this a chance to try out The Idea?

"I've opened my heart to you, Di, because I suspect
that you are playing with the temptation to marry a man
you don't love—Larry Crane to be exact. There's nothing in
it. You've just referred to the tragic example practically next
door. Patty-Lee Lovel, married to a man for his money.
Naked passion in her eyes when she looks at Mac Cameron.
I've heard that she threw him over for his stepfather, threw
over a man who would be all tenderness, all devotion to the
woman he marries."

The strain in her voice was a knife thrust in Diane's
heart. Merry was seeing him with a halo. She didn't know
that he had come here to be with the girl to whom he had
once been engaged. She plunged.

"'The time has come, the Walrus said' . . ." Her voice
was perfect, light with a hint of emotion. " . . . to confess
that my remarks about marriage were phony, that I've gone
off the deep end about Mac Cameron myself." That would
do the trick. Merry wouldn't allow herself to love a man
for whom her sister had confessed she cared.

"Di! Stop playing jackstones with those pebbles. Look at
me. Do you mean—that he is in love with you?"

"That's the general idea. We came to a—an understanding
on the way to the dinner." That much was true. She had
told him she didn't like him, hadn't she? She didn't dare

look at Merry for fear of what she would see in her face.
Was she too late with The Idea?

"Di! Don't be so exasperatingly cool about it! For a girl
just engaged—"

"Practically, Merry, only practically. We—"

"Where do you get that practically," inquired a cool voice
behind them.

Diane jumped to her feet and turned with a speed which
sent the foraging sandpipers scurrying out of sight. Mac
Cameron, seated on a boulder, was regarding her with spec-
ulative eyes. At the same moment Merry caught the wheels
of her chair and whirled it to face him.

"Mac! Mac! Is it true? I'm so—so—happy—I—" Her voice
caught in a sob.

He came to her and clasped the hand she extended.
"Then that makes it unanimous," he said gravely.

"But, but, Merry, you misunderstood. I didn't say we
were really engaged. I—I—said 'practically' and that's a
long ways from *really*," Diane protested breathlessly.

"Not in this case. Come here." Mac caught her hands
and drew her close. "I think Merry would like to see the
bargain sealed."

Arm about her shoulders, he pressed his lips on hers in
a long, hard kiss. Diane fought the temptation to close her
eyes and glared at him. The reckless gleam in his sent
a wave of fury through her veins. Dopey, in a frenzy of
welcome, dashed up and planted his wet paws on the sleeve
of his white cardigan. Diane twisted free.

"You see, even Dopey gives us his blessing," Mac observed lightly.

"It—it isn't true. I was—" The look in his eyes checked
her furious protest. "I—I—mean, that I'm not sure—you
won't speak of it to anyone yet—promise, lovely."

Merry glanced from the man to the girl and back to him,
where her eyes lingered.

"Of course I won't, Di. It is your business and Mac's.
I'll be silent as the grave until . . ." Over her face swept
a startled wave of emotion. Her eyes were wide with incredulity.

"Jim!" she breathed. "Jim Brewster! Where did you come
from?"

The man in white, who had been standing in the path
between the boulders, laughed and approached her chair.
Color crept back into his face, which had been pale.

"Hello, everybody." He caught Merry's impulsively extended hand and held it tight.

"Couldn't seem to condense all I wanted to tell you in one letter in answer to yours, so decided to run down and talk shop. Good lord, Di, you've grown to be a big girl since I saw you last." He released the hand twisting free from his tight hold.

"Merry, just to keep the record straight, I won't be sent back now, so don't try it."

"I shan't send you back, Jim. Why didn't you let us know you were coming?"

"If I had, you would have refused to see me. I can't afford to take chances. Sometimes surprise will dynamite a barrier when nothing else will."

"Your dynamiting has been a huge success. I'm glad. I'm terribly glad to see you, Jim."

"That's one step forward." Brewster cleared his voice of huskiness. "I left a manuscript at the house I want to talk over with you, Merry. Let's go."

He turned the wheelchair toward the path, as if it were his daily custom.

"No, Jim, no. Please. I—I couldn't bear it. Di will do it. I'm used to her. The path is steep. You may tip—"

"Tush! Tush, gal!" He flexed his right arm. "Regard that muscle. It's terrific. I'm just back from a month at training camp. Do I look so puny that I can't get you to the house without an accident? You live too much with fear."

Merry would hate having Jim touch her chair; hadn't she fought against his seeing her? Diane took a quick step forward, stopped as he shot a look at her which had the arresting quality of a bullet reaching its mark. Mac laid a detaining hand on her arm. Side by side they stood till man and chair, preceded by the frisking, barking dog, disappeared beyond the rise.

"You're staring at that path as if dazed." Mac Cameron regarded Diane above the lighter he was holding to a cigarette. "What did Brewster mean by implying that he hadn't seen you since you've grown up? I saw him kiss you at the Manor."

She explained Merry's attitude; added:—

"He was not to come until I phoned him. But as it turned out his sudden appearance worked like a charm."

"I'll remember his theory that surprise will dynamite a barrier when nothing else will. Before we close the subject of your sister—and take up you—Doc Reynolds thinks you make her helpless."

"I! *I* make her helpless! I live for her. She hates to have anyone but Freda or me push her chair and as for having Jim Brewster touch it—she'll be stabbed to the heart."

"Sure about that? Listen."

Even above the splash of rollers breaking against the ledge sounded a gay little laugh—Merry's. Dopey's excited bark drifted back. Diane's spirit soared. Jim had come and Merry was laughing.

"Now that your sister is temporarily off your mind we'll turn our attention to our own affairs. Looks as if we'd come to the pay-off. What's it all about?"

The wings of her spirit folded like a quickly closed fan as she met Mac Cameron's keen eyes, noted the determined line of his mouth.

"What's what all about?"

"Don't stall. You're going to explain if we stay here all night. You told your sister that you loved me, didn't you?"

Diane put her hand to a burning cheek and dropped it quickly. Why give him the satisfaction of knowing that she was panicky inside? Bluff it out. That was her best bet.

"Conceited as you are, you can't believe that—that—I—I—love you, can you? I asked you to keep away from Merry because—because—"

"Her heart has been broken once. That's right. I got that. Go on."

"You refused, asked in your cocky way, 'What are you going to do about *that?*' Later I had an inspiration—it seemed a perfect answer then—I thought if I pretend to—to care for him, if Merry has begun to she'll stop at once."

"Good as far as it goes. Perhaps you'll go a little farther and tell me why your sister shouldn't love me—if I love her?"

"Because you're here to get back your stepfather's wife, aren't you?"

His pallor, the flames in his eyes sent Diane's heart to her throat. She recoiled a step.

"So that's what you think of me." Anger in his voice changed to caustic amusement. "And *you, practically* my fiancée."

"You know that isn't true. You know that I was trying to save my sister from unhappiness. If you hadn't been snooping—"

"Just a minute. I wasn't snooping. You and Merry had

pitched your voices to make them heard above the rollers. I started to hail you. Caught my name and listened to your coy declaration of love."

"You know I don't love you. You know I detest you. More than ever since you took advantage of what you overheard and—and—"

"Kissed you? Advantage? I take *advantage* of a girl who acknowledges five fiancés? You must have been kissed many times by your four heartthrobs—my mistake—five."

"Why did you laugh when—when—"

"When I kissed you? I was thinking that I had forgotten in the last three years how wonderful a kiss could be and asking myself why I hadn't done it long ago."

"You don't mean *me?*"

"Why not? You're rather sweet. But no more fiancés for you. All that will have to stop now that I'm elected."

"What do you mean, *elected?* You don't think for a minute that I'll go on with this—this stupid farce, do you?"

There was a disturbing light in the eyes that met hers.

"Sure you'll go on. You don't intend to stop saving your sister from my devastating charm, do you?"

He held the lighter to a cigarette before he added: "Lady, you *are* in a spot."

XIV

THAT night Diane tossed and turned, counted sheep, went over all the poetry she knew but sleep wouldn't come. She stared into the dark. Whichever way she looked she met Mac Cameron's eyes blazing at her. The room seemed to echo with his cool voice saying:—

"All that will have to stop now that I'm elected."

He elected! Maddening. . . . As if she had proposed to him. Hadn't she, practically? Could it be true that he hadn't kissed a girl for three years? Suppose it were—what difference did it make to her? At that stage of her reflections she jumped out of bed and went to the window to escape her thoughts.

The world was ghostly with mist, fragrant with the clean scent of wet leaves and pine. If only the wind would change and blow the fog bank off to sea. Foggy weather depressed Merry.

Curious sound. . . . The clink of metal on metal. . . . It came from the direction of the Musgrave Manor field. Nearer now. Was that a shadow creeping through the whiteness? Was someone moaning? A swinging light like a hazy opal. A glint of wet oilskins.

Icy shivers feathered through her veins. The wraith of the wrecked sea captain was walking! *Imbecile!* Of course that drifting figure was a tree swaying and didn't the buoy moan?

She was glad when morning came and her mind and time were full to the brim of the day's work. In the glittering sunshine the imaginations of last night seemed nothing short of fantastic. She must have been emotionally unbalanced. She had been, hadn't she? She had pretended she was in love with a man whom she detested. He had heard her fatuous declaration. Had kissed her. It was his way of retaliating for her snubs. Would she ever reach the stage when she could remember it without burning with fury at her stupidity as she was burning now?

She left the herb garden and Asaph, to pace the terrace. Suppose she explained to Merry—how could she confess that she had made the crazy declaration because she suspected that her sister was beginning to love Mac Cameron? That she had warned him to keep away from her? She couldn't. The only chance of extricating herself from this mess was that Jim Brewster's entrance into Merry's monotonous life, bringing with him his intense enthusiasm for his business, the atmosphere of a world of which she had been a part, work in which she had been vitally interested, might break the spell of Mac Cameron's attraction.

How had she dared beg him to keep away from Merry? *Brainstorm* was the answer. . . . Yet, had the suspicion that Merry was strongly attracted to him been so crazy? She had put away Pete's ring. Her voice when she had said "You have a gift for straightening out spiritual tangles" had been a little unsteady.

Since she had launched The Idea yesterday afternoon on the shore she had avoided being alone with her sister. It hadn't been difficult. Jim had remained for supper on the terrace and she had excused herself before he left, saying that she had an article to finish. She had stopped only for a minute at Merry's door this morning. She couldn't dodge her forever. She must think up a plan.

"What is on your mind, Di? I've been watching you from my window. You have been pacing the terrace as if you were qualifying for a marathon."

Diane turned with a start. Freda Swenson was pushing her sister's chair through the doorway.

"My word, Merry, you made me jump. What have you in that swank turquoise-satin bag?"

"*Regardes-tu!*" Merry held up a slip of knitted khaki wool a few inches wide. Her brown eyes sparkled as she looked at Diane, who had dropped into a chair, her bare arms crossed on the back.

"Snap up your chin, dearie. Surprise has been known to dislocate a jaw. I'm knitting for the Red Cross at the same time that I limber my fingers to hold a pencil. Jim is sure that I can do the work he wants. Isn't it wonderful? This must be our happiness week, Di. I'm so thrilled about you and Mac—"

"Please, lovely. Let's forget that."

"What do you mean, forget it? You said you loved him—"

"I did, but—" she swallowed *I don't*—"but you see, neither he nor I want anyone to know it for the present. We're neither of us really sold on the idea. It's a sort of trial arrangement. You see—"

"I see more than you think I see, dearie." Merry's tone was dry. "I'll be silent as a dummy model. After all, perhaps it would be wise not to let the Lovels in on your tender secret while he is their guest."

Diane regarded her in consternation. Merry sarcastic? . . . She never had heard that edge in her voice before. After the mess she had gotten herself into to save her had she hurt her more?

"You have the right idea, lovely," she agreed because she didn't know what else to say. "Perhaps Patty-Lee—Golly! There they are!"

She ran into the house and dashed out with a rifle. She slipped in cartridges and explained as she crossed the porch:—

"A hawk in the chicken yard! There he goes with something yellow in his claws. There's another about to swoop. Life on a farm is certainly just one thing after another."

She ran down the ramp. Aimed. Fired. The hawk fell.

"Dandy shot!" a voice shouted.

It came from under a clump of white birches at the southeastern corner of the Vernon land, the boundary to which the Lovels claimed their estate legally extended. She unloaded the gun and dropped the shells into a pocket in her slacks as she approached it.

"What are you doing here, Luigi?" What she could see of his eyes, under the drooping lids, was charged with insolence.

"I'm diggin'. M's Lovel's orders is for me to dig for that bound," he said, spat out a cigarette and raised the pick.

"Stop! My orders," Diane countered crisply.

He leaned on the tool and regarded her with a saturnine grin.

"Guess ya got the right of it, seein' you've got a gun. I never argue with a guy that's got a gun. Guess you was about to shoot me, wasn't ya?"

Diane frowned at the rifle in her hand. In her anger at the intrusion had she made a threatening motion with it? Certainly not. The thought hadn't entered her head.

"Don't talk nonsense, Luigi. You know that I had no intention of shooting you."

"That day I brought the berries for Miss Merry I heard ya brag you wouldn't let the Major or none of his folks dig on your land, that you'd get your gun." He sneered through the pulled-down corner of his thick lips. "So when ya come hot-footin' across the field, I figured you were out on a shootin' party an' was goin' to let me have it. Practisin' for that Civilian Defense stuff his nibs was gettin' off his chest in the barn?"

Diane's throat tightened. You're not letting that tough frighten you, I hope, dumbbell, she derided herself and the tension eased.

"I'm glad you heard the Major. You may be able to help. Now that you know there will be no shootin' party, shoulder that pick and run along home."

He regarded her with flat, expressionless eyes, eyes which always made her think of the surface of a stagnant pool, beneath which crept and crawled slimy, poisonous life.

"'Run home.' Cut out talkin' to me as if I was a kid. I'm twenty-two years old. Guess ya was goin' to shoot me. Guess p'r'aps I'd better put the sheriff wise to you an' your rifle."

Diane's face burned with anger. Did this—this moron dare threaten her?

"Having 'guessed' so much, Luigi, you'd better guess that it's time for you to be on your way."

"Sore, ain't you? Say, I'll make a deal. You quit turnin' Trudy Budge against me an' I'll keep your gunnin' for me to myself."

Diane disciplined an almost uncontrollable urge to slap his swarthy face. She shook her head.

"No deal with you, Luigi. Tell the sheriff whatever you like. I'll handle my own business without your advice—that reminds me, while we are on the subject of advice, I'll hand you a bit. There's a rumor that that same sheriff has a pretty good idea where to look for the leaders of the gang which broke into the summer cottages last winter."

She caught her breath. His face had flushed purple-red. Sparks of hate stirred the stagnant surface of his eyes. Her shot had apparently hit a target. He doubled his fists and took a threatening step toward her.

"The sheriff! It's that dope of a Major Lovel, I'll bet. What d'ya mean by that dirty crack? You accusin' me of leadin' the gang?"

Diane shrugged indifference, though she kept her eyes on the flashy green stone on his pudgy hand.

"I was taking my turn at 'guessin',' Luigi."

"You stop your guessin' about me, quick, see? Or I'll—"

"You'll what?" a savage voice demanded behind her.

Mac Cameron! . . . Where he had come from Diane had time only to wonder before Luigi bragged:—

"I said I'd knock her block off if she didn't quit pickin' on me, first with my girl an' now 'bout s—somethin' else. An' can I do it? She an' his nibs the Major tryin' to run the world. Defendin' the county. Nuts. I'll fix 'em both. I'll show you, first, wise guy. Ya've got it comin' to you for butting in between me an' Danny Stark." He brought up his fist, squared his shoulders and thrust out his chin.

"Is that so? Ready!"

Mac's quick left laid the swaggering Luigi flat. He stood over him.

"Manchusto, if I were you, I would go slow on the tough-guy act. The Government is on the warpath for aliens like you who have slipped into the country without passports. You're due for a voyage. Exciting on the ocean, just now. Plenty of mines, E-boats and bombs to keep you on the jump."

Luigi's face had turned a dirty yellow. He sat up, tried to speak. His eyes were venomous. He mumbled something from the corner of his mouth. Mac caught Diane's arm.

"Come home before the gentleman gets up. He's brave

enough to stab in the back or shoot a defenseless person —always with a gang supporting him. Give me that gun."

She took three running steps to his one, to keep up with his stride.

"How did you know that he entered the country without a passport?"

"I didn't. I guessed it. Sometimes a guess is as good as a certainty for locating a machine-gun nest. I have a hunch that your wish will come true, that fear that he will be checked up on and fingerprinted will railroad the blowhard Luigi out of town."

"And Danny would be free of him. Marvelous. What did he mean when he said you had butted in between him and Danny Stark?"

"I've given the boy a job. Heard him say he was crazy to be a photographer. I picked up the camera bug myself in South America. The Major has made me chairman of the air-defense subcommittee of his Defense Group. I'll cruise over the county to pick out air-defense spots. I have engaged Danny Stark to come along. I'll teach him to be an aerial cameraman—and what I know about developing. All this on condition that he considers it a regular job, for which he will be paid. No short-changing on hours; no serving two masters. He's got to choose between me and Manchusto."

"And he has chosen you. Wonderful! You don't know what a load you have taken from my mind. If only we can keep Luigi from interfering."

"You're forgetting that a grand person named Uncle Sam will take care of that unless I have the wires completely crossed. You keep out of it and let me manage Manchusto. Why in thunder did you start an argument with that rough-neck? What did you say to make him ugly?"

"When he accused me of threatening to shoot him because he was digging on our boundary line—"

"*Did* you?"

"Of course not. I never even thought of it."

"I wouldn't put it past you. Why did you have this gun?" He leveled the rifle and squinted along the barrel. "It's a beaut."

"I was after a chicken hawk, Doctor I.Q. I got it. There it is by the barn if you don't believe me. Why should I want to shoot Luigi?"

"I don't know. I don't know why you do a lot of things you do. Like telling your sister that you love me."

"I explained that."

"Not very satisfactorily. On thinking it over I've decided that you must like me a lot or the scheme never would have bobbed up in your mind."

For a split second she was speechless, as her eyes met his, alight with mockery. Then her words came with a rush.

"*Like* you! That's too amusing. I admit now that my plan wasn't worth the powder to blow it but no harm has been done. Merry alone heard my—our passionate declaration of affection—and I have begged her not to mention the matter to anyone as neither you nor I are quite sure of—of—"

"Love? Why stumble over a simple word of four letters? I'll make a trade with you. I'll pretend that the little scene I interrupted on the beach yesterday never occurred—"

"Thanks. I—"

"Hold everything. Let me finish. So long as you appear friendly. The armistice is for the duration of good behavior only. It better be good. I can be pushed just so far. The first time you slip I'll remind you that we are 'practically engaged' and collect the perqs that go with it."

"You wouldn't dare."

"Wouldn't I? Want to make a test case of it? I can see that you don't. Now that that is finally settled, we'll return to our blowhard Luigi. What did you say to him?"

She told him.

"The Major will be glad to know that the sheriff is on the job. Bringing those hoodlums to justice is getting to be an obsession with him. Having heard at first hand the damage they did to that superb house, I don't blame him. That isn't all. He has another grievance chalked up. Last night both planes were put out of commission. Someone broke into the hangar."

"Last night! I wonder—"

"Why are you shivering, soldier? Cold in this sun?"

"No. I suddenly remembered that I thought I saw the ghostly sea captain, wet slicker, sou'wester, swinging lantern and all, stealing across our lawn last night in the fog. Do you suppose . . ."

He glanced down at the slender, rosy-nailed fingers she had impulsively laid on his sleeve. He forced his eyes back to hers.

"What is this? An act?"

She thrust her hands into the pockets of her slacks.

"Is what an act?"

"This pretense at friendliness. If you—"

"O Di!" Asaph Hicks's shout interrupted. "Cripes, did

you git this hawk? . . . You did a mighty fine job, Di," he approved as she and Mac joined him. He stirred the feathered body with his clumsy foot. "I couldn't done better myself."

"Thanks, Asaph. I don't like thieves. That reminds me, were you prowling round our place in the fog last night?"

His beady, weasel eyes flashed from her face to Cameron, who was regarding him intently.

"Heck, I was out last night, but not on this place. Marthy was certain she heard something in the barn. Wouldn't give me no peace till I got up to see."

"Did you find anyone?"

"Neither hide nor hair. 'Twas jest her nerves." He shifted his pipe from one corner of his platter mouth to the other.

"Don't you never git married, Mr. Cameron. Take it from me, a wife's a blamed nuisance."

"Asaph Hicks, you ought to be ashamed to say that when you have a wife like Martha. Everyone thinks she's a grand person."

"Glad to hear it, Di. It just happens that I don't like her."

XV

MAC CAMERON cut the engine of the black roadster in front of the village fruit shop. The morning glittered with sunlight. The air was scented with the smell of peaches, pears, early apples, plums and oranges colorfully displayed on the outside counter. The rotund, oily, white-suited proprietor, dark-haired, swarthy-skinned and smiling bustled through the doorway.

"Good morning, *signor*. I have the nectarines you ordered. They are beau—tiful—" he clasped pudgy hands in ecstasy—"but verra hard to get. Verra high price."

"Then I'm in luck. Knew you would find them for me if anyone could, Manchusto. Arrange them in one of your attractive baskets and I'll take it along."

"*Si. Si, signor*. I have already that done. I knew you say that as always. I get them. Quick."

He bustled through the doorway, barely escaping collision with two saucer-eyed, black-pigtailed little girls in bright-print aprons, who were coming out. They squatted on the doorstep and licked at ice-cream cones as they stared at Mac.

"Morning, kids. How's tricks? Those your children, Manchusto?" he asked as the proprietor returned, with a flat basket, in which row upon row of rosy-cheeked, satin-skinned nectarines were arranged with military precision.

"Si, signor. Sure, they mine. You like these nectarines, yes?"

"Finest ever." Mac set the basket on the seat beside him. He reached into his pocket for money.

"Any other children?"

"Si, signor. Seven, an' one more comin'. They go like thees." He moved his pudgy hands to indicate steps.

"Luigi the oldest?"

"Si, signor." The fat, pleased smile vanished. "But he not have the same mother. She die in Italia when he was born. I stay there four years after. Then I come to thees country, leave baba with wife's mama eighteen years ago. I thought Luigi always stay there, then one day two year past, he walked in that door an' say, 'Hello, Papa.'"

No doubt that his hunch a week ago had been correct, when he had accused Luigi of slipping into the country illegally, Mac decided.

"You didn't know he was coming, didn't send for him?"

"No, signor. I have all I could feed here already. He come here from Mexico. Smart, Luigi is. He speak verra nice American. He mak much money. Has nice log house on bluff. Fish. Clams. Lobsters. Good business."

"I presume you're an American citizen by this time, Manchusto?"

"Not yet. Not yet, but I hurry. I hurry much. I thought that someday I go back to Italia." His voice dropped to a confidential whisper. "Now I not think so no more. My money in the bank here. My children in the schools. My home is here." He pointed to the Stars and Stripes, floating from the town library. "I fight for that flag, if I fight. Last week I took out what you call my first papers."

"Last week! And you've lived here eighteen years! Pretty late in starting, Manchusto. Better late than never, though. Keep on the watch for more nectarines. Good-by."

He has lived here eighteen years and is only now applying for his first papers, Mac reflected, as the roadster slid smoothly forward. The registration-of-noncitizens act has given him a kick in the pants. So Luigi got in via Mexico.

Wonder what he was thinking as he leaned against the barn door while the Major was speaking? That guy will stand watching—and how. More than ever now it occurs to me that the Department of Justice might be interested in his career.

That evening, in the loggia of the Manor, Asaph's words recurred to him as he regarded the woman stretched in a wheel chaise—"Don't you never git married, Mr. Cameron. Take it from me, a wife's a blamed nuisance."

Patty-Lee Lovel had a nuisance value all right. She was pulling the ears of the Pekingese, whose eyes glinted like beads, in its black mask, as it curled in the violet-chiffon lap of her evening gown, while she listened with insolent indifference to her husband, slumped in a deep chair beside her.

With unseeing eyes on the two, he relived the meeting with Diane on the morning that Asaph had taken that crack at the holy estate of matrimony. He considered the truce with her, if it could be called a truce. He hadn't seen her since she had gone into the house carrying her rifle, though he had dropped in on Merry daily. Usually Brewster was just coming or going. When that day at the brook she had sobbed in his arms he had felt that he would give his life to shield her from trouble. Then she had accused him of trying to get back his stepfather's wife.

"I've told you, Patty-Lee, and I repeat it, that this fight may antagonize the townspeople," the Major's impatient voice cut in on Mac's indignant conclusion. "Didn't I buy this estate because I was born in Maine and decided that this was the logical place for me to start in politics? Haven't I begun by taking an interest in village affairs? Haven't I hunted out the leaders of that gang of vandals who robbed and defaced the summer cottages, with especial attention to this one? The suspects are to be hailed into court tomorrow. I stand an excellent chance of being nominated for Governor when the election comes again in two years. I've got to work for it; so have you. How do you like the sound of Governor Seth Lovel? Would you risk losing all this for a dinky fifty acres of land? The village won't stand for it. The Vernons are liked and respected. They are popular."

"Speech! Speech! Are you practising on me, *Governor?*" The ridicule in his wife's voice brought the Major to his feet in impatient protest.

"The village! The Vernons!" she mimicked. "I'm sick of hearing of the *Vernons*. It's ridiculous to argue that two women can keep you, with your money, your war record and your colossal charm from winning all the votes you need when you want them."

Mac wondered if her husband sensed the sarcasm in that "colossal charm."

"Even if they can't, I tell you again, I don't like it." The Major paced back and forth, like a shadow crossing the bar of light which shone from the living-room windows on the flagged floor. "I don't like to fight women."

Mac could see the glint of malice in Patty-Lee's eyes as she glanced at her husband who had stopped, hands thrust hard into the pockets of his white dinner jacket, to stare unseeingly into the dusk of the patio. Was Diane's youth, her grace, her beauty responsible for his reluctance to fight for the land? He remembered the Major's tenderness and devotion to his first wife and was hotly ashamed of his doubt of him.

"Especially if they are pretty women." Apparently Patty-Lee was following the same line of thought. "Noble of me to acknowledge that they are. If it were that chinless Budge female who owned the land I want would you fight her? I'll say you would."

"I don't fight women," he repeated doggedly.

"But *you* aren't fighting them. I am. This is *my* land, *my* home, isn't it?"

"That's right."

"Then can you be blamed if I insist upon having what is mine?"

The Major wheeled and towered above her as she lay in the long chair.

"Which do you want most? The Vernon land or my success in politics?"

With a lithe twist she was on her feet facing her husband. The abandoned dog barked shrilly.

"I want them both and I intend to have them and while you're dickering you'd better buy the emeralds Diane wore the other night. They were superb. I've made inquiries and discovered that they were her grandmother's. Costume jewelry is good enough for a girl in her position. She doesn't need the real thing. She needs money."

"I'll make a deal with you. Give up trying for the land and I'll buy the emeralds."

"I shan't give up the land. It belongs to me by law. We'll locate that bound but I will concede this much: We won't claim it till you feel you are solid with the voters.

After that I'll take what belongs to me. It does belong to me. Haven't you copies of the old deeds in your desk to prove it?"

"My lawyer claims they prove it. Mac, you're land-wise. Take a look at those deeds and the blueprints of the estate and give me an opinion on the justness of our claim, will you?"

"Glad to, Major. I'll give them the once-over the first thing in the morning."

"And plan to go to court with me. I have a feeling that when we jail those vandals we'll find out who put the planes out of commission. By the way, the mechanic has them in order again for you to use."

"Now smooth out those deep lines, Sethy." Patty-Lee drew her jeweled fingers across her husband's forehead. "Everything is going to be all right. You can wash your hands of the old land. *You'll* help me get it, won't you honey boy?" She smiled confidently at Mac, who was leaning against a vine-covered column.

"No! I'll look at the blueprints for the Major but I will have nothing to do with your land grab, Patty-Lee. Count me out. Don't think for a minute that the voters in this village won't get wise to your plan. You're in New England and a New Englander can see through a pine board. The Major has the right idea. Listen to him."

Even in the dim light he could see her face whiten with anger.

"You, too, are going in for oratory, are you? It's quite evident that you have fallen for the Vernons. First Larry Crane, then the Major, now you. I *haven't* and I tell you now, I'll have that land." Her voice rose to a shrill note and broke.

"Patty-Lee, Patty-Lee," her husband chided sternly. "Behave like a woman, not like a spoiled child. I'm glad to have your backing, Mac. Makes me feel less like a whip-cracking tyrant. We'll stand together, boy."

"Not in this house. If Mac Cameron stays here I leave."

"Patty-Lee! You—"

"She's right, Major," Mac interrupted his stepfather's shocked protest. "I've had my plans made—been waiting since dinner for a chance to tell you. Doc Reynolds and I have taken a house in the village—"

"You and Doc Reynolds! Where has he found the money to buy—"

"We've leased it," Mac interrupted her furious question.

"He has decided to open an office here. I have hired a boy to help me with aerial photography when I hunt air-defense spots. Major, do you suppose the wrecking of those planes was to prevent the checkup?"

"I hadn't thought of subversive activities in this small town. After this we'll watch out. I don't like to think of you leaving, Mac."

"I don't like to go, but that boy I have engaged will be tramping in and out at any hour of the day. This sensational house is no place for that sort of thing. I intend to move in with Reynolds in the morning. I'll explain to you about it later, Major. Meanwhile, I will leave you two to fight to a finish about the land."

"You can't leave. People are coming in for cards after the movie in the village. Don't go, honey boy—I didn't mean—"

Mac ignored the penitent cry, crossed the patio and ran down the steps of the three terraces to the shore.

Sea smooth as dark-green glass. . . . Tide flowing in wistfully. . . . Air, pine and sea-scented, soft as velvet fingers against his cheek. . . . After an unusually hot day the water coming in over warm rocks and pebbles would be perfect for a swim. That was an idea! It might wash away the memory of the infernally unpleasant scene in the loggia. He hated to be let in on family dissensions.

In the commodious bath-boathouse he stripped and pulled on trunks. He closed the door cautiously when he stepped out. The world was so still that the click of the latch might reach the loggia. If Patty-Lee heard the sound it would be quite in character for her to suspect where he was and follow. He wouldn't chance it. Experience had taught him that maddening as were her angers, her penitences were more to be dreaded and—sidestepped.

He stopped. . . . Sounded as if someone were moving in the shrubs at the lowest terrace. . . . The ghostly sea captain? Why should Diane's mysterious wraith in oilskins and sou'wester flash into his mind? Had it been he who had put the planes out of commission? Was there a person or persons in this county who had been hired to block the Civilian Defense Group? He strained his ears to listen. It might be no one more sinister than Patty-Lee. Not the rustle of a leaf to be heard now. Imagination, plus.

He plodded along the shore, flinching with a muttered "Ooch!" when he stepped on a sharp clamshell or a jagged stone. His bare feet sank deep into the pebbles and sand, leaving prints which quickly filled with water. The smell of briny kelp was in his nostrils; the hushed murmur of the tide smoothed out the tangle of conflicting loyalties in his mind.

He was fond of his stepfather, but not fond enough to help him grab the Vernon land,—that was what he would be asked to do. The Major would fume and protest but in the end would give in for, after all, the woman was his wife and he had been desperately eager to marry her.

When he was sure that he was out of sight and sound of the Manor he waded into deep water. Soft as he had known it would be, it was as full of chilly prickles as an iced effervescent drink. He flung out his arms and dived. The plunge set his blood dancing.

He swam for a while, turned on his back and floated. The gold-stippled purple sky seemed so near he had the feeling that heaven itself was bending low to hear his thoughts.

He smiled grimly at the stars. If they were listening they would hear plenty. The manner in which he had flung his decision to spend the rest of his Maine vacation with Reynolds had been pretty crude; he owed the Lovels more courtesy for their hospitality. He had intended to tell them later in the evening but Patty-Lee's spitefulness had been a spark to his explosive temper.

He thought of his plan to interest Danny Stark in photography. The boy had been shaky with excitement when he had made the offer. Could he interest him enough to break Luigi Manchusto's hold? It promised to be a fight in which a look-see into the manner of the Bad Boy's arrival in the United States might help. Whether he held Danny or lost him he had "taken a load" from Diane. That was worth doing if only for a short time. Her slim shoulders were carrying too heavy a burden. Why did she dislike him?

He thrust her out of his mind, and substituted the memory of Doc's talk with him before he decided to establish practice in this Maine town; he thought of his own offer to furnish offices with the latest instruments and equipment and to pay the salary of a nurse that a clinic might be started; of Reynolds' stunned surprise, of his protests, his incredulous gratitude when it had been made clear that it would be given by a son as a memorial to a mother whose life, in these latter days, could have been saved by science.

Curious that Reynolds had so quickly impressed him with

a conviction of his skill and power and the certainty that he would soon be a higher-upper in the profession he had chosen. He needed a boost *now*. By giving that equipment he, himself, was helping to prevent pain, helping to save lives. How better could he use part of the money his mother had left him? Only yesterday he had read an editorial which set forth the tragic need of rural hospitals, and emphasized the fact that there were large sections in New England where the nearest doctors were miles distant. He wasn't financing a hospital but it might well be the beginning of one.

He would put it up to the Major to help. He'd hang round long enough to be sure the offices were running on greased wheels, then beat it for New York and the position waiting for him when he was ready to claim it, that is, if he weren't called into the army. Nothing to keep him here. He had felt a passionate desire to help Merry Vernon, but she didn't need him now that Brewster. had come to encourage her in her work. As for Diane—why think of her? Hadn't she said she detested him? She had miscalled that *inspiration* she had had to keep Merry from liking him too much; *brainstorm* was the word.

He swam slowly, raised his head. Where was he? A diving raft ahead. Must be the Vernons'. He remembered seeing one. He increased speed, pulled himself up on it. He would rest and then walk back along the shore. Boy, what wouldn't he give for a cigarette.

Behind him the tide laved drowsily against the ledge. The solitary pine stirred lazily. In front, the white house bulked dark against the starry sky. He could smell the mixed scent from the herb garden. A light burned in one of the lower rooms. Would that be Merry's? Probably not. In the hall, maybe.

He crouched cross-legged fashion, on the raft. As he looked at the white house he wondered, as he had wondered when Doc had told him that he intended to settle here, if Merry Vernon had influenced that decision? Did he feel that he could help her, perhaps restore her to normal living? That if he succeeded he would win more fame and fortune than years in a big city would bring him? He was seeing her every day.

Merry. Di's passionate "Won't you please keep away from her?" swept back into his mind. He should have been more understanding. Hadn't the Dominie declared that she was fighting for her sister? If instead of ridiculing her and accusing her of attempting to play God he had been sympathetic, had gently talked her out of her anxiety, that absurd declaration of hers at the shore a week ago wouldn't have happened. He had tried to make her see that her sister had been friendly to make up for her own marked unfriendliness, but he hadn't put it across. . . . Why—why go all over that again?

He shivered. Getting colder. He'd better start back. Walking would set his blood circulating. Running would be better. A dog barking! . . . A sharp warning yelp. . . . Was it the English setter? Was something or someone lurking round the Vernons' chicken yard?

He slid soundlessly off the raft. Swam cautiously, waded to shore, listened. No extra lights had flashed on in the house. Perhaps the occupants were accustomed to the dog's bark in the night. Perhaps he, himself, had had an attack of jitters when he suspected prowlers.

He started along the shore. The faint boom of a clock striking the hour drifted from the village. He counted. Only ten. Seemed a lifetime since he had left the loggia. The dog was barking again. He stopped. Turned back. Experience had taught him to heed his hunches. Something was wrong. He knew it.

As he stole up the path to the house, between pale blurs which were flower borders, he chuckled. He would be better fitted to cope with trouble if he had on a few more clothes. All he needed was a knife between his teeth and huge rings dangling from his ears to give a Grade-A imitation of a pirate. He flattened himself against the bole of a tree and listened. The dog barked shrilly from inside the house.

"Dopey! Dopey! Stop! It's Di!" The warning whisper came from the porch. He was near enough now to locate it. "Have they come yet, Asaph?"

Why was Diane Vernon prowling round her own place at night? About whom was she inquiring so breathlessly?

"No, they ain't come. Prob'ly gone to a dance. By heck, you're back safe. You shouldn't have did it, Di. Terrible risky."

In spite of his attempt to keep it low, Asaph Hicks's voice rasped through the still air.

"Risky or not, it had to be done. And it's done! Tell you what happened tomorrow. Good night, Asaph. Thanks for keeping watch."

A door was opened and closed softly.

Mac waited till Asaph had passed him in the dusk, muttering to himself. Why wasn't he carrying a lantern? He watched a light flash on in an upper window. Diane was safely in her room. There had been tense excitement in her. "And it's done!"

He'd better get back. Patty-Lee had said that a crowd was coming in for contract. She counted on him to make up a table. She would have forgotten—or would pretend to have forgotten—her anger at him by the time he returned. He sprinted. Didn't even waste breath on "Ooch!" when shells cut his feet. Broke his record for quick dressing.

As he left the boathouse he could hear laughter and voices drifting from the great living room. The card game was on. From the cruiser off shore came a radioed voice singing:—

"Can this be love?"

He had a sudden vision of himself crouched on the raft watching the white house, stealing up the path keeping vigil till the light in the room he had assumed was Diane's flashed on.

"Can this be love?" he hummed and laughed at the absurdity of the suggestion. Hadn't his experience with Patty-Lee inoculated him against a recurrence of that fever? He ran up the terrace. . . . Stopped. On the top step, as if dropped in haste, lay a ship's lantern, the wick still burning. He looked from that to the patio. What was lying in a rift of light from the house? His body turned to ice. . . . A man? . . . A man in white?

He brushed his hand across his eyes. He was awake. Blood coursed through his veins again. He ran forward. His brain whirled. The Major. A stream of red stained the breast of his white coat. Mac lifted him till the silvery head rested against his shoulder. Who had shot him? He looked around for a weapon. A bit of metal glinted in the dim light. A rifle. As clearly as if broadcast from a radio Asaph Hicks's voice echoed in Mac's memory.

"You shouldn't have did it, Di. Terrible risky."

The Major's wide-open eyes burned into his.

"Don't—try to f—find who—shot—mistake. I don't fight—"

His lids fell; his weak voice died away.

XVI

On her knees, Diane swished cups and plates in the frilly white water that lapped almost to her feet, bare in their straw beach shoes. Gulls mewed and screamed, swooped to forage for scraps in the green water, soared and circled. A kingfisher flashed by, a streak of blue. Against the purple horizon two white sails shone like mother-of-pearl. Her tomato-red swim suit made a gorgeous splash of color against the panorama of sea and sky. Behind her a thin pillar of smoke rose from a bed of graying coals between two rocks, and drifted on the salty breeze, slightly denatured with the scent of bacon, till it resembled nothing so much as streaks of matrix against the huge turquoise that was the heavens.

From her chair in the shade Merry watched her dry the dishes and pack them in the capacious hamper. Diane had been fitfully gay while she prepared the luncheon. She hadn't appeared like a girl who recently had discovered that she was in love with a man who loved her. She ought to be radiantly happy. Mac Cameron would be everything a woman could possibly desire; he reminded her so much of Pete that his smile tightened her throat.

Was it only a little over a week ago that Di had confessed her love for him, that Jim Brewster had made his surprising re-entry into her own life? It seemed now as if he never had left it. It was grand to have him back; she hadn't realized how much his encouragement had meant in her work. She was glad that she had not let him come before. Now she could use easily the hands which had been so helpless, now she could—

"That's done!" Diane strapped the hamper. She adjusted white-rimmed dimmers before she flung herself flat on her back beside her sister's chair. Dopey, who had been sniffing for titbits among the rocks, galloped up, and flopped down beside her.

"Even though we can't see it, how clearly we can hear that plane, lovely. It growls like the M.G.M. lion. One went over the house at dawn this morning. Sounded as if it grounded at the Manor—my imagination, doubtless: Guests wouldn't be likely to arrive at daybreak."

"They might. Flying breakfasts are the latest fashion. Ever long to fly again, Di?"

"No. It's a lonely sport. I like to motor, better. I love the smell and color of the earth; people fascinate me. I'm glad I had the training, though. Someday I may be needed to fly small ships for reconnaissance work, even to rush supplies across the country. Now that we have compulsory military training for men, women must do their part. In this world crisis personal problems seem inconsequential, don't they?"

"Measured by the importance of the ramifications of each life, no. Individual morale must be kept up for the good of the whole."

"Let's forget problems. Did you ever know a more typical Maine day? Here come a lot of little puffy white clouds."

"Gorgeous is the word for it. I love that ballerina-skirted swim suit you're wearing, Di. The color is perfect for you."

"Nothing wrong with your dusty-pink frock." Diane stretched lazily. "My swim made me sleepy. The water was grand. Prickly as 'pin-point carbonation.' Made me ravenous, as you must have observed at luncheon."

"I didn't do so badly myself. I love our weekly picnics here. I was tempted to invite Jim to join us today, but I knew it would mean more work for you."

"Me? Work when there is a man in the party? You done me wrong. I know how to keep the lads busy." She rolled over and began to erect a pebble fortress. "Has Jim told you anything about his girl?"

"Not much. My fault. When we have been together I have had the subject of my work on my mind to pretty near the exclusion of everything else. I was unselfish enough —note the tinge of satire in 'unselfish'—to ask her name, age and type. She's Aurelie Leonard, twenty-three, a tall blonde."

"I get you—divinely-tall-and-so-divinely-fair type. Too young for Jim; altogether too young, if you ask me. He's forty, isn't he?"

"Yes, but seventeen years isn't much if they love one another. There is ten between you and Mac. That's all right, isn't it?"

The question was tinged with amusement. Diane realized that Merry suspected there was something queer going on. Had she better confess and get it over? Not yet. Not until she was completely immersed in interest in her work and

—Jim Brewster. Somehow that engagement yarn of his didn't ring true. His eyes when he looked at Merry belied it. If it were true, his "Aurelie," if she really wanted him, had better recall him at once.

"Anyone would think *I* was Mac's heartthrob. You never are visible when he comes," Merry observed, still with the amused note in her voice which Diane distrusted.

"I'm too busy with herbs and the articles my contract calls for to have time for him. You've taken that—that—understanding is a good word for it—between Mac and me too seriously, Merry. I have no intention of marrying for years and years *and* years—if ever."

"Exciting prospect for Mac. Is it because of me, Di? If that is your reason, it's wrong. I must battle my own way out of grief and loss and helplessness. With all your love and devotion you can't do it for me."

"I know that, lovely, but I can help." Diane cleared her husky voice. "Now that I think of it, none of our 'boy friends'—cribbed from Trudy, in case you care—not even Doc Reynolds, has appeared today." She yawned prodigiously in an attempt to change the subject. "My word, but I'm dopey."

"That's because you were prowling round the house last night instead of being in your bed asleep."

Diane sat up on crossed bare legs with a speed which sent two floating gulls soaring. Did Merry suspect? Did she know where she had been? How could she? It was a secret between three persons, none of whom would tell. Why would a resident of this small village conceal a radio and store "explosives"? Only one answer. . . . She had thoroughly distrusted the man but she hadn't suspected him of being a traitor. She must make one more trip to be sure she was right before she reported the discovery. She impatiently pushed aside the conclusion to answer her sister.

"What do you mean? I never go to bed until eleven-thirty. I do my writing when the house quiets down. You and Freda are such noisy persons. . . . Those tide pools reflecting the sky look like patches of blue mirror set in the rocks."

"Don't try to sidetrack me with a word picture, Di. I know that there was a lot going on outside the house between nine and ten. Dopey barked. I listened. The night was so still I would be willing to swear that someone slipped from the raft and swam to shore, that the swimmer came up the gravel path toward the house."

To hide the startled color which burned her face Diane bent for a handful of pebbles. Had someone been on the raft last night? Had he seen her return? Could it have been Luigi? No. Asaph had reported that he had taken Trudy to a dance.

"Were you out for a moonlight swim after I have asked you not to go alone?"

Diane dramatically crossed her throat with a pink-nailed forefinger.

"'Hope to die' I wasn't, lovely. You know I wouldn't go after I promised you. Just to keep you from worrying I'll own up. I did steal out the back door, hoping you wouldn't hear me, because—because Asaph flung some pebbles against my window. I suspected at once that Martha had had an attack of hysterics and he didn't know what to do."

"Why didn't you call Freda?"

"Freda has enough on her hands; besides she has no patience with the woman. I like Martha. Asaph is always cracking at her about her nerves. I have a feeling that it isn't all nerves. Also, I have a conviction that living with crabbed Mr. Hicks isn't a joy ride."

"Asaph's bark is worse than his bite."

"A barking dog might be toothless but it would still be a barking dog. Who wants to live with one?"

"What is it, Dopey? Did you think I was talking about you, old lamb pie? Not much. You don't speak out of turn. What are you all gaga about?"

The setter was brushing Diane's shoulder, plumed tail waving, nose quivering, eyes intent on the path which sloped easily between two large boulders to the shore, a slope which had been graded to accommodate Merry's chair.

"I hear voices. Who can it be? Both Freda and Trudy know that we never see callers when I'm here for a swim. I'll wring that girl's neck if she has let anyone come."

"Don't be so excitable, Di. You're adorable in that bathing suit, so don't be sorry about that; as for me, I must overcome my hatred of being seen wheeled about. That's another bogy to fight. I—"

"So here you are! Hiding out on us, were you?" Mac Cameron hailed them from the path. Jim Brewster followed him to the shore. With no respect for their white cardigans and slacks, Dopey jumped first on one, then the other in frenzied welcome.

"Oh, it's only you!" Merry exclaimed.

"Cameron, was there a tinge of disappointment in that voice? Have these gals heavy dates with two other guys?" Brewster demanded theatrically.

"If they have we'll break it up. You take Merry to the terrace and I'll guard Di here."

"O.K. with me. I'm taking Merry for a drive, Di."

"Jim! It's impossible. I haven't been off this place since I came here three years ago!"

"No foolin'! Then it's high time you made the break. Give you ideas. Can't have my top illustrator going small-town on me. We're off."

Brewster turned Merry's chair. With a queer tightening of her throat Diane noticed that her sister made no further protest. She was laughing. Had accepting Jim's dictatorship become a habit so soon? What would happen when he left to marry blonde Aurelie? Had she better warn him not to hurt Merry? *No*—her recent attempt to protect her sister hadn't been such a spectacular success that she would try again.

"The Dominant Male—in person. Does he really think he can inveigle Merry into his car? I have begged and begged her to let Freda and me drive her for a change of scene if only to the next village, but it was like beating my wings against iron bars."

"Brewster didn't beg. He just told her she was going. She'll go. What were you doing last night beween nine and ten o'clock?"

Surprise switched Diane's thought to the man frowning at her. Incidentally, it took the stiffening from her knees. She sank to the pebbly shore. His voice had been grave. Now that she really had looked at him, she noticed lines in his face she never had seen before. His eyes were unsmiling. His bronze skin was drained of color.

How had he heard? What did he know? If anyone else had seen her, the risk she had taken might prove useless. Each person who shared a secret jeopardized its chance of remaining a secret. You never can tell, she thought, twisting a scrap of skirt between her fingers, when Bully Boy Bad Luck will take a wallop at you.

"Was it you on our diving raft last night?" she demanded as he dropped to the rug beside her. "Did you swim ashore and gumshoe up the path to the house?"

"I object to that word 'gumshoe' but we'll let it pass for the moment. How in thunder did you know that?"

She told him; added: "Why were you spying on me?"

"I wasn't spying." With the caution and tact of a man skirting a wasps' nest, he explained how he had happened to arrive at the raft. Even as he talked he knew that she was chalking up another score to the already staggering total she thought she had against him.

"When I heard the dog bark—I've owned dogs, I can detect the difference between warning and welcome—I concluded there was trouble afoot and rushed to the rescue. A week ago you had had a showdown with Luigi. I suspected he might be out for reprisal. I don't see how a man under the circumstances could have acted otherwise."

"So what?" she asked and treated him to a cocky little smile.

"Don't rock the boat, soldier. Even girls who aren't 'practically engaged' have been kissed for less provocation than that perk of your brows."

The gay recklessness of his eyes sent her scrambling to her knees. He caught her bare arm and pulled her back.

"Sit down. You are perfectly safe."

"I presume you mean that you wouldn't care to kiss anyone so dis—agreeable as I?"

"That's the underlying idea. But I didn't come here to fight with you. Our disagreement seems unimportant at the moment. I came to ask what you know about the—the accident to the Major last evening before ten-thirty."

"*Accident!* What accident? What do you mean?"

"Someone shot him."

"Shot the *Major?* Why? *Why* would anyone shoot him?"

"That's what I'm asking you. What did Asaph mean? I overheard him warn you:—

" 'You shouldn't have did it, Di. Terrible risky.' "

She doodled in the sand with one finger while her thoughts ran hither and thither like a mouse looking for a hole through which to escape. She couldn't tell him where she had been last night before ten-thirty. Thank heaven, there was no ground for her recent suspicion that he knew.

His eyes hardened with sudden doubt.

"You do know something about it. Be quick. Tell the truth."

"You—you don't really believe that I know anything about the accident to the Major, do you?"

"I'm trying to give you a break. If the Major dies—"

"*Dies!*"

"It will be murder."

"Murder!" She shivered. "Why should anyone murder him?"

"Because someone wanted papers in his desk."

"You're practically accusing me of shooting him."

"I'm not accusing you. Of course I don't think you did it. I think you may know something about those papers."

"What papers? Perhaps you'll tell me why *I* should be interested in anything in Major Lovel's desk."

"I'll tell you why. Those papers contained all the data his lawyer had worked up from old deeds about his claim to your land. Your rifle was beside him."

XVII

My RIFLE! Impossible! How would it get there? I didn't have my ri—" Diane snapped off the sentence and swallowed the last syllable of the word. "Where is the Major now?"

"At home. The nearest hospital is one hundred miles away. They didn't dare take him there. Luckily Reynolds was at the Manor for contract; so was Sally Arnold, who is a registered nurse. The Doc phoned the Major's physician. Told him who he was; gave his credentials. Declared that because of the position of the bullet the incision to follow it must be made at once to stop the hemorrhage or the wounded man wouldn't live an hour. The New York doctor said 'Go ahead.' Doc sent the butler for his instruments and ether; then, with Sally and me to assist, probed for the bullet and got it. The New York man flew here at dawn with a noted surgeon and two nurses. The big shots agreed that they couldn't have done a better job themselves."

"What a break for Doc Reynolds, if not so good for the Major. Apparently it's true that if you're worth it Opportunity will tag you whether you're in a big city or in a Maine village. That explains the early-morning plane. What does the surgeon think?"

"He refuses to commit himself yet. I must get back. I told Brewster that I had something important to say to you. That's why he took your sister to the house so quickly. It was to give me a chance to—"

"To warn me that I am suspected of shooting the Major?"

"To warn you not to talk. No one knows the rifle was found beside the Major—no one, that is, but the person who used it and myself."

"How do you know it is mine?"

"It's a hunch. It looks like the one you used the day you shot the hawk; it has the same bright trim. Is yours missing?"

"I don't know. Wait. I'll look."

She dashed up the path; prayed as she ran into the library that she would find her rifle. It wasn't there.

Mac Cameron took an eager step toward her as she raced back.

"Well? How about it?"

She shook her head and put her hand over her thumping heart.

"Gone. Where is it?" she asked between harshly drawn breaths.

"I'll produce it when it is needed as evidence. Meanwhile—"

"Miss Di! Miss Di!" Trudy sent her voice ahead of her. Her round face resembled nothing so much as the full moon in a halo hat as she appeared between the boulders. "The Dominie phoned he guessed you'd forgotten you were to meet him at the church to select the hymns for Sunday service. He's holding the line."

"Good heavens, I had. Tell him I'll be there in twenty minutes, Trudy."

"O.K." The little maid's eyes bulged till they looked like blue glassies. "Gee, did you know that Miss Merry went off in that Brewster guy's super roadster? I 'bout had heart failure when I saw Freda an' him lifting her into the car carefully as 'a baby, an' she all smily as if she went speedin' every day. I'll say he was white as a sheet, though. I'll bet he was scared. After they drove off Freda just dropped in a heap on the front steps. I could see her shake. She kept sayin': 'I t'ank I done goodt. I t'ank I done goodt to let her go.' As soon's I phone the Dominie you're comin', Miss Di, I'll get goin'. You know it's my afternoon off." She flung the words over her shoulder and disappeared.

"Trudy should go in for monologues," Mac observed. "She didn't stop to breathe. Sorry I can't drive you to the church, but I must get back. I shouldn't have left the house. Patty-Lee collapsed, but I had to see you. In case you care, I think your fifth fiancé is a grand guy. Don't worry about Merry. He'll take care of her. Good-by."

He was out of sight before she could answer. What answer could she have made, except to agree with him about Jim? Would she be forced to explain where she was last night between nine and ten? His eyes had sharpened when she had breathlessly left the word *rifle* unfinished.

As she went slowly up the stairs to her room to change to a frock the house seemed terrifyingly still. She felt Merry's presence whichever way she turned; she could almost hear her gentle breath. She hadn't been away from the place since she was brought here on a stretcher three years ago. It must seem like this after the death of a person whom one has loved and watched over.

She indignantly shook off the morbid mood as she slipped into a lettuce-green linen. For the first time in years Merry was having a change of scene. Why let imagination turn it into tragedy?

What would Asaph say when he heard about the Major? What would the members of the gang who had despoiled the Manor say when they heard? Perhaps they had known when it happened. As if radioed she heard Luigi Manchusto's sneer: "It's that Major Lovel, I'll bet." As on the screen she saw his chalky, sinister face as he had listened to the Major's plans that night at the barn. Had he shot the Major?

How had her rifle come at the Manor? She hadn't used it since the day, a week ago, when she had placed it in the gunrack in the living room after she had left Asaph and Mac Cameron measuring the stretch of the chicken hawk's great wings. Who had taken it? For an instant she had thought that Mac suspected her of shooting his stepfather. Apparently he was as allergic to Diane Vernon as she was to him. How had the aversion come about? Looking back at those few moments by the brook she knew that she had liked him then; but she had become suspicious and everything had gone haywire. They never could be friends now.

Who had taken her rifle? Had Luigi used it? The questions echoed through her mind like a refrain as she drove the decrepit yellow station wagon toward the village. She tried to remember if she had noticed it in the rack at any time during the last week. Why would she, when she was used to seeing it there?

In spite of her troubled preoccupation she felt the usual thrill when she passed the swinging sign at the crossroads. She had designed it, had superintended the painting in brilliant enamels; and the town blacksmith had contributed

the wrought-iron frame. It presented the legendary sea
captain in yellow oilskins and sou'wester, swinging a ship's
lantern which showed a red light. She had brought the idea
from England where the then Duke of York had initiated
the erection of village signs of symbolic or historic interest.
Not one of them was standing now.

The sign brought back the vision of a ghostly figure stealing through the fog. It brought also the memory of her
trip last night with Nicols; the icy shivers creeping up her
spine and tobogganing down, as she had kept watch while
he hid his sedan among the bushes; the *thump-thump* of
her heart as they stole noiselessly along the path; the way
it had stopped when they found the hidden key.

"Terribly sorry to have kept you waiting, Dominie," she
apologized as she entered his study in the church. He looked
hot in his clerical black. Why didn't the woman whose brilliant blue eyes had watched her, from the Manse window,
as she hurried up the path, see that he had comfortable
clothes to wear in summer? Too absorbed in herself, was
the answer.

"Quite all right, my dear." The Dominie patted her shoulder. "'Ill blows the wind that profits nobody.' I polished
my sermon for Sunday while I waited for you. My text is:—

> Eye hath not seen, O God, nor ear heard, neither hath
> it entered into the heart of man, what good things thou hast
> prepared for thy children.

"Although our own Government policies, our speeding-
up defense preparedness and the tragedy overseas are the
topics uppermost in everyone's mind, I shall endeavor to
turn the thoughts of my congregation toward hope, toward
glimpses, hints and promises of goodness. . . . Shall we
go into the church and try out the hymns?"

Seated at the organ in the gallery, Diane could see how
the sunlight, shining through the stained-glass window which
was a memorial to her grandparents, gemmed the white
backs of the pews with ruby, emerald, sapphire and topaz;
fretted with gold the mahogany railing of the stairs which
mounted each side of the pulpit; set the letters on the
cover of the closed Bible glinting and rested like a benign
hand on the Dominie's silver hair.

While her fingers softly pressed the ivory keys, while
"In Heavenly Love Abiding" set the old church pulsing
with its fervor and its music, Diane half closed her eyes

and let her thoughts return to Merry, who was faring forth into what must seem a brand-new world. Was it the beginning of a fuller, richer life for her? Were her own prayers about to be answered? Was her sister commencing really to live again?

She thought of Mac Cameron and his tense concern about his stepfather. A man had been shot, wounded perhaps fatally, with her gun. If he died it would be murder. Who had shot him—Luigi Manchusto? The possibility made it more important than before that she follow the trail she had started on last night.

She shook her head, as if by the motion she could clear away the haze of incredulity. It was unbelievable. It had happened somewhere else. Not in this lovely village. She had been bitter toward the Lovels. Had she radiated an aura of hate which had reached out and poisoned the sensitive mind of a person who had a real or fancied grievance, until his mental balance was upset and he had done this horrible thing?

No, no, *no!* Why should she think herself in any way responsible? She wasn't, even though her rifle had been used; *if* it had, she still couldn't believe it. Who had stolen the gun? It might have been taken at any time during this last week.

The organ notes thinned into the solemn silence of the church. The Dominie's voice rose from the center aisle.

"Thank you, my dear. The hymns are perfect. They will tie my service together. I like unity in the speaking and music. Come down to the study, Miss Diane. There are a few things about which I would like to consult you if you have time."

Time! She had time to burn. She dreaded to go outside the church, to face questions and gossip about the Major, which by now would be rolling on every tongue like a delectable titbit. Mrs. Lovel's attitude toward the community had been aloof and tainted with disdain. There would be no sympathy for her.

"We'll give Trudy Budge the solo on Sunday." The Dominie indulged in the chuckle his parishioners loved as he opened the door of his book-lined study. "I believe it would be called 'featuring' her in the movies."

"I'm glad you have decided to let her try, Dominie. She has a sweet voice. If we can get her interested in improving that, we will have a weapon with which to checkmate her mother who is trying to force her into an early marriage. It would be nothing short of a crime for the girl to be cheated out of a few happy, carefree years."

"You have great influence with Trudy, Miss Diane. You are helping her as you would want a child of yours helped. Jesus Christ, who knew the needs of humanity, set an Eternal Light in the world by which our lives may be guided when he gave us the Golden Rule. I know from the talks I have had with Trudy that you are teaching her honor and self-discipline, those two enduringly valuable elements in character."

"Sometimes I think the progress I make—if you can call it progress—is one step forward and two back."

"Don't be discouraged. Trudy admires and loves you and your sister. That affection will keep her from backsliding until personal integrity has become a habit. Your life here for the last three years has ramifications more extensive than you imagine. Because of your Young Voters' Club new power is stealing through the village. I notice fresh energy, and a return to the standards of decency, and a certain decorum that has been missing during late years.

"The young people are even showing a slight interest in church." He chuckled. "Of course it may be that they look upon it as a fashion show while the summer people are here, but who am I to complain about why they come, if they come?" He smiled with the tolerance and sympathetic understanding which made him so dear.

"Dominie, you're a darling and I love you," Diane exclaimed impulsively.

"So that's what goes on here."

The spiteful words came as if forced between pursed lips by a malevolent demon behind them. The woman in the doorway drew her magenta shoulder shawl tightly across her polka-dotted breast and stared accusingly at her husband with hard, brilliant eyes.

"Why Violet, my dear." The Dominie was beaming, her acridity apparently unnoticed. "It's a long time since you have walked from the Manse to the church and you're not breathless. You must be better."

His wife became at once noticeably short-breathed. Her blue eyes glittered as they flashed to Diane.

"Quite time I came, David. But we'll let that go for the present. I risked my life when I walked here—my heart might have stopped—to tell you that one of your parishioners is in dire need of your spiritual ministration. But perhaps you already know. Perhaps Diane has told you that Major Lovel has been fatally shot."

For one horrible moment Diane despaired of restraining a hysterical laugh. The woman was melodrama in person, as a cartoonist or a humorist would caricature it. She bit her lips hard to steady them.

"The surgeon hasn't said 'fatally' though the Major *is* seriously wounded, Mrs. Richards. I had not told the Dominie, we have been so occupied selecting hymns for Sunday service."

"Hymns!" The woman's shoulders almost touched her ears. "That's a new name for it. David, why are you lingering here when Mrs. Lovel needs your spiritual aid and comfort?"

"I will go at once. I'll see that you get safely back to the house first, Violet, my love. Thank you for coming, Miss Diane. Please close the study door when you go out."

Diane waited until she saw the Dominie leave the Manse before she kicked the starter of the station wagon into action.

"Cat! If it wasn't too ridiculous, I would think she was accusing me of trying to ensnare her husband, putting on the irresistible Patty-Lee's *femme-fatale* act. The old dear didn't for a minute sense what she meant."

The smile the thought flashed to her lips faded as she looked about her. This was the loveliest summer she had known since she and Merry had come here to live. Clear days. . . . Abundant showers at night. . . . Except for an occasional flame of maple and the darkness of spruce and pine and cedar, the woods were as freshly green as they had been in June. Never had the hills been more purple, the sea more like sparkling sapphires, the islands more emerald. The roadsides, all faint violets, pinks and yellows, where asters and goldenrod were just coming into flower, had the delicacy of coloring of a Fragonard panel. The sun shone warmly on white houses, like a huge floodlight turned on a painted city.

A gorgeous world and in its midst a man had been shot and a vicious-tongued woman had sprayed venom through tightly pursed lips. The poet was right—"Where every prospect pleases and only man is vile." In this case it was a woman who had taken the beauty out of the afternoon. Cheerio. It wasn't all to the bad. Merry was motoring with Jim Brewster. Perhaps he would break the spell of Mac

Cameron's attraction. If only that could happen. She stepped on the gas as she saw a bicycle ahead.

"Wait, Dominie," she called. "I'll give you a lift."

"Thank you, my dear. I'm quite out of breath." His face was red above the clerical collar; his black suit was dusty. "Violet hurried me so; she was afraid I would be too late." With a sigh of relief he lifted his wheel into the back of the station wagon.

As she drove on, with the Dominie silent beside her, her thoughts switched back to her own problems.

Who stole my rifle? Who shot the Major? Nicols may have views as to who did it. Nicols! . . . Her heart spiraled to her throat. *Nicols!* Why had that hideous suspicion of him bobbed up? He had been with her, hadn't he? But the shooting might have occurred after he had said good night and added, "I'll carry on."

"Carry on." What had he meant by that? Why was a man of his evident breeding and education serving as a valet? Would the answer to that question solve the mystery of the shooting of his employer?

XVIII

$\mathcal{A}$ s HE stood before the mirror in his dressing room at the Manor, Mac Cameron's thoughts were far away from the brown hair he was furiously brushing. Why had Diane been so mysterious as to her whereabouts, last night between nine and ten? Who had dropped her rifle beside the Major? Who had borrowed or stolen it?

He hadn't told her of the ship's lantern, or that he had left it where it lay on the terrace step for someone else to find, or how he had kicked the rifle into the shrubs and had returned for it after the Major had been carried into the house. Why the dickens had he been so sure it was her rifle? There must be dozens like it in the village. That was a thought. He shook his head. Hers was missing. Was she engaged to Brewster? She had intimated that she was, but he appeared devoted to Merry. If so, how about that kiss the night of the dinner?

"Will you wear this, sir?"

It was Nicols' voice, Nicols beside him with a white dinner jacket in his hand.

"Yes. But later I may have to pilot the plane if the doctors want another specialist from New York."

"Very well, sir. I'll lay out your flying suit; then you won't be delayed a moment. I shan't leave the house this evening in case my help is needed. I was told to inform you that dinner will be served in the loggia, sir."

"The loggia! What's the idea; aren't the surgeons dining here?"

"They are to be served in the breakfast room, Mr. Cameron. The Madam felt that she could not see them. She is still suffering from shock." Nicols repeated the words as if by rote.

Mac's brows met in a frown. There was something wrong with the picture of Patty-Lee and him tête à tête and the surgeons dining by themselves while her husband lay in bed, perhaps mortally wounded. It might be all right with any other woman but with her—He remembered how she had clung to him, had collapsed in his arms when the Major had been carried upstairs. He had delayed moving in with the Doc just twenty-four hours too long.

"Isn't Doctor Reynolds here, Nicols?"

"Yes, sir. He was wonderful last night, wasn't he, Mr. Cameron? I saw great surgeons operate in the World War but never one more expert than he. Miss Arnold knows her business. I felt it a privilege to be allowed to help. You were rather wonderful yourself, sir, the way you handled the ether."

"I had to anesthetize while in camp several times, when the doctor needed an assistant. Isn't Doctor Reynolds dining with Mrs. Lovel?"

"No, sir. The Madam thought it would be better if he dined with the New York men. She said she couldn't bear to see anyone but you. Curious that the weapon with which the Major was shot wasn't found; don't you think so, sir?"

"Curious! What's curious about it?" Mac felt the betraying blood prickle under his skin. Did Nicols suspect him of having taken the gun? Guilty conscience . . . Why should he?

"As a rule men who attempt murder don't leave their tools behind them, do they?"

"No, sir. Of course not. A stupid question of mine, Mr. Cameron."

Something in the man's voice set suspicion blazing. Nicols was a mysterious person. Why had a man of his type taken a position as valet? By his own admission he had served in the World War. So had the Major. Could their paths have crossed and tangled? Was he here to settle an old score, or was he a Fifth Column agent checking up on this Maine shore? Others beside Englishmen had acquired the Oxford accent. Was he implicated in the shooting? A crazy supposition but one worth following up.

"Curious that no one heard the shot last night, Nicols. Where were you at the time?"

"I don't know just when it happened, sir. After Major Lovel dressed for dinner I was free for the evening. I went out as usual. To the cinema. Jolly good show, too."

"You reported that the Major's desk had been rifled, didn't you?"

"I did, sir. I returned to the Manor shortly before eleven. I motored with an—acquaintance after the picture. I should say between nine and ten-thirty. It was a perfect night, if you remember, sir."

"I remember." He had reason to remember. Hadn't he been swimming at about that time? Had Diane been with Nicols during the hour for which she wouldn't account?

"You came back to the Manor shortly before eleven. How did you happen to go to the Major's study if you were through your work?"

A ghost of a smile played round the valet's lips and was gone.

"No matter what time I come in I always lay out Major Lovel's lounge robe and his slippers in his study, sir. If he's a bit edgy he likes to slip into them. Sometimes he reads until morning. Last night when I entered the drawers of the desk were open and papers were strewn over the top."

"Did you know then that important documents had been taken?" Suddenly he remembered that the deeds and blueprints of the Vernon estate were the ones he had promised the Major he would look over this morning.

"No, sir. How could I? I am not the Major's secretary. I am his valet. If you remember I came to you at once and reported the condition of the room."

He answered a faint knock on the door.

"Dinner is served in the loggia, Mr. Cameron," he announced as he returned and picked up a coat.

"Just a minute, Nicols. If you didn't know and tell what papers were missing, who did?"

A dull color suffused the valet's face. His eyes were on the garment he was brushing.

"It might have been the Madam, sir. She was trying to tidy up the desk when I entered the room."

"Mrs. Lovell! In the study when you came in at eleven? Impossible. She was in a state of collapse when I carried her upstairs after the Major had been taken to his room."

"Mrs. Lovel was there, quite angry and excited. She accused me of stealing the papers. That's one of the things I've felt a bit down about. Lately, she has resented my being here. In fact, the Major had given me notice that he would not need me after the first of next month. Dinner is served, sir."

There was a slight suggestion of steel running through the smooth, cultured voice. So Nicols had received his walking papers. Would he take his revenge on his employer for that?

"Oh, all right, Nicols. Keep what you've just told me about the study under your hat. We've been so concerned about the Major that we haven't notified the sheriff to follow up the gunman. We'll have him here tomorrow and we'll bust this case wide open."

"If I may presume to suggest, every moment of delay means that the trail is cooling, Mr. Cameron. Why wait until tomorrow? I'll leave your flying outfit ready in case you need it, sir."

That didn't sound as if the man had anything to conceal, Mac concluded as he walked slowly along the corridor. He hadn't considered it necessary to explain to Nicols that it hadn't been concern for the Major that had delayed the appeal to the sheriff, it had been the wounded man's broken command.

"Don't—try to f-find who—shot—mistake. I don't fight . . ."

Did that word "mistake" mean that he had recognized his assailant and was trying to protect him? Him! . . . Hadn't he tried to say that he didn't fight women? That last word struck at the pit of Mac's stomach. Diane's rifle had been beside him.

Reynolds stepped out in answer to his light tap on the door of the Major's room. His coarse red hair was rampant, as if electrified; his keen eyes were sunk in deep, dark hollows; his face was drawn.

"How is he?"

"Not so good, Mac. The big shots have decided not to send for another surgeon. They've discovered that I know my stuff. You won't have to take off tonight."

"I'm ready in case you need me. What can I do to help?"

"Stick around. The Major tried to say something; we

thought it was your name; but he drifted off again. We'll call you the minute he rouses. One other thing you can do: Keep that woman away from here."

"*What* woman?"

"His wife. We let her into his room for a moment and she began excitedly to whisper questions—we couldn't hear what they were, but we feared the Major would slip away before we could get her out. Viper, if ever there was one."

Mac let that go. He had a sudden vision of Patty-Lee in her husband's study "tidying up" his desk. It was she who had reported that papers *in re* the Vernon land had been stolen. Had he hold of a time bomb which might explode at any minute? The Major had tried to say his name. Did he want to tell what he knew about the shooting?

"I'll be on hand if you need me, Doc."

Two tall, hurricane-shaded lamps shed a soft light in the loggia. Patty-Lee pouted and turned an unblemished, satin-smooth expanse of creamy back on him as he stepped out. The halter of her violet-net evening frock was studded with amethysts which shot out little crimson sparks when she moved.

"You took your time," she complained as he drew out her chair.

"I'm late because I stopped to talk with Doc Reynolds about the Major's condition."

He sat down opposite her at the exquisitely appointed table. . . . Glint of silver. . . . Sparkle of glass. Fragrance of white sweet peas. Flames of candles that matched in color the crisp balls of iced pink watermelon heaped in individual crystal baskets at each place.

"What did he say?" she asked eagerly. The candlelight set a million colored sparks dancing from the jewels on her fingers, red lights in the depths of her eyes.

"Not too good." And then because it hurt unbearably to talk of death or danger menacing the man who had been the only father he remembered, he suggested:—

"Look behind you, Patty-Lee. What a sky! All crimson and gold, green and lemon-yellow. Gorgeous as it is, that ragged purple cloud looming above it looks uncommonly like the vanguard of a storm."

She shivered and glanced over her shoulder.

"I hope it isn't. They are terrific here and scare me out of my senses. Wasn't that thunder?"

The butler served the dinner, course after delectable course. The two at the table kept up a give-and-take of small talk. Mac made a pretense of eating, but with his mind on the man upstairs who had tried to say his name he found it difficult to swallow. "Stick around," Doc had said. "We'll call you the minute he rouses." The delicate porcelain-and-silver coffee cups were filled.

"You may go, Barnes. Don't come for the tray until I ring."

"I understand, Madam."

Mac thought he detected an ironic twist to the man's mouth before he backed into the shadow.

"Now we can talk, honey boy. Come here." Patty-Lee indicated a chair beside the wheel chaise.

The very chair the Major had occupied last night, he remembered.

"Like to sit where I can watch the water." He dropped into a deep wicker one at the edge of the loggia, held a lighter to his cigarette and wondered how soon he could decently break away.

"Then if it's a case of Mahomet and the Mountain, here comes Mahomet," Patty-Lee declared and settled herself cozily on the arm of his chair, in an aura of expensive perfume.

He sprang to his feet. She gripped the back to steady herself.

"I almost lost my balance, honey boy," she pouted. She stood up and clasped her hands about his arm.

"Mac. Mac. I didn't mean what I said last night, that if you stayed here, I wouldn't. You know I'm crazy about you. Have you ever thought that if the Major dies—that you and I—with his money—I really loved you all the time, Mac, but I was so poor—" She pressed her head against his sleeve.

He jerked his arm free. Hot, nauseating revulsion swept through him like a tide. His face burned. His head felt light. This was the woman he might have married. He caught her roughly by the shoulders.

"Listen to me, Patty-Lee." He administered a shake by way of emphasis. "You've lost your mind. The Major won't die. Get this: *I wouldn't marry you—*"

"Honey boy. Don't be cross." She laid her head against his shoulder and flung a bare arm about his neck. "Love me—"

"I'm terribly sorry to trouble you," a breathless voice behind them interrupted, "but I must have—" It broke with a horrified "Oh—h."

XIX

Merry vernon withdrew her thoughtful gaze from the glory of crimson, green and yellow in the western sky to look at her sister, as she stepped from the hall to the terrace. Her eyes were brilliant with tears.

"Di, I'm an absolutely different person. Since that drive this afternoon I feel as if I had been born into a new and glorious w—world." Her husky voice broke.

With her hands deep in the pockets of her rose-and-white–print frock Diane leaned against the terrace wall. She mustn't let Merry know how the sight of her on the chaise instead of in the wheelchair, how her flushed, eager face, tightened her throat. She must treat this great step forward as a matter of course, not as the miracle it seemed to her.

"Sure, it's a great world. You and Jim certainly looked like a million when you drove up to the door in that sensational roadster of his. The publishing business must be on the way up. Didn't get overtired, did you?"

Darn. . . . That was a bad break. Why suggest that she might be?

"No. Jim's a marvelous driver. Smooth as velvet. When we came to a lovely view we would stop. He would cut out the engine. He even had a tea basket along. I was shocked to hear over the car radio that Major Lovel had been wounded."

"Mac Cameron told me about it after you and Jim left. I feel as if I were struggling under a load of bricks which had been dumped on me. I can't get the events of the last twenty-four hours out of my mind. Much as I disliked Major Lovel, I can't bear the thought that he may die. And then my . . ." She caught back the word *rifle* and wondered if it could possibly be true, as Mac Cameron claimed, that her gun had been found beside the wounded man. It was true that it was missing from the rack.

"Go on," Merry prodded. " 'And then my' you began and stopped as if you had bitten off the sentence."

"And then my set-to with that poisonous Richards woman," Diane continued, with a breathlessness occasioned by the realization that she had almost told something which must not be told. "I was so hot about it that I boiled over the minute you reached home and dumped all the harrowing details on you, you may remember. Doc Reynolds warned me about her the first day I met him. He said 'Vitriol can escape from between lips as tightly pursed as Mrs. Richards'.' "

"Sometimes I think John Reynolds is a wizard who can read minds. Was that thunder?"

Diane turned to look at the western sky.

"The cloud above that gorgeous coloring looks like a gunmetal–gray horse on the rampage. See its ragged mane? There are a lot of colts and younger fry scampering up to join the veteran. However, we may not get the storm. Sometimes it follows the river. In case it decides to drop in on us I'll make the rounds of the windows. It's Trudy's afternoon off and Freda is clearing up after supper. What had I better do about the Dominie's wife, lovely? Give up playing the organ and training the choir till her brainstorm passes?"

"Not for a minute. Charge it up to sunspots—they are being blamed for everything unpleasant in the world—and forget it. Jim is coming in later to decide upon the parts of the story I am to illustrate. I hope he will get here before the storm breaks."

"Mees Di," Freda Swenson spoke from the doorway. "There's a storm comin' an' Trudy's gone to the Islandt vith that Manchusto an' the tide iss running out fast. She iss scaredt to death of thunder an' lightning."

"She hasn't gone alone with him, has she?"

"Ya. She toldt me he said the place vas lousy vith blackberries an' she vas goin' to bring home a svell lot for me to can for Mees Merry. I t'ank you never make that girl to talk lak a lady, Mees Di."

"When did she start?"

"Yoost after Mees Merry went. That Manchusto fella coom in his car. She said they vas goin' first to the next town to buy pails to pick in, didn't have 'em in our village, then they vas goin' in his 'Evenrudt,' I t'ank she call it. She said she'd be back here by seven."

Seven. . . . It was eight o'clock now. Diane glanced at the gathering clouds. Thunderheads, every one of them. To her troubled fancy, Luigi Manchusto's face, with its leering mouth and heavy-lidded eyes, appeared to be superimposed on their sullen purple-blackness. She came to a swift decision.

"Freda, phone the Budge house and ask if Trudy is there."

As the woman disappeared in the dusky hall, she paced the terrace.

"Merry, if Trudy isn't at home, I'm going to the Island for her. If they haven't started back yet, Luigi may frighten her about the storm and persuade her to wait in that empty fisherman's shack till it's over. It may last all night. I must find her."

"No, Di! *No*. I'm as anxious about the child as you are, but use your head. We have nothing but the rowboat, which isn't seaworthy. By the time you reach the village to hire a launch the storm may be raging. Hear that?"

A low, ominous roar rumbled away beyond the hills, and sent the shivering setter crawling under Merry's chair.

"That's a long way off. It may go round. Don't worry about me. I'll borrow Larry's motor launch at the Manor; he told me to use it while he is away. I know every bar and ledge in this bay. I ought to. At one time or another, I've been hung up on each one of them. Is she there, Freda?"

The woman in the doorway shook her head.

"No. She not coom home. Her mudder say she vas comin' right here from the Islandt. She say something 'bout Trudy not likin' home no more but I hung up on her. So!"

"Bring my tweed topcoat, Freda. Quick!"

"Di! You mustn't go. You're crazy to think of it."

"I'll be crazy if I don't. We've taken that girl into our home, Merry, and I feel responsible for her safety. Lucky I left the station wagon in the drive."

She slipped into the plaid coat Freda held for her and dropped a hasty kiss on her sister's shining hair.

"Don't look so scared, lovely. We can't sit here and take even a chance at cruel gossip for Trudy, can we? I can get the launch without disturbing anyone at the Manor. I'll ask the butler for the boathouse key and get away without being seen. I'll be back before you can say 'Jack Robinson.'"

"'Jack Robitson'! So! Mees Di, she sure have her little joke. Don't you vorry about her, Mees Merry. They t'ank she crazy at the Manor. They say 'No' 'bout the boat. You see." Freda's soothing voice followed Diane as she raced through the hall.

The yellow station wagon shook in all its aged joints,

snorted when she wrenched it into gear. Would they think she was crazy when she asked for Larry's launch at the Manor? She wasn't and she would get the boat. That settled that.

Much as it irked her, she drove slowly when she entered the drive. With each distant streak of lightning, trees stood out like black smudges in a charcoal sketch. This was not the psychological moment in which to come to the Manor in quest of a boat. In the great house ahead a man might be dying. The atmosphere must be tense with anxiety.

The car sighed faintly when she cautiously stopped it, some distance from the entrance steps, behind a shabby jalopy—Doc Reynolds'. It wouldn't do for him to see her; he might try to stop her. It would be a break if she ran into Nicols. She had reason to know that she could count on his help. The epoch-making trip last night about which she was being so mysterious wouldn't have been possible if it hadn't been for him. For a moment this afternoon she had been suspicious of him. Pretty ungrateful of her.

Step by soundless step she followed the grass border along the drive. Even the crunch of gravel might disturb the wounded man. The front door was wide open. She slipped into the hall. Voices. In the loggia. Luck was with her. The butler and waitress doubtless were clearing away after dinner. She would speak to Barnes there.

Did her heart *have* to pound till it shook her body? One might think she was breaking and entering. *Ooch!* What a clap of thunder. The storm was coming and she was wasting time. Thank goodness it was light enough to see someone standing in the loggia. Whoever it was, she must get that boat. She dashed out between the open French doors.

"I'm terribly sorry to disturb you, but I must have— Oh—h!"

With a little shriek the figure divided.

Mrs. Seth Lovel in Mac Cameron's arms! . . . Her husband perhaps dying upstairs! . . . For an instant the world went round and round and churned Diane's stomach with it.

"What are you doing here?" The woman's shrill question restored equilibrium.

"Sorry—sorry to intrude—" that wasn't tactful—"but I must have the key to the boathouse. I need Larry's launch."

"The launch! Anything happened to your sister?" It was Mac Cameron's hand gripping her arm. Was that hoarse voice his? Perhaps he did love Merry. Perhaps that was why he had been so furious at her attempt to interfere. Silly. Hadn't she just seen him with Patty-Lee in his arms? Hadn't Merry said "naked passion in her eyes when she looks at Mac Cameron"?

"No, no, she's all right. I must get to the Island."

"The Island! With a storm coming up! You're crazy."

"I'm not. I must get there. It's a matter of life and death." He stared at her from beneath frowning brows. Nodded.

"Sure. Pretty desperate aren't you? I'll get the launch out myself. The boathouse isn't locked. Helpful Mac, that's me."

His voice infuriated her. So he might speak to a child he was trying to comfort, to a crazy woman or to a drunk.

"I don't need you—I want—" A rumble of thunder drowned the end of the sentence. His hand on her arm tightened.

"Come along, if you really must get to the Island."

Mrs. Seth Lovel came to sudden, protesting life.

"Honey boy, don't humor that insane girl. She . . ."

Mac hurried Diane across the patio. . . . Down the steps of the three terraces. To the boathouse. At the door his fingers bit into her shoulder.

"Wait a minute. Now what's it all about? Tell me and I'll help you; if you don't—I'll lock you in here. Take your choice. I mean what I say."

She knew that by the set of his jaw. She explained breathlessly. Concluded: "You said yourself that Luigi was a bully, that he would stab in the back or do worse things. I've just got to find Trudy."

"I get you. Wait here."

It seemed but a moment before he slid the launch out beside the pier.

"Hop in!"

"I don't need you. Go back to Pat—" She broke off the word. If she antagonized him he might flood the engine so she couldn't use it. "I'll run the boat myself."

"Like fun you will. Are you coming? Do you want to get to that island or don't you?" She hadn't known that a voice could be so hard. The clean, strong line of his jaw made her think of bronze.

"I *do*."

"Then jump in and be quick about it." He glanced up at the clouds. "We'll make it before the storm breaks. There's always a chance it may go round. Take the wheel. You know where you're going—I hope." He pulled off his white coat and waistcoat, flung them on a seat, ripped off collar

and black tie, turned back his shirt till his throat was free. . . .
Rolled up his sleeves and started the motor.

"I know every bar and ledge in this bay; if I didn't, it is
still light enough to see the buoys that mark the channel.
I'm terribly sorry to take you away from—from the Major."

"Forget it! We'll take that up later. Keep your mind on
the course if you expect to get there. If you ask me, it's get-
ing dark as Hades."

The launch shot through roughening water. Dusk settled
down quickly like a faint, violet mask. Purple clouds
threaded with fiery streaks rolled up behind a hill and shook
more thunder from their folds. Something splashed near by.
Ripples spread in quicksilver rings. A jagged line of fire
slashed open the heavens. In its light the Island showed
just ahead.

"Here we are," Mac called from the bow. "Wait for another flash. Then we can make it."

She hadn't long to wait. For an instant the world was light
as day. The boat slid neatly to the landing. She stood up.

"I'll go ashore—"

"Nothing doing. Sit down! I'm captain of this expedition.
You'll wait here until I come back. Don't get out of this
launch, understand?"

"But you don't know the Island."

"Not this one, but I've seen a few in my time." He sprang
out and tied the painter to a ring in the rough pier. Looked
around. "Any other landing? There's no boat here."

"Sometimes it's dragged up on the shore. No other landing."

"I'll take a look-see to make sure they aren't here. Unless
I miss my guess I'll have plenty of light to guide me."

He vanished into the dusk. She heard pebbles crunch
under his feet. . . . Silence. Uncanny silence. Suppose he
lost his way? She peered over the gunwale. Not any too
much water. The tide ran out fast when it started. If only
she could grip it and keep it from ebbing until he came.

"Trudy! Luigi! Manchusto! *Trudy*—Trudy—y!" His shouts
trailed away in the distance.

She held her breath that she might hear an answer. Nothing but the faint call repeated and repeated came back to
her.

She sat there while distant lightning flashed and thunder
rolled, remembering Luigi's face as he had cursed at her
that night in the drive. Hearing Trudy's laugh: "Gee, I'll

bet you were a lot of fun when you were young, Miss Di."
Remembering Maw Budge's whine to Freda about "Trudy
not likin' home no more." Thinking of the dash into the loggia, Patty-Lee's shriek. Her own horrified realization that
the woman had been in Mac Cameron's arms. His hoarse
voice. The boathouse. His harsh commands. The charged
silence between them as the launch cut through the water.

It seemed hours before she heard the crunch of feet on
the shore. She held her breath. Had he found Trudy?
Across the water drifted the boom of the village clock striking nine.

"Guess what? Not a sign of anyone," he reported as he
untied the painter.

"Are you *sure*? Did you go into the hut?"

"I did. No sign that anyone has been there today. Any
use to *put-put* round the Island?"

"No. This is the only stretch of fields and beach. Jagged
rock, everywhere else."

"Then let's get a move on. There's mighty little water under us. Take the wheel. Quick!" He jumped in. . . . Pushed
off. Started the motor. The boat shot ahead at full speed.

"Sure you didn't have a nightmare? Didn't dream all this
horror stuff about Trudy and her caveman Luigi?"

"I did not. She told Freda she was coming here for black-
berries, that she would be at Honeywort House at seven.
When she didn't come, and she wasn't at home—*Ooch!*
What a flash. I . . ."

With a suddenness which almost pitched them overboard, the launch shuddered to a stop.

"Wh—what happened?"

In answer Mac went forward to the bow.

"I'll say that as an adventure this fool expedition is going
well. We drove into a bar. You said you knew them all. What
was the big idea? Anxious to see this old friend again?"

Lightning turned night to day. He whistled.

"There's a boat length of mud between us and water. The
tide is on the run. *Miss* Vernon, with your panicky hunt for
a girl who probably is safe at home, you're given this situation the works. Sheer cinema. It's a masterpiece of direction any way you look at it. We'll be stuck here for
hours."

XX

DIANE did not answer. A flash of lightning revealed her clutching the wheel and staring at the mud beyond. Her wavy hair had been blown like a dark cloud about her head. The soft rose and white of her print frock showed under her open tweed coat.

"It has the Hollywood touch all right," she agreed in a singularly faint voice and made an effort to flex stiff lips.

He shouldn't have cracked at her like that, Mac told himself as he threw the engine into reverse in an unsuccessful attempt to back out. He'd been brutal; but his nerves were raw. When Patty-Lee had purred ". . . if the Major dies . . ." he had felt perilously near the edge of the slimy underworld. He had seen the horror and loathing in Diane Vernon's eyes when they had met his in the loggia, and had known of what she was accusing him in her thoughts when she had stopped with the startled "Oh—h!" Why not, when she had seen a dying man's wife in his arms? It was maddening. . . . Unbearable.

"Don't stand there like a lookout on a ship. I expect every minute to see you shield your eyes with your hand, hear you shout 'Land! Land!'" Her voice had recovered its strength and color. "What do we do now, Captain?"

She hadn't forgotten that only a few moments ago he had announced himself as head of the expedition. That held. He picked up an oar.

"'Land' isn't the word. If I shouted, it would be 'Water! Water!' There is still a little under us. I'll try to float the launch. If we could only tie the tide and hold it."

She leaned over the gunwale.

"It's running out fast."

Again and again he thrust the oar deep into the mud and pushed.

> "Ol' Man River, Ol' Man River,
> Don't go away from my door,"

he sang in a lusty baritone. Letting his voice out had eased the furious certainty that he was fighting not only the tide but a girl's contemptuous distrust. The song had its effect on Diane.

"Can I help?" she asked eagerly. "Just sitting here I feel as useless as—as a picture postcard without a one-cent stamp. As I told you, I've been hung up on a mud bar before."

The relief, the incredible relief to hear the friendliness in her voice, as friendly as it had been the afternoon he had held her close in his arms by the brook. . . . Had she forgotten that scene in the loggia, or because she was a sport of sports was she ignoring it during this crisis? Whichever it was, he would make the most of it.

"I'm waiting for orders, Cap."

"Sure you can help. Grab an oar. Push on the other side. We'll try rocking the boat. That may start it."

They pushed and rocked. Overhead sounded the high-pitched, eerie laugh of a loon.

"I'm not crazy about that shivery sound. Makes me think of a buzzard hovering over the spot marked X where the dead body lies."

"That's a cheery thought. Snap out of it, gal."

"I'm sorry. I'm terribly sorry I said that. It sounded so flippant when the Major—"

"Stop a minute," he interrupted curtly. The heavens split to reveal a red inferno. In the weird light they looked at each other as they stood resting on their oars.

"Let's make a peace pact. Let's agree while we're stuck here to forget everything that happened before you and I stepped into this boat; that fake love affair of ours, the Major's condition, everything; will you? Let's pretend we've never met before; otherwise it's going to be—unbearable."

The dark-blue eyes met the gray eyes steadily. Mac saw the muscles of her throat contract.

"O.K., Stranger." She peered over the side of the boat. "I can't see that we are an inch nearer that adorable water ahead; on the contrary, it is leaving the mud flat—that's a wisecrack, in case you care. Good heavens, what a crash! That struck somewhere. Listen! The siren!

"One! Two! Three! The fire is in East Village. For one horrible moment I feared it might be our barn. Barns are lightning's meat."

"Forget the fire. Keep pushing."

"I will, though something tells me we'll spend the night just where we are. At least I have the satisfaction of knowing

that Trudy isn't on the Island, and if she isn't there, I'm
sure she is safe."

"We won't spend the night here. At the most we won't
be hung up more than a few hours. I'll make another stab at
moving the boat. Drop that oar. Sit down."

Elbow on knee, chin in hand Diane watched him as he
pulled off shoes and socks and rolled his black trousers above
knees that were as bronzed as his face.

"*Mac!* Mac! You *mustn't*," she protested, as he eased
over the side of the boat and cautiously tested the mud
under his bare foot. "You may go through."

At her frantic "Mac! Mac!" his heart spread wings. She
had forgotten that scene in the loggia. . . . If only he
could have a chance to explain to her that he loathed
Patty-Lee Lovel; if only he could make her listen.

"Through! To China!" Hope had set his voice vibrating.
"If I do, I'll bring you back a string of crystal beads; or would
you prefer an embroidered Mandarin robe—they do them
rather well in the Orient? Stop worrying. Do you think I
would take a chance of leaving you alone here? When I
shove, push with that oar. Ready?"

"Aye! Aye! Cap! I'll do my darnedest. Mind if I laugh?
The mud sounds so—so *squishy* under your feet."

In the tense stillness between rumbles he could hear the
chirp of crickets on the Island, the piping of frogs near a
small pond he had noticed. The *puff-puff* of a distant motor
grew louder.

"A boat. Have they seen us? Are they coming to pull us
off?" Diane asked eagerly.

They held their breath to listen. The engine beats grew
softer and died away.

"Wrong number. Not for us," he said.

From out of the darkness drifted a man's rich voice:—

> "Through the leaves the night winds moving
> Murmur low and sweet."

"Who is singing the Schubert Serenade?" Mac inquired
as he yanked at the launch without moving it an inch.
"That song coming out of this storm is uncanny."

"It's probably from the radio in Larry Crane's cruiser. He
motored to New York and left the big boat here. He phoned
he would be back tonight."

Larry Crane. Larry Crane, who was legal counsel for the

Vernons. He had forgotten him. That only made what he had to do in the next few hours harder. So what? Most of his time during the last three years had been spent doing things that couldn't be done, hadn't it?

As the final exquisite note died away he swung into the launch, dragged his muddy feet after him and dropped to the stern seat. His breath came as if it were being pumped from his lungs by a hundred-horsepower engine.

"Drop the oar, soldier. We haven't moved the boat half an inch. We were going at such speed we drove deep into mud. No use trying to get back to the shelter on the Island; even in this dim light I can see the flats between us and the shore. Buck up. The tide must be dead low, and like luck, when it has done its worst it's bound to turn and give a hand up. In other words, there's a gate in every wall. We don't need an awful lot of water to float us. Think you can stick it out?"

"And what would you suggest my doing if I can't? The walking looks messy."

The unsteady gaiety of her voice started the *tom-tom* of drum beats in his blood. A passionate tenderness for her surged through him. He had admitted to himself that he admired her before his mouth on hers had set his pulses racing. Now he knew he loved her from the top of her dark head to her sandal-shod feet—and she had seen Patty-Lee in his arms. For an instant fury tightened his throat. Desperately, he cleared it.

"You're a gallant fighter, aren't you? You've got the idea," he approved huskily and became absorbed in removing the mud from his feet.

"What shall we do while we wait for that precious water?" she asked and answered before he could:—

"Let's talk. Tell me about yourself—before this summer," she amended. "That won't break our pact. Tell me about engineering below the Equator."

When he appeared to be absorbed in pulling on socks and shoes, she prodded:—

"Go ahead—South America!"

He laughed.

"*This*—is South America. Mackenzie Cameron speaking."

He described the picturesque side of life in an engineers' camp; the mountains of Peru sharp as paper cutouts against a blue sky; the harbor of Rio at night, set in a rim of sparkling lights; the streamers, horns, balloons and floats of the Buenos Aires Carnival; the flowers and sunshine of Santiago; the silver shops, the Spanish-colonial buildings, the pre-Inca textiles and the pottery of Lima. He told of the three snow-capped volcanoes which formed the background of the Little Town of a Hundred Churches, seven thousand feet up in the Andes. Described its Inn, where breakfast is served on the roof, tea in the palm-shaded garden and dinner by candlelight in a great paneled room. It had been his favorite resort when he broke away from camp for a change of outlook. He commented on the festivities at the smart country clubs.

"The fashionable native women wear black, black, black. Perhaps there is North American Indian in my blood. I like color," he admitted, as he slipped on his wrinkled white dinner jacket.

"Most men do. They're pushovers for blue or red."

"It is subtly indicated that you're a pushover for yellow, yourself."

"I love it. It means concentrated sunshine to me. Are you planning to go back to South America?"

"No. My place is in this country at present. I'm a captain in the Engineer Corps of the National Guard. Also, I'm a pilot with the credit of many thousand hours in the air. I'm unmarried—all of which means that I'm likely to be called for service in case—"

"The United States is drawn into the horrible war overseas, or into the defense of this continent. That's the mental reservation of every thinking person to any statement he or she makes, isn't it?"

"It is. Meanwhile I have a job in New York which will take all I can give it."

"New York. You're lucky. Divine place. I adore it! The lights. Music. Theaters. Churches. Pictures. Lectures. Shops. Contacts. There are always celebrities, living there or going through, who are doing big things. We entertained so many in our home, met so many through friends. Sometimes I'm so homesick for it all that I feel as if I must smash my way out of this impasse and . . ."

The break in her passionate voice hurt him.

"Eminent persons appear even in Maine," he reminded lightly. "There's that author Newcomb, and from all I hear I'm beginning to think I picked one out of a brook a few weeks back. They tell me that as a writer you have what it takes."

"Forget what I said, *please*. I didn't mean to turn sobsister. I like my life as it is; really I do."

A jagged line of fire tore open the heavens. *"Ooch!* What a flash! The storm is nearer. I hoped it might cut across-country."

"Looks as if it meant to give us the works. Do you mind a storm?"

"I'm not one of those starry-eyed females of fiction who *loves* a thunderstorm. But since Merry's accident I've had to be a sport; I can't let her think I'm frightened about anything. Just between you and me I'm as jittery as Dopey. He hides under the bed if he can't find an open closet."

"Sit here." He caught her hand and drew her to the seat beside him. He buttoned her long coat from chin to hem. "That won't save your pretty frock much but it may help. We'll pretend that my shoulder is a closet. Hide your eyes against that."

He shouted the last word to make it heard above the crash which shook the universe. The very mud under the launch trembled as if shaken by the vibration of countless army tanks driving relentlessly forward, intent on destruction.

"Thanks but I'll take it with my chin up. Must grow into a big girl sometime," Diane shouted in return.

A blinding flash ripped open the sky. A ball of fire plunged into the water. The air smelled of sulphur. There was the sense as of mountains crashing, heavens torn to tatters. The sea ahead was a lashing ocean of immensity. Mac put his arm about her and drew her close. He felt her tense resistance, then shuddering surrender as pandemonium broke loose.

It must be what the end of the world would be like. The wind came up. The storm battled on with increasing fury. . . . Came a glare that set the sky on fire, a crash that sent her face burrowing into his shoulder, his lips against her hair. Every nerve in his body tingled as if in contact with an electric charge. The boat shivered. He held her closer. . . . Shouted:—

"That one is behind us. Don't move. You've proved yourself a soldier. Keep your head where it is. Here comes the rain! If only there were a slicker for you! This will finish your frock."

"Never mind the frock. This isn't rain; it's a deluge. That last flash must have ripped the bottom out of a water tank overhead."

"We've been yelling for more water and here it is. Stick close to me."

Rain came down in whirling sheets. Lightning turned it to streamers of silver tinsel. It hissed. It beat. It lashed. It drummed. It whined. Always to the overtones and undertones of thunder crashing and rumbling its way to some distant center of activity.

"Here comes the hail." Mac's voice rose above a sound like machine-gun bullets rattling against the boat.

"It shimmers like a shower of crystals against the distant flashes. I don't mind this. It's beautiful."

She moved away from him and he promptly withdrew his arm. Pulled off his coat and threw it over her head.

"This is soaking wet but it may break the force of the hail. It's as big as robin's eggs. The Storm God certainly is putting on a show for us tonight."

It seemed hours before he exulted:—

"Cast your eyes on that pale light. It's the moon breaking through clouds. Blue skies follow storms as surely as day follows night. Now I'll be able to see you."

"Then you'll see something closely resembling the tattooed lady of song and story. My face feels as if it had been beaten black and blue. It *is* the moon! The storm is over!"

This one, Mac thought, and wished the night could last forever. The moment the boat was off the bar he would tell her that Seth Lovel's wife was nothing to him, hadn't been since she had broken their engagement.

A breeze, soft as "the voice that breathed o'er Eden," wafted thin mists like opalescent wraiths along the bay. The moon tossed down a shower of gold till every dancing little wavelet wore a sequin in its cap. In the coves the water gleamed black and mysterious. Far away a clock struck. The air smelled as if it had been shampooed and balsam-scented. Crickets chirped. Frogs piped on the island. Peace had descended on the world.

"Hear that *lap-lap?*" Mac sprang to his feet and grabbed an oar. "The tide has turned! Take the other oar! Push and rock like the dickens! That's telling 'em! We're due for a break. We'll float her off!"

They pushed and rocked. Diane's oar snapped with a suddenness which tumbled her off her feet.

"Never mind, darling. I can manage alone. We're moving. Eureka! We're moving."

Did she realize that he had called her *darling?* If she did she had not resented it. She was watching him breathlessly as he poled first on one side, then on the other. Once the oar bent almost double. He heard her sob of sheer excitement.

The launch shot forward into deep water, tilted and cavorted as Mac crept toward the engine and started the motor.

"That is the end of that adventure. Someone has defined adventure as that which happens without design. We certainly didn't know what lay ahead when we started on this expedition, soldier."

He could see the winking lights at the Manor. Had the Major been asking for him again? During these last hours he hadn't given the condition of his stepfather a thought, he remembered guiltily.

"Our boat landing is lighted. Merry must be wild with anxiety. Will you take me home, please?" Diane asked eagerly.

"Sure; you didn't think I would take you back to the boathouse, did you? We'll be there in five minutes. I know I'm sticking out my neck, but before we dock I want to explain that scene in the loggia you—you—"

"Our 'pact' still holds." Her voice was iced. "We were to speak of nothing which happened before we stepped into this boat. *Nothing.* You flatter yourself when you think that what you and Mrs. Lovel do interests me. You see, it just happens that I don't like you. The words are Asaph's but the sentiment behind them is my own."

If her first words had chilled him the flippancy of the concluding ones sent a wave of fury like liquid fire surging through his veins.

"That washes up the subject very nicely." His voice was hoarse from his effort to keep from shaking her.

Neither spoke again till the launch slid up alongside the Vernon boat landing, which was floodlighted by lamps from two cars. Oilskin figures glistened in the light. Mac sprang out; his shirt, now a sodden gray, and his black trousers dripped like a leaky gutter.

Jim Brewster held the gunwale while Larry Crane helped Diane out. She stood there a slim, tense figure, her dark, drenched hair curling undefeatedly at the ends, each curl gemmed with a diamond drop sparkling in the light. Her eyes were black with excitement; a crimson bruise stained one colorless cheek; her tweed coat was soaked and shapeless.

"Golly, Cameron! Why did you take Di out in this storm? Why didn't you pull the slickers out of the locker?" Larry Crane demanded and tenderly brushed back a wet lock of her hair. "Hurt, dearest?"

She twisted free from his possessive arm.

"We were drenched before we thought of slickers. He didn't take me out. I went to find—Trudy! I've been looking for you. Where have you been?" she demanded as the girl ran on to the landing.

"O Miss Di! Did you go to the Island for me? Gee, I'm sorry. We didn't get there. We were goin' for tin pails in Luigi's car an' he turned on the radio and a fella was saying that Major Lovel had been shot an' was goin' to die. He swore something terrible. Pushed me out, an' told me to walk home, he'd got to get goin'. It was a long walk, Miss Di, an' then I stopped for supper with my girl friend. I didn't mean to stay so late. You'd better hurry up an' see Miss Merry, she's fit to tie about you."

"So you didn't go to the Island, Trudy." Diane's eyes flashed to Mac's. "Sorry I broke up your evening by crashing the party, Mr. Cameron."

"The pleasure was all mine. Now I'm bowing out. You—"

"You're wanted, Cameron," Jim Brewster interrupted. "Doc Reynolds has phoned every half hour. The Major's losing his grip but is holding on desperately to see you. Something on his mind he wants you to know, apparently. My car is here. Let's beat it."

XXI

In the short, fast drive to the Manor it was Jim Brewster who talked, Mac who listened, while he was seeing Diane as she had stood on the boat landing with Larry Crane tenderly smoothing back her hair, calling her *dearest*. Was it Crane or the man beside him for whom she cared? What difference could it make? She had only contempt for Mac Cameron.

Occasional words kept slipping into his consciousness, adding up to something he could understand. The Major had emerged from the coma, had kept muttering brokenly, "I want—want—must—tell—" Had closed his eyes and moved his head restlessly from side to side when asked if he wanted to see his wife. Twice his lips had formed the word "Mac." Then, as if the exertion had been too much, he had relapsed into stupor.

Did his stepfather want to tell him again that the shooting was a mistake or had his brain cleared sufficiently for him to realize that his assailant must be found?

Brewster left him at the front door. As he entered the white house he realized that except for the Major's, there was no sleep within it. The butler whispered a message to him. A maid flitted by with a tray of sandwiches. Patty-Lee, in a lacy violet negligee, crouched on the top step of the great stairway, stared at him without speaking. From a room a white-uniformed nurse made a ghostly exit, passed another making an equally ghostly entrance. There were little uncanny sounds, with more uncanny silences.

Reynolds was waiting for him in the plant room at the end of the corridor. Through the long open windows came the clean, spicy smell of washed leaves and earth. Beyond them he could see illimitable depths of purple sky extravagantly freckled with gold, the moon like a gigantic neon golf ball teed on top of a mountain; and in the east the first lovely pink of dawn flushed the horizon.

As he listened to the Doc's low voice, the time on the mud bar seemed as far away as the end star in the handle of the Big Dipper, pointing the way to Arcturus.

"You're wet to the skin, Mac. You can't go in to the Major like that. Beat it. Change. Come back here."

Nicols, who was waiting in his room, helped him peel off the soaked clothing.

"The storm finished this suit, sir."

"And what a storm. Nicols, pack my bags tomorrow and have them sent to Doctor Reynolds' office. The woman in charge will tell the chauffeur where to put them."

"You're leaving us, sir? I'm sorry."

"I'm not going far. But with—with nurses and doctors in the house, my room may be needed."

"I understand, sir." The valet carefully folded a scarf about Mac's throat.

Confound him, how much did he understand, Mac asked himself as in a black-brocade lounge coat he returned to the conservatory. . . . And why was he "sorry" when he, himself, was leaving shortly by request? . . . Reynolds stopped pacing the floor and pulling at his eyebrow.

"Quick work. Go to the Major's room. Find out what's on his mind, Mac. He's holding on to see you. Perhaps he wants to tell you who shot him. Then again he may know and not want the person followed up. Let him talk. With what he's trying so desperately to say bottled up inside it will do more harm to stop him. Come on."

Patty-Lee was backed against her husband's door when they reached it. Reynolds' face, which had been relaxed in drooping, tired lines, stiffened into a stone mask.

"You can't go in, Mrs. Lovel."

"Why not? If he is able to see his stepson he is able to see his wife." Her voice was low with fury. "Who are you to dictate to me?"

"I'm the physician in charge of this case and what I say goes. The Major wants to see his stepson. He does not want to see his wife—at present." Reynolds caught her shoulders and lifted her away.

"Go in. Quick!"

As Mac slipped across the threshold he heard her harsh whisper.

"If he cuts me out of the money—"

He closed the door softly and shut off her infuriated protest.

A nurse came forward.

"Mr. Cameron? Sit beside the patient. He'll rouse in a few moments. Let him talk. I will be just outside in the corridor in case there is a sudden change."

Thank the Lord she hadn't whispered. Her low, controlled voice restored his composure, which the sight of the motionless figure on the bed had shaken. He stepped lightly across the room; sank into a low chair.

The light from a shaded lamp on a stand silvered the Major's hair. His usually full, smiling mouth was a trifle drawn. His eyes were closed. His once ruddy face was an ash-gray mask, smudged with blue shadows. Was this the special quiet before the end?

All at once the man lying there stood for the person he had loved the most—his mother. In a surge of emotion he gently touched the white hand on which the seal ring looked like a drop of dark blood.

"I'm here. It's Mac, Pop." The name he had called his stepfather as a boy slipped out.

The heavy lids lifted, dropped. Lifted again. The drawn mouth twitched in an attempt at a smile. The glazed eyes met his. Mac's hand closed tightly over the groping fingers.

"Good—to have you—boy." The lids dropped; lifted. "You
—mean more—You're—true."

The silence lasted so long that Mac started to call the
nurse, but the hand under his moved as if in protest.

"Don't—go. Resting. Much to say—"

"Take your time, Pop. Take your time. I'm here for as
long as you want me."

He wondered if his hushed assurance had reached behind those closed eyes. After a minute which seemed an
hour the Major said faintly:—

"It was ac—ci—dent—boy. Shot myself. Get it? Shot—myself. Say that." The eyes, which had been closed, opened
wide. He struggled as if for breath. "No—one is—to be ac—
cused. No one. Someone—went—hay—haywire—for a minute. Under—stand?"

For one horrible second Mac wondered if he suspected
his wife.

"No in—vestiga—ga—tion. Promise! You'll be boss, boy—
if—I go. All ar—ranged. Promise."

The darkly intent eyes met his. With unbelievable strength
the Major's fingers gripped and held.

"Promise." The word was a gasping whisper.

"I promise, Pop."

"You—you could al—ways be trusted to—keep your word
—" His eyes closed, as if he were marshaling every atom of
strength. "She said—that night—after you left—you loved her
—had—begged her to—leave me." His voice trickled away.
Mac bent closer. Had it gone forever? No. . . . Faint, but
desperately determined, it went on:—

"She may tell—you—after—after—I'm gone that—that I
believed—her. I didn't. Not—for—a minute. I know—you. I
—know—her."

The last word thinned into silence. Mac started to rise.
The nurse should be here. The Major's fingers tightened
again on his. His eyes opened. His attempt at a smile was
heartbreaking.

"Now—that's settled I'll rest—really. I'm better. Can't k—
kill me till—my work's—done. Got ideas—to help the state—
the country. Couldn't—let go and sleep—until—you ca—"

The word shattered like a fragile glass dropped in the
still room. His lids closed. Blue shadows spread. The taut
fingers relaxed.

Mac bent over him. Tiptoed to the door. The nurse slipped

in. He followed her to the bed. She laid her hand on the Major's forehead.

"Has he gone?"

"No, Mr. Cameron. Call Doctor Reynolds."

Back and forth, back and forth Mac paced the loggia. Thinking of Patty-Lee's lie. She must have told the Major that yarn when he had left them together and gone to the boathouse. She had been white with anger because he had refused to help her grab the Vernon land, and had taken her revenge by attempting to make her husband believe that his stepson had "begged" her to run away with him. She had lost Nicols his job. Why?

He thought of the Major's insistence that no investigation of the shooting be made; of his own promise. That had been wrong, dead wrong, even—which of course was unbelievable —even if in a frenzy of temper his wife had shot him. "Someone—went—hay—haywire—for a minute." If the person who had committed the crime got away with it this time, what would prevent his going "haywire" the next time he—or she—had a grievance? He might use Diane's gun again.

Diane. He remembered her as she had stood on the boat landing; he could see her wide, incredulous eyes as Trudy had said—what the dickens had she said? The emotion of the time since had swept it from his mind.

He stopped pacing. Shut his eyes to bring back the scene. Trudy had run on to the boat landing, had said—he had it—

"We were goin' for tin pails in Luigi's car an' he turned on the radio an' a fella was saying that Major Lovel had been shot an' was goin' to die. He swore something terrible. Pushed me out an' told me to walk home, he'd got to get goin'."

"He'd got to get goin'." Mac resumed his restless pacing. Why did Luigi Manchusto have "to get goin'" when he heard that the Major would die? Because he had shot him? Shot him with Diane's rifle? Hadn't he threatened to "fix 'em both" the afternoon Di had shot the hawk? Hadn't he sneered that "she and his nibs the Major" were "trying to run the world"?

Hands hard in his pockets, he stopped and stared at the powerboat riding at anchor. The port light glared back like a great red eye. . . . That conclusion was all right as far as it went, but why would Luigi steal the data about the Vernon land? He couldn't use the papers. Why should the Major shield him? It didn't make sense. He had disapproved of him and his gang, had declared that the leaders should be locked up. Fright that he might be apprehended could account for Luigi's crime, if he did the shooting, but not for the Major's attitude toward the suppression of investigation.

"Mac."

He turned at the hushed voice.

"What is it, Doc? Has he—has he gone?"

"No. The change you saw was sleep. The surgeons have decided that they are no longer needed. They want to leave. Will you fly them back?"

"Sure. How soon?"

"They'll wait an hour to be certain there is no relapse. I've sent word to have the Major's plane fueled and ready. Did he talk?"

"Yes." He told what the Major had said, deleting all mention of Patty-Lee; added, "This is strictly between you and me."

"You don't have to tell me that. I'm a physician." He linked his arm in Mac's. "Come out in the patio. These posts may have ears."

They stopped beside the pool speckled with gold from the reflection of the sky. Reynolds tugged at his bushy right eyebrow.

"You found the Major, Mac. You must have seen the lantern. We have that but there's not a trace of the gun with which the Major was shot."

It seemed as if even in the dim light Doc must see the hot color which burned his face. Should he admit that he had that rifle? No—not until he had had it tested for fingerprints.

"A person out to murder wouldn't be likely to drop his gun for an exhibit, would he? I'll get into my flying togs at once."

"There's not a trace of the gun with which the Major was shot." The words kept recurring to Mac as he piloted the plane, with the surgeons as passengers, above the rose-tinted clouds of early morning. Whose fingerprints would be found on Diane's rifle? He was glad that, stunned as he was, he had taken the precaution to carry it by the tip end of the barrel when he had smuggled it to his room. It was now riding the sky in a golf bag.

He resolutely pushed aside the memory, and concentrated on radioing to the operator at the control tower for directions to land at La Guardia Field. The surgeons left him there with hearty handshakes and the assurance that his stepfather had every chance of pulling through. He'd had a narrow squeak; if Reynolds hadn't been on the spot he would have passed out, they declared. He had done a splendid job. It was good to hear these two big men praise a man with his foot on the lowest rung of the same ladder on which they stood at the top.

He breakfasted at the Kitty Hawk restaurant, at a table with a view of the field, and watched the constantly changing panorama of great silver transport ships tuning up, landing as lightly as birds, disgorging passengers; while departing planes loaded for flight. Even so early men, women and children were making for the observation deck, the balcony several hundred feet long which overlooked the field. He phoned the Manor. Barnes replied to his query that the Major still slept.

"To Police Headquarters," he said to a waiting cabby and braced the golf bag containing the rifle against the seat beside him. His other important business would have to wait till he had this washed up. . . .

The officer in charge looked at him curiously, as he returned the rifle he had been testing for fingerprints.

"Nothing doing. That gun has been wiped clean as a whistle. You can't hang anything on the last person who handled it."

XXII

I T SEEMED years—instead of days—to Diane since she had walked along this road to the Hicks's cottage. Was it only last evening that she had set out on that mad trip to the Island, to rescue Trudy, who hadn't been in the slightest need of rescue? From the time she had left home till the moment she had returned it had been sheer nightmare.

Patty-Lee in Mac Cameron's arms! . . . She bit her lips to steady them. Before she had blundered on that hideous scene she had begun to wonder if possibly she had misjudged him, if perhaps she had been wrong when she had jumped to the conclusion that he had come to the Manor to help the Lovels grab the Vernon land. Then the storm. Her inner turmoil during it—all the time reminding herself that the man in the boat, who seemed so strong and efficient, so competent to grapple and conquer any danger, was treacherous to his stepfather, to himself; with every inch of her body fighting against the warm security of his arms, desperate for the feel of them.

For a time his tenderness and care had drugged her into forgetfulness of his falseness. Then he had said:—

"I want to explain that scene in the loggia," and the memory of it had swept over her in a flood of feeling so bitter, so intense that she had stopped him with deliberate, insulting coldness which had whitened his face, set flames in his eyes.

She had wakened this morning from a troubled dream that she was sobbing, with her head against his shoulder; saying over and over, "That washes up the subject very nicely"; crying as never in all the heartbreak of the past three years had she cried before—and all because she had tried to help a girl she had taken into her home. As she had prophesied to Merry, Trudy had become woven into the very fabric of her life.

She arrived at the annoyed conclusion and the Hicks's cottage at the same moment. Except that the August air shimmered with heat, it was all so like the afternoon she had come here days ago. The sun slanted in through the windows of the sitting room, picking out the tight-lipped mouth of Asaph's side-whiskered grandfather on the wall, the framed waxed funeral wreaths flanking the portrait; lighting up the thin, tense face of Martha Hicks. Like that other afternoon even to the fragrance of Rosy Dawn petunias drifting in from the windowboxes, and a hummingbird exhibiting his aerodynamics above them, the scent of balsam, the lingering aroma of frying doughnuts and the unwelcome presence of Maw Budge rocking furiously in the chair by the fireplace, as she had rocked then.

Not quite the same. . . . That day Martha had been knitting a dark-blue sock; now the idle fingers twisted and untwisted nervously in the lap of her soft-gray cotton dress —of the exact shade of her hair. Her face was white, her worried eyes more sunken; the lines at the corners stood out as if inked with a pen; the left lid twitched incessantly.

"How are you, Martha? Good afternoon, Mrs. Budge."

The woman in the rocker stopped rocking and answered with a sniff which might mean anything. Mrs. Hicks rose quickly.

"Miss Diane! I'm glad to see you. When you stood in the

doorway in that yellow dress, I thought for a minute you was a patch of sunshine. Sit down and I'll put the kettle on."

Diane perched on the arm of the chintz-covered wing chair. "Don't trouble to make tea for me, Martha," she protested and immediately wished she hadn't, as Maw Budge clamped her lips in a thin line of approval, settled back in her chair and resumed her monotonous rocking. It was evident that the woman had decided to outstay the recent arrival. Let her try. She had come here to talk with Martha Hicks about Danny, to urge her to encourage him to keep on with his job with Mac Cameron and she would stay until she had.

"On second thought, if it won't be too much trouble I would like tea, Martha," she declared. "I've been on my knees picking herbs for hours today. Tea and one of your crisp doughnuts—I can smell 'em—will turn the world, which had been taking on a tinge of gun-metal gray, to luminous rose color."

"Don't seem possible you can ever get down-hearted, Miss Diane. Asaph says you're a great hand at work an' you never whine about what you have to do, like I do. I guess it's partly because you're strong and well."

"Cheerio, Martha. I may be able to pick herbs for hours on end but I can't make doughnuts like yours. Asaph brags about your cooking. Says you're the best cook in the village. How about that tea?"

"Sure, Miss Diane, sure." Mrs. Hicks drifted into the kitchen like a gray wraith. . . . Followed the sound of the lid being lifted, of wood being poked into the stove.

Maw Budge's eyes, the tint of faded-blue bachelor's-buttons, than which there is nothing more faded, had followed Mrs. Hicks, had come back to Diane in the winged chair.

"More lackadaisical than ever today," she volunteered, in what she fondly believed to be a whisper. "Her eyelid hain't stopped twitchin' a second. Danny lit out a couple of nights ago."

Diane's heart turned a cartwheel and settled back. "Lit out." Did that mean that Luigi had forbidden him to take the job with Mac Cameron? She must find out the facts before tonight. His whereabouts was the information she had come for, but Maw Budge mustn't suspect it.

"He's always lighting out, isn't he?" she commented indifferently. "And he always comes back to home and Mother's cooking."

"Well I guess this time it's for good. Marthy said Asaph

give him a powerful trouncin' when he come in a couple of nights ago. I'll bet if he was his own son he wouldn't a done it. Let's see, 'twas the night I see you, an' that fella at the Manor they call the valet—I'll bet he ain't no valet, I'll bet he's one of them foreign spies—gettin' out of his car at the Swingin' Lantern Crossroads." There was slyness in her voice and malice in her eyes.

This time when Diane's heart jumped it remained in her throat. If Maw Budge had seen her, the fact that she had been in Nicols' car must already have been broadcast, with an especially lurid version for the Dominie's wife. That meant that their plan, their carefully worked-out plan for this very night, might be suspected. It mustn't be. Too much depended on its execution. Even more since the Major had been shot. She must get in touch with Nicols, must consult with him. If she went to the Manor, could she see him without her visit becoming known to the household?

As if she had followed Diane's train of thought the woman leaned forward:—

"I ain't told *nobody* I saw you an' that valet out on a neckin' ride an' I won't if you'll give your word to stop turnin' my Trudy against Luigi Manchusto," she bargained.

Diane's heart dropped from her throat to its original position. "A neckin' ride." It was maddening to have the woman think that but better, a whole lot better, than for her to suspect the truth. What should she say? If Nicols and she put their plan across tonight she wouldn't have to promise. The Trudy–Luigi complication would be nicely taken care of. If it failed—before her eyes flashed the illuminated card that hung above her typewriter:—

MANY PERSONS FAIL BECAUSE CONQUERING
DIFFICULTIES HAS NOT BECOME A HABIT

Their plan mustn't fail. Hadn't she made conquering difficulties a habit during the last three years? She leaned forward and laughed—if a sound so drenched with anger could be called a laugh.

"Mrs. Budge, that conclusion of yours about 'neckin'' is what a psychiatrist would call a 'misobservation.'"

Her face and voice hardened.

"That isn't all. If you repeat a word of that silly story, I'll go to the sheriff and tell him that you know who put Major Lovel's planes out of commission."

It was a desperate, blind shot in the dark, taken on the

chance that Luigi had been the figure in the glinting oil-skins who had been on the business of crippling the planes, that Maw Budge knew it. The woman's chinless face grayed. Her slack mouth gaped.

"I don't know what—what you mean, Miss Diane." She knotted the shawl about her stooped shoulders. "Tell Marthy I had to go. I can't wait for tea."

Diane stared unbelievingly at the screen door that slammed behind her. Why such haste? The jitters? Snapping down the legs of the cutting table for the tea tray helped work off a little of the excitement seething within her. She much get in touch with Nicols at once. She must tell him of Maw Budge's reaction to her threat. . . . At once. That meant that she must go the Manor to find him. What would Barnes assume when she asked for Major Lovel's valet? She couldn't afford time to think of that. Minutes counted.

Mrs. Hicks came from the kitchen with a laden tray.

"Where's Maw Budge?"

"She said to tell you she couldn't wait for tea. She acted as if she had suddenly remembered something · she had to do."

The chance had come to talk with Martha. Diane lifted the brown-stone teapot.

"I'll pour your tea first, Martha. It's fun, just us two by ourselves, isn't it?"

There was no hint of mirth in the haggard eyes which met Diane's in answer. For Martha the life-saving spirit of humor had gone back to never-never land.

"Miss Di," she whispered, "Miss Di, Danny's gone." Her lumpy-knuckled hand shook as she lifted her cup.

"When did he go?"

"Must have slipped away after Asaph went out two nights ago."

Two nights ago. After Asaph had come to stand watch for her. That very evening the Major had been shot.

"I thought Danny had taken a job with Mr. Cameron, that he was very happy about it. Why did he leave?" Diane wondered that her ordinary voice could come through her tight throat.

Tea spilled over as the woman set her cup down with a crash. If that eyelid doesn't stop twitching I shall scream, Diane thought.

"Danny was happy; he was tickled to death about the job. It was Asaph. Asaph give him a terrible lickin'."

"Why, Martha?"

"Because—because he said Danny'd stolen your rifle."

"*My* rifle?"

"Don't get mad, Miss Diane. You're white as a sheet. Please don't get mad. Danny didn't steal it. He told Asaph he'd borrowed it, that he'd went up to your house to ask you fer it an' when you wasn't there, he just took it, he was that sure you wouldn't mind. You'd let him take it before. He wanted to get a fox that's been stealin' the geese he's raisin' for a prize at the County Fair.

"Asaph didn't believe him an' blasphemed somethin' terrible. Said folks in town knew that my Danny an' Luigi Manchusto was the leaders of the gang that broke into the summer houses, that Major Lovel, up at the Manor, knew 'twas him an' he was goin' to swear out a warrant for their arrest the next day which would land Danny in jail for years, maybe. An'—an' then he picked up a whip an'—an'—"

She covered her eyes with her hands and shuddered.

"It was terrible! Terrible. I watched him do it." Her hand dropped. Her head came up. She spoke between clenched teeth. "I could have killed Asaph, feelin' as I did, I could 'ave killed anybody who hurt my Danny."

Diane laid her hand gently on the fist clenched on the woman's knee.

"Try not to think of it, Martha. Try to forget it. Where is the rifle now? Did Danny say?"

"I don't know, Miss Diane. Things went kind of hazy."

"Sure it isn't here?"

"I haven't seen it." A crafty look narrowed the haggard eyes. "You ain't reckoning to have Danny arrested because he borrowed it, like Major Lovel's threatening, are you? That man better have stayed away from this village. Accusin' the young folks here of takin' things from his cottage while all the time he's tryin' to steal your land. I hate him. Hate him."

"Don't get excited about it, Martha: The Major won't trouble anyone for a time. Haven't you heard what happened to him?"

The woman tried to speak. Licked dry lips. Shook her head.

"What?" The word was a hoarse whisper.

"He was shot—with a rifle."

Martha Hicks's eyes were wide with terror.

"A rifle! How'd they know 'twas a rifle? They ain't accusin' my Danny, are they? You don't think he did it because he took your gun, do you, Miss Di?"

"No, Martha, no. Of course Danny didn't do it. Don't

worry about him. He'll come back. He always does. He
has run away before."

"Yes, but before he's always taken some clothes and
food. This time the only thing that's gone is Asaph's swingin'
lantern."

XXIII

Who had carefully wiped Diane's rifle free of fingerprints
before dropping it beside the Major?

On the return flight the question went round and round
in Mac's mind like an anchor chain spooling over its metal
runway. It was still puzzling him when in the late afternoon he
brought down the plane at Musgrave Manor. As he walked
from the hangar to the house, he remembered the day he
had arrived at his stepfather's home. Color now glowed from
every foot of the visible world as it had then; the sea was as
sparkling, the islands as green, the distant hills as purple.
His memory of the tall, erect man, in blue pull-over and
white slacks, who had hailed him from the steps under the
portico faded into a picture of the quiet figure on a bed
with closed eyes and drawn face.

"Glad you've come, sir."

The butler's voice broke the spell of memory.

"How's the Major, Barnes?"

"Still sleeping, sir. Doctor Reynolds has gone to his office to
get a little rest."

"That sounds encouraging. Have my bags gone?"

"All but one. Nicols left an outfit in your room in case you
stopped here after your flight."

"Where is he now?"

"Somewhere about, sir. Shall I tell him you want him?"

"Yes." Mac started up the stairs.

"Just a minute, sir. The Madam gave orders that you were
to come to her morning room as soon as you returned. She is
driving to the village later."

"All right." He added to himself, "Not if I can make
my getaway without being seen."

Shaved and showered, he dressed in the white clothes
Nicols had left for him and dropped into his suitcase the re-

volver he always carried when he flew. Now if he could slip out of the house without meeting Patty-Lee he would consider that luck was with him. Barnes had said she was to drive to the village. He would watch from the window. As soon as she left he would phone the garage to send round his roadster.

He couldn't see the front steps, only the curve of the drive and the great iron gates. Near one of them, in the shadow of a shrub, a man and girl stood close together in earnest conversation.

His heart went into a tailspin. The girl wore yellow. It was Diane. The man was—Nicols. She was leaving. Nicols was coming toward the house.

He stood at the window smoking, thinking. Remembering his suspicion that Nicols had been with her the night he had heard Asaph warn: "You shouldn't have did it, Di. Terrible risky." Reflecting that Merry Vernon wouldn't have asked the valet to motor Di to the dinner at the Manor unless she had been seeing him often; and how could she see him unless he went to Honeywort House? He visualized the man's hesitation when he had come to him that evening and asked him to go for "Miss Diane," as he was needed by the Major. What was it all about? What the dickens was it all about? Did it tie up with the mysterious shooting of the Major or was it just another romantic adventure in Diane Vernon's life? He answered a knock.

"Come in!"

Nicols entered with a tall, tinkling glass and a plate of sandwiches on a tray.

"Barnes said you had returned, sir. You've had a stiff forty-eight hours. I know you don't care for whisky-and-soda or cocktails. It's pretty hot for tea; I thought iced coffee with plenty of cream might taste good, sir."

"Thanks, Nicols. Coffee is O.K. I learned years ago that there isn't room for even a drop of liquor in an engineer's brain or in a pilot's."

"You're right, sir." He set the tray on a table and placed a chair. "You'd better take it easy. You're likely to feel let down after the emotional strain. Major Lovel roused and took some nourishment and is again sleeping quietly."

"Thanks." Mac broke a sandwich. "It was infernally hot in the city and I had a lot of errands." The word city sent suspicion bubbling up from his subconscious.

"Nicols, did you touch the rifle I had locked in that closet?"

The man who had been folding the blouse of the flying suit straightened.

"A rifle!" His thin, distinguished face flushed and paled. He appeared to grow several inches taller. "It is not my habit to open locked doors, Mr. Cameron."

"I bet it isn't. Sorry, Nicols. I'm haywire with anxiety."

Suspicion of the valet in some miraculous way had been changed to confidence. "I know I can trust you. I'll come clean. It was Miss Diane Vernon's gun. No possible doubt that it is, because hers is missing. It was beside Major Lovel when I found him in the patio."

"Miss Diane's rifle! Impossible. Where is it now?"

Mac told him of his visit to Police Headquarters.

"Of course the person who cleaned that rifle of finger-prints was the person who shot the Major," he concluded.

"I'll be glad to help follow up the investigation, sir. I wonder: Would it have been the same person who stole the papers? Madam Lovel, at the wheel of her roadster, passed me in the drive as I came in, sir. She had the dog with her."

"The person who stole the papers. Madam Lovel. She had the dog with her." Had Nicols mentioned them in the same breath purposely? Was he intimating that the missing data might be found in Patty-Lee's possession? She had been "tidying up" the Major's desk when Nicols had entered the study. As a suggestion it had its merits.

"Gone already, has she? I'm out of luck. Barnes reported that she wanted to see me. I'll scribble a note of explanation before I shove off to Doctor Reynolds' office."

At the desk he wrote hurriedly. Slipped the sheet into the envelope.

"You might give it to her maid, Nicols—"

"The maid will be below stairs at this hour, sir."

"Then I'll leave it in her morning room myself. And while I'm leaving it, you might stroll in the corridor to be sure that the maid *remains* downstairs, Nicols."

"I understand, sir. I'll be there."

"Nicols. The rifle is in my roadster. Get it and keep it in your room, will you? I'll pick it up there when I want it."

"Very good, sir."

Mac stood on the threshold of Patty-Lee's morning room. It was decorated in all the shades of iris; *moderne* with blond mahogany, silver and mirrors. Which article of furniture would a woman select as a hiding place? . . . Dressing

table? Desk? Thick-cushioned windowseat or a tall bookcase
with glass doors? Cushions were out. The maid would remove them when she dusted.

Steps in the hall. He slipped in and softly closed the
door behind him. He felt like a thief. Takes a thief to
catch a thief, he reflected, and met his own grin in the
mirror.

The desk was the best bet. If Patty-Lee had taken the
papers she had figured that she would be the last person
suspected. He opened unlocked drawers, tugged at locked
ones. . . . Pressed panels. Nothing doing. The bookcase?

He pulled books forward soundlessly. Mounted a foot-
stool to reach the top shelf. The crackle of paper. He drew
out a sheaf of blueprints and a long white envelope. DEEDS
RE VERNON ESTATE. He read the typed words to make
sure that what he saw was not a hallucination.

He stepped cautiously to the floor, thrust the papers
inside his coat. Now if he could get away—His heart went
into a tailspin. Voices in the corridor. The Peke barking
furiously. He was caught with the goods. Patty-Lee had
arrived. So what? She had left "orders" with Barnes that he
was to come to her morning room, hadn't she? He could
say he was waiting for her.

"Nurse Skinner left a message that she would like to
see you in the Major's study immediately upon your return,
Madam." It was Nicols' voice, cool, unhurried. Good old
Nicols.

"What are you doing outside the door of my room, Nicols?
Had a change of heart? Stop barking, Precious. Why does
the nurse want me? Is the Major worse?"

"She didn't say, Madam. Only that you must come at
once."

"Oh, all right. I suppose I'll have to go. Take Precious.
The doctor said he must be kept in the garage when he
wasn't with me for fear his barking might disturb the Major.
Don't come here again. In future send your messages by
my maid, understand?"

As Mac listened he thought, You're small in every way,
Patty-Lee. You're built on a small pattern with a skimpy
soul, if any. He heard Nicols' "Yes, Madam. I understand."

He listened. Was the valet muffling the Peke's bark with
his hand? It sounded smothered. Did the dog know there
was someone in the room of his mistress who didn't belong?

It seemed ages before the door swung open softly. He

waited a moment, then stepped into the corridor. Nothing human in sight.

Back in his own room he tucked the blueprints and envelope into the suitcase and locked it. With the caution of a man treading a mined road, he ran down the stairs, broke his own track record to the garage, and with the relief of a prisoner escaping from a concentration camp shot his black roadster along the highway.

Why had Patty-Lee taken those papers? Did they show up a flaw in her claim that the Vernon holdings belonged with her land? Had she been afraid he might find it when he examined them as he had told the Major he would do? Whom would she suspect when she missed them? Nicols of course. Hadn't he been in the corridor outside the morning room when she came up the stairs? Hadn't he told her that the nurse wanted to see her in the Major's study? Her voice had lashed when she spoke to him. The valet had admitted that she had turned her husband against him. Why? All of which figured up to the fact that he must return to the Manor, explain that he had found the deeds and blueprints she had hidden and force her to confess why she had taken them from the Major's desk. . . . He would see the Doc for a moment before he returned for the showdown.

He had landed himself in an infernally unpleasant mix-up. He had no choice but to save Nicols from the heat Patty-Lee would turn on when she missed the blueprints and deeds. If she had disliked the man before she would go to any lengths to discredit him now. Who was he? Why had Diane been talking so earnestly with him in the drive a short time ago?

Now what, he asked himself, as he stopped the car in front of the white cottage he and Reynolds had hired. A convention in town? Automobiles of all sorts lined the street.

The gate of the picket fence stood open. He passed along the nasturtium-bordered path to the front door, by the side of which glittered a brand-new brass plate that informed a more or less interested public that JOHN REYNOLDS M.D. might be found within.

"Hi, Mac."

It was Cecily Cole, in Red Cross uniform, who hailed him from the threshold. Her hair gleamed like copper where it strayed from beneath the white headdress.

"For the love of Mike what are you doing here, Cis?"

"Receptionist for the already famous Doctor Reynolds.

The news spread that he had opened an office. People with kids and without kids have been arriving since early morning and few of them look like paying patients to me."

"Is he seeing them?"

"Yes. He looks tired enough to drop, but he's on the job though the equipment I hear you have presented hasn't arrived. You rate a mammoth Oscar for that performance, Mackenzie Cameron. Sally and I heard of the rush of patients and came to the rescue as our contribution to the good work. She's in there taking case histories. She's an honest-to-goodness nurse and I've had Red Cross training. It's a good thing for us to get practice here in case . . ."

She left the sentence unfinished. Mac never before had seen her so grave. Di had been right. In the back of every mind flitted the grim shadow of war.

"You two girls are aces, Cecily. Let me know when the Doc has a spare minute, will you?"

"There ain't goin' to be no such animal, but I'll tell him you want to see him. A boy was here inquiring for you half an hour ago."

"What did he look like?"

"Death and destruction. White as a ghost. Lock of hair dangling over one eye. Shaky as a mold of jelly, wild-eyed as a mustang. He left a note. It's in your room."

"O.K. I'm going up to unpack."

Must have been Danny, he decided, as he ran up the stairs. Probably his overlord Luigi had turned thumbs down on the job. If the inquiries he had set in motion in the city this morning panned out as he thought they would, the overlord stuff would be plain hooey.

As he entered the comfortable room, his taut nerves relaxed for the first time in forty-eight hours. It was staid with Victorian, marble-topped, black-walnut furniture; gay with enormous crimson roses splashing the wallpaper; spicy with the scent of nasturtiums drifting in at the open window. It banished the sense of nightmare which had had him in its grip.

Nicols not only had sent his luggage but had unpacked and arranged the contents. His fishing tackle and tennis rackets were prominently displayed. A soiled pink envelope was propped in front of the black-marble clock on the mantel. . . . Danny's note. He pulled out a scrap of brown-paper bag. Read:—

"Be at log hut on bluff at ten sharp tonight. Leave car at Swinging Lantern Crossroads. Come alone if you want to know who shot Major Lovel. Knock twice."

No signature. Too melodramatic a communiqué for Danny. He wasn't the type to send a message like that. Was Luigi Manchusto behind it? His father had boasted that he owned a log house on a bluff.

He read the scrawled lines again before he held his cigarette lighter to the scrap of paper. Was it a trap or was someone trying to make easy money by selling information? Through his mind echoed Luigi Manchusto's threat:—

"Remember you've got it comin' to you, buttin' in between me an' Danny Stark."

His narrowed eyes rested on the suitcase he had brought with him. Should he take his revolver? Certainly *not*. A gun sometimes bred trouble. He laughed . . . Said aloud:—

"You almost had me jittery, Luigi. I'd like another twenty-four hours leeway before we meet, but I'll be there as the clock strikes."

XXIV

A MESSENGER boy on a bicycle shot out from between the iron gates of the Manor, when Mac Cameron drove in. He stopped the black roadster in the drive. He had come to clear Nicols in case Patty-Lee, having discovered that the papers she had taken were missing, were to accuse the valet of stealing them.

He was primed for a fight with one who, from previous experience, he knew to be a knife-in-the-back adversary. The blueprints and deeds he had found hidden in the bookcase in Patty-Lee's morning room were in his pocket. He had gone over them before leaving his room. . . . Looked to him as if the Lovel advisers had located the V rock on the wrong line. He would follow up his hunch tomorrow. That wasn't all he had discovered. To his amazement there had been also a document labeled LAST WILL AND TESTAMENT OF SETH LOVEL.

So that was what Patty-Lee really had been after. The papers relating to the Vernon estate had been taken as a blind. Had she planned to destroy the will if the terms were not satisfactory to her? She ought to have enough business sense to realize that what she had stolen was but a copy, that the original was probably in her husband's deposit box in a city bank.

"How's the Major now, Barnes?" he asked as the door opened.

"Seems better; we are much encouraged, sir."

"Good. Ask Mrs. Lovel if she will see me."

"She's expecting you to dine with her in the loggia, sir. She's there now. She is talking to Nicols."

"I'll find her. I shan't stay for dinner, Barnes. As you see, I'm not dressed for it, have an important date as soon as I have seen Mrs. Lovel."

That would explain the dark-blue serge he was wearing at this hour. He had put it on as being less conspicuous for the log-hut rendezvous.

"Would you mind giving this telegram to Nicols, sir? It came just a moment ago. I was waiting until he was through talking with Madam before delivering it, but the boy said 'Very important.' I think he ought to have it at once."

"I'll take it." The envelope the butler handed him seemed to prickle with electricity against Mac's fingertips as he passed through the living room to the loggia. "Very important" the boy had said. Would this message solve the mystery of the real identity of Nicols?

"If you didn't take those papers, explain what you were doing in the corridor outside my door this afternoon or I'll have the sheriff here and accuse *you* of shooting your employer."

Patty-Lee's voice, charged with venom, was low, but not too low for Mac to hear, as he stepped from the long window opening on the loggia. The woman looked even smaller than usual as she stood between him and the tall light with its hurricane shade. Haggard lines showed under the unusually heavy make-up. One hand was twisting the double chain of amethysts about her white throat; the other was clenched on the shimmering violet satin at her hip. She shook back her soft yellow hair and took a step toward the valet, whose eyes were like glowing coals in the white mask of his face. Behind him silver and crystal, on the table set for two, gleamed in the flickering light of pink candles flanking the bowl of matching sweet peas.

"Answer me, Nicols. Where are those papers?"

Mac stepped from the shadow.

"What's all the shootin' about, Patty-Lee? Are these the papers you want?"

She snatched the deeds and blueprints he offered.

"Where did you get them? Did you catch Nicols red-handed?"

"Hold everything." Mac handed the telegram to the valet. "This came for you a moment ago. Better open it at once. Messenger said 'Very important.' "

"Thank you, sir. If you will permit me, Madam."

Mac caught Patty-Lee's arm in a grip of steel as she opened her lips.

"Keep quiet. Let him read it."

Nicols, whose face was whiter, if that were possible, than it had been before, looked up from the slip of paper he had been reading.

"I shall be obliged to leave at once, Madam."

"Oh no you won't. It isn't so easy as that. You arranged to have that wire sent so you would have an excuse to get away, I presume. Suspicious. Very. Now I believe that you did shoot my husband. You won't leave till you have explained where you were when he was shot and why you were snooping round my morning-room door this afternoon *just* before I discovered that these papers were missing."

"I will explain about the papers." Mac tightened his grip on Patty-Lee's arm. "Hope it's not bad news, Nicols."

The valet straightened. A new man appeared to emerge from the old self. There was a mocking light in the eyes that rested, for an instant, on the woman, whose face was unbecomingly flushed with anger; there was the faintest flash of a grin on his lips.

"Bad news in a way, Mr. Cameron, and yet not too bad for me. The two cousins who stood between me and a title and estates were killed in the Battle of France. I never knew them. I am now Nicols Clifton Perley, Viscount Darnsford. With castles in England and Scotland—if they still stand."

The silence which followed was broken only by the swish of the tide, the monotonous chant of crickets, the hiss of a meteor which lighted the heavens like a tracer shell.

The man's head was silhouetted against the pale blue of
the sky above the pink still lingering on the horizon. His
squared shoulders were black against the afterglow as he
stood there, still with that curious smile on his lips, still
with his mocking eyes on the woman who had been ren-
dered speechless by his announcement.

Mac was the first to shake off the spell of surprise.

"Congratulations that you have come into your inheri-
tance, Ni—"

"Always Nicols to you, Mr. Cameron. As you will understand I must leave at once. I had only two weeks more to
serve here. I can be of use on my estate. Major Lovel will
not need me now."

He bowed formally to Patty-Lee, who had dropped into
a chair. Mac followed him into the living room.

"How will you get to England, Nicols?"

"Only one way. Clipper to Lisbon and from there—well,
it's on the knees of the gods. I'll telephone at once to
New York to find the exact time the plane leaves. No
matter what the hour I must keep an engagement before
I go. If you will come to my room while I pack my bags
I'd like to explain a bit my reasons for being in this house
in this country."

"I'll help you get your traps together. You may not believe
it from what you've seen but I'm an A-1 hurry-up packer."

While Mac folded clothes and laid them in a suit-case,
he was wondering if the engagement was with Diane. Would
she be implored to become the Countess Darnsford? Nicols
and she had been friendly. There had been unmistakable
warmth in his voice when he had spoken her name. Why
let that worry him now? The man couldn't, wouldn't take
her with him into that conflagration across the water, not
if he really loved her.

"Leave out the tweeds, Mr. Cameron. I'll wear those."

Nicols' voice brought his thoughts of Diane up short.

"Cut out that Mr. now. I don't want to seem inquisitive,
but you said you would give me a few facts that would
explain your hurried departure to the Major—when or if
he recovers."

"Cheerio, he'll get well. Here's my dossier in tabloid
form. My father was the youngest son of Viscount Darnsford; he had five older brothers. There were so many
between us and the title we never gave it a thought, even
after the World War had taken its heavy toll of the family.
I had four years at Oxford where I read hard and widely,

accumulating an amount of knowledge which was of no help to me later when I needed a position. After that I joined a regiment composed of men from families like mine. Came War '14. I was gassed. My father died. I lived with my mother and sister on our country estate, a gentleman farmer. We had our flat in London and our social life there.

"Three years ago our family solicitor killed himself. We discovered that because of mismanagement and enormous taxes the fortune upon which we had been living was gone. I tried to get something to do to bring in an income. No success. My sister, jolly sporting of her, took a position as a secretary. I came to this country, having heard that the cinema wanted English actors. I wasn't an actor, as I soon found out after having played a gentleman's gentleman twice. That experience gave me an idea. I must help support my mother. Why not *be* a gentleman's gentleman? No one knew me here; I had taken the name of Nicols. I had not gotten in touch with the Americans whom I had met socially at home. I knew all the requirements and the pay was good. So here I am and my mother has lived in comparative comfort." He closed and strapped a suitcase.

"Packed and ready to start out on a new life. They didn't want me in the present army. I'm good with a gun. I can pick off—things in the air and now I will be able to help with money and devotion to my king and country." He cleared the huskiness from his throat.

"Natural enough that Mrs. Lovel should suspect me of taking those papers, I presume. I was trying to protect you when she accused me in the loggia, and she took my silence as an admission of guilt."

"Forget it, Nicols. I'll take care of that. You'd better get a move on and phone about the Clipper. You may have to make a quick getaway. I'll fly you to New York if you are short on time."

"Thanks, Mr. Cameron. I shall have time to drive there."

"How about money? I'll be glad—"

"No thanks. I shall have plenty. The solicitor of the late heir has placed to my order in a New York bank what seems to me now a princely sum. I'll find out at once about the Clipper. Off with the old and on with the new," Nicols said, squared his shoulders and swung along the corridor.

From valet to Viscount. . . . Reminded him of the Horatio Alger stories, belonging to his father, that he had devoured when a boy, Mac thought as he ran lightly down the stairs. He had left unexplained Mrs. Seth Lovel's aversion to him.

What was behind it? He'd better forget Nicols, concentrate on slipping out without being seen or heard by Patty-Lee and fare forth on the next adventure of this melodramatic week.

Doubtless she was still dazed by Nicols' news. No use in seeing her again. She had the papers. Unnecessary to explain at present how he had come by them or that he had examined them. Lucky he had had the chance to look them over. He would take up the matter of the right location of the rock with Diane in the morning.

He looked back at the house before he drove between the iron gates. "Curtain on Act I," he said under his breath. "Let the show go on."

The sound of a bell brought him back to the immediate present. . . . Nine o'clock! At ten sharp he was to be at the log hut on the bluff. He had forgotten that when he had offered to fly the new Viscount Darnsford to New York. He'd better get a bite before he set out to keep the mysterious date. The iced coffee and sandwiches Nicols had provided had been all right at the time, but they didn't take the place of dinner. This was movie night; there would be a restaurant or teashop open in the village.

As he stepped into his roadster a half hour later, the world was shrouded in a white mist, punctured by dark blotches which must be chimney tops. Mist like wisps of down from a white swan's breast clung to tall trees; distant lights shone like opals in a haze.

The shore was a solid mass of fog. "And that's where I'm going," Mac thought as the car slid forward. "Boy what a night for the ghostly sea captain, oilskins, swinging lantern and all, to put on his act."

He drove slowly. The windshield wiper swung rhythmically but it accomplished nothing. It was like flying through a thick cloud. Was he headed right? Shouldn't he have reached the Crossroads long before this?

Was that a post or a tree ahead? He left the motor running, stepped from the car and snapped on his electric torch. Luck was with him. It was the sign of the mythical Captain, complete with yellow oilskins and red-flamed lantern. . . . So far so good. Now to locate the log hut. There must be a road leading to it. He ran his light over the ground at his feet. There it was, with a footpath beside it. Better walk the rest of the way.

He backed his car into what looked to be an old logging road. Thanks to the fog it would be invisible to a passerby.

He groped back to the path. After what seemed hours a dark bulk loomed in front of him. The log hut at last. He heard the oily lash of the tide below. A clock struck. He counted the strikes, muffled by the fog. Ten. On hand to the minute. He knocked twice on a heavy door.

After what seemed an interminable silence came a hoarse whisper from the other side.

"Who's there?"

"Cameron."

The door was opened cautiously. He slipped into the cabin, which was lighted by a lantern. Log walls chinked with moss. Lobster pots. Fishing tackle. Clam forks and cradles. Yellow oilskins and sou'westers hanging from pegs. A shelf with swinging lanterns like the one burning on a rough table. . . . Why so many? . . . In one corner an iron sink with a pump. . . . A closed door at the back. . . . Two small square windows covered with dark cloth. . . . A boy staring at him with enormous eyes. . . .

"Danny!" His surprised whisper echoed from log wall to log wall. Only Danny, and he had thought Luigi Manchusto was behind that note.

The boy's face was starkly white above his yellow slicker, which crackled as his slim figure shook with fright.

"O Mr. Cameron—" his lips twitched convulsively—"I got you to come here 'cause Luigi said he was goin' away for a couple of days an' we can talk. I got to tell someone. I shot—the—the—Major."

"You! Danny! Why? Why?"

"Because—I didn't mean to—I—Listen! Someone's coming. The sheriff's followed me!"

"Quiet!"

Tense and motionless, they stood side by side. Mac's hand gripped the boy's shoulder. The stillness was broken by a scratching sound outside.

Danny shuddered.

"It's Luigi, feeling for the key," he whispered. "He's come back, sudden. He'll beat me up for bringing you here. He's —he's terrible when he's mad."

XXV

THE EVENING was cool, with a damp breeze stirring the sheer curtains at the windows of Merry's sitting room, where lamplight and firelight glinted on the silver bowl of pink Perfection roses and set the facets of the tall, crystal vase of lilac gladioli sparkling like diamonds.

Curled up in a deep chair, Diane kept her eyes on the licking scarlet-and-orange flames while she counted the strokes of the tall clock in the hall. . . . Nine. Zero hour. Nicols would stop in the road at the entrance to the drive at any minute now. They must go tonight. The coast would be clear. Luigi never missed the movie.

Slivers of ice coasted down her spine. Little chills slithered through her veins. Were Nicols and she setting out on a crazy expedition, or would it prove a *Blitzkrieg* against the powers of evil? Whichever way the battle swung it was too late to back out now. He had vigorously objected to her going with him, had declared that he would carry on by himself, but he was following Luigi's trail to help her and she couldn't let him go alone into what might prove to be, if not danger, annoying complications.

From under her lashes she glanced at her sister's reflection in the pier mirror between the windows. Merry was braced up in the chaise longue by lacy pillows; her lips were curved in a faint smile; her eyes were on the khaki sweater she was knitting. What excuse would serve in place of the truth when she slipped out to meet Nicols? Merry looked up and met her intent eyes.

"A penny for your thoughts, Di."

With lightning rapidity Diane withdrew those thoughts and hustled up reserves.

"I was thinking that you reminded me of nothing so much as a slice of harlequin ice cream. The white pillows are vanilla, your pink frock strawberry and that brown wool chocolate. On top of that I was thinking that you looked slap-happy."

Merry Vernon dropped the knitting and clasped her hands in tense earnestness.

"I am happy. I am, Di. I wonder if I can make you understand that seeing Jim Brewster was like suddenly emerging from smothering fog into brilliant sunshine. All I had accomplished in my work, all I had planned to accomplish, spread before me in a new, gorgeous, technicolor world. I had a chance at real life again. I—I can't adequately describe the spiritual experience; it—it was like a divine vision; it—was like resurrection after death." The last word was a whisper.

The space between them pulsed with Diane's silent sympathy.

"Doc Reynolds has been a tower of strength, and Mac Cameron has given me courage by his refusal to believe that I wouldn't someday be my active self again," Merry went on dreamily. "He's such a grand person. You just feel that he is everything that is fine, that he has loyalty, courage and strict standards of decency in human conduct."

The picture of Patty-Lee Lovel in the arms of the man "with strict standards of decency" flashed on the screen of Diane's memory. All day she had been battling to forget the tenderness of those same arms, had been trying desperately to thrust the remembrance of that scene in the loggia out of her mind, and here it was back again large as life and twice as hideous.

"Oh, Mac's all right—in his way," she countered indifferently. "He was my hero-for-a-day but now that Larry's back the spell is broken. Our—our 'understanding' is on the rocks."

"On the rocks! It never was anywhere else, was it? You needn't keep up the deception, Di. You thought I was falling in love with Mac Cameron, didn't you? You invented that yarn 'I've gone off the deep end about him' to warn me off, in the romantic movie tradition, didn't you?"

"I was so afraid you would be hurt, lovely."

"I'll forgive you this time, but see that it doesn't happen again—" Merry's laugh was infectious—"because I'm likely to be exposed to many fascinating males next winter—if, as I hope, we can have a small apartment in New York. Freda is in Seventh Heaven at the mere suggestion. Can we manage to afford it, Di?"

"*Merry!* Do you mean you'll go?" Diane was on her feet. "We'll afford it some way. We can sell this place to the Lovels. The Major offered to buy it—to save a fight. If that fails there are Grandmother's emeralds—I—did you hear something? Did a car stop?" she asked breathlessly.

It couldn't be Nicols coming to the door. She was to

meet him at the entrance of the drive. Larry had explained that much as he hated to spend an evening away from her he was committed to cards at the Newcombs'. Jim was in on that party too. That counted *them* out.

"Cars have stopped here before at nine P.M.," Merry reminded dryly. "What have you on your mind, Di? Except for a moment ago, when I suggested wintering in the Big City, you just haven't been here for the last twenty-four hours. I'm not referring to your body, dearie. Your spirit has been miles away and—why *Nicols*—"

Diane echoed the astonished greeting. Consternation tightened her throat. The man's eyes glittered with excitement in his pale face. Had their plans for tonight gone haywire?

"Nicols, what has happened?" Her voice seemed to belong to someone a long way off.

He told them, added with his eyes on Diane:—

"The Clipper is scheduled to leave New York sometime tomorrow. I am starting for the city at once."

"It's like a fairy tale. I can't begin to tell you how much you have helped me carry on this summer." Merry smiled through tears. "Good luck and all happiness to you, Nicols Clifton Perley, Viscount Darnsford."

He raised her hand to his lips. "Good-by," he said huskily. "Will you come to the car and wish me Godspeed, Miss Diane?"

Without answering, she left the room with him. In a world white with mist beside the sedan he said earnestly:—

"You understand, don't you, why I can't keep that date with you tonight?"

"Of course I understand. You shouldn't have taken the time to stop here."

"I couldn't go without seeing you again. If ever the hatreds and conflicts, the unleashed savagery which are convulsing Europe cease, I will come back. Meanwhile I want you to know that I think you are the loveliest, gamest girl I have ever known."

"I shan't forget that, Nicols. You have meant a lot to me. Without your help—"

"About that help. Promise you won't carry on tonight. It isn't safe. Promise. It would be so like you to go alone." He seized her hands in his desperate earnestness.

"Alone! I'm not *that* adventurous. I'll have to think of some other way to get our proofs. You really ought to start, Nicols."

"I'm going." He turned her hands over and pressed his lips to each rosy palm. "That's a flashback to the days before I was a valet." There was a touch of gaiety she never before had seen in his eyes, a hint of emotion she never before had heard in his voice.

"Good-by—my dear."

"Just a minute!" hailed a gruff voice.

With one foot on the running board, Nicols Clifton Perley, Viscount Darnsford, turned to look at the man who suddenly materialized out of the fog.

"Sheriff Martin! Why are you here at this time of night?" Diane's question was drenched with surprise.

The red-faced man, broad as he was long, shook his shock of black hair and blinked eyes which resembled nothing so much as currants stuck in the face of a gingerbread boy. With his thumbs, he snapped the green-and-white suspenders which so nobly supported his mammoth trousers, and swelled with importance.

"I'm here, Miss Diane, to arrest this valet for shooting Major Lovel."

"You're crazy!" Diane's explosive protest drowned Nicols' colorful exclamation.

"Who makes this charge?" he demanded.

"Mrs. Seth Lovel. She found a rifle in your room of the same make used when her husband was shot."

"The lady is mistaken. I haven't owned any kind of a firearm since I came to this country."

"You'll be given a chance to prove it. She's offered a big reward for the capture of the guy who shot the Major. Come along."

"He can't go. He's got to get to New York; he's going—"

"With the sheriff," Nicols curtly interrupted Diane's breathless protest. "Will I be permitted to travel in my own car to—to jail?"

The amused contempt in the question turned the sheriff's face a lively purple.

"Gettin' fresh, are you? You'll go in mine. It's parked at the gate."

"Keep my sedan in your garage, Miss Diane, until I call for it. Forget the story I told you tonight. That goes for your sister too, understand?"

Diane nodded. Of course she understood. Even with more war headlines than they had space to print, papers would go to town on the news that Viscount Darnsford had been arrested for attempted murder.

"Get in touch with Cameron at once. Tell him that a rifle was found in my room and of our discovery at the log hut. He'll know what to do." Nicols added the last sentence in a whisper.

Diane watched till the two figures, one with its rolling gait, the other springy, alert, vanished in the mist. Her mind felt almost as woozy as it had after her crash in the brook. . . . A reward offered for the capture of the man who had shot the Major! Nicols accused of shooting his employer. Patty-Lee had found the rifle in his room! Her rifle. The rifle Danny had borrowed. But Mac had said *he* had it.

It didn't make sense. Perhaps Patty-Lee had lied. Why try to implicate Nicols unless she *knew* who had shot her husband? That was an idea! Nicols needn't have made her promise not to put through their plan for tonight. His arrest spiked any chance of her setting out alone. Her first business was to find Mac Cameron and tell him what had happened. Nicols must be freed to reach the Clipper in time.

"Mees Di. Mees Merry says to bedt she is goin'. She vants to say goodt night." The light in the hall behind her turned Freda Swenson's straw-colored hair to gold, her white uniform to silver as she stood at the open door.

"I'll come." She must tell Merry at once what had happened to Nicols, warn her not to mention the story he had told them. Had it been true? For an instant doubt of the validity of the Viscount Darnsford title tightened her throat. Suppose he had shot the Major? Suppose his sudden accession to the English estates was merely a ruse to make his getaway possible?

"Mees Di, you coom now? Vy you standt staring oop at de sky?"

"I—I—was thinking that—that this is the thickest fog we have had this summer. It drips from the trees like rain. I'll say good night to Miss Merry, now. Leave us alone for five minutes, will you, Freda? I have something important to tell her."

"I never heard anything so absurd," Merry protested when Diane had poured forth her news. "Nicols would no more shoot the Major than I would. Stop walking the floor. Sit on the end of the chaise while we plan to help him."

"Of course he didn't do it."

"I don't like the doubt in your voice. You've been seeing

and liking that man for weeks. How can you accuse him of crime even in your thoughts?"

"I'm not accusing him, lovely. I don't believe for an instant that he did it, but why should the rifle be in his room?" She had omitted the fact that it was her rifle which had been found beside the Major.

"Page Patty-Lee Lovel."

"What possible reason could she have for wanting him arrested?"

"A personal grudge, probably. Perhaps Nicols didn't admire her sufficiently. She's the type which would exact tribute even from her husband's valet. What was she doing in his room? Phone Mac, quick. Try the Manor first. He's probably dining there."

"Probably." A vision of the last time she had seen him in that loggia set Diane's teeth deep in her lips as she dialed.

"Left before dinner? Thanks, Barnes." She cradled the telephone. "He's not there, Merry. I'll try Doc's office."

"Doctor Reynolds' office. Miss Cole speaking—you, Di? Oh, I'm helping with the patients. We don't have union hours at this office—Who?—Mac isn't here. Left after he unpacked—Yes, before dinner—Isn't he at the Manor?—No. I haven't the faintest idea where he was going. Hold on, maybe he's gone to meet the wild-eyed youth who left a note for him today. He had a dangling lock of yellow hair and was white as a sheet and—"

"Thanks a lot. Good-by."

Diane banged the instrument into its cradle.

"Mac is somewhere with Danny," she announced breathlessly. "The boy left a note for him at the Doc's. Martha told me today he had run away. Asaph had whipped him because he came here and took my rifle without asking if he might borrow it."

"Why should Mac be mixed up in that family row?"

"He had hired Danny to work for him and—"

"And Danny has turned to him for help. We all turn to Mac for help. Now if we knew where to find him—"

"I know."

"Where are you going?"

"To find Danny. Find him and I find Mac."

"Di! Di! Don't go. Remember that useless trip you took to reach Trudy."

"This won't be. This is simple A B C. I know where Danny's hideout is. Nicols *must* go on that Clipper, lovely.

Don't worry. I'm bound to find Mac with Danny; then everything will be all right and Viscount Darnsford will be en route to his estates." She dashed into the hall before Merry could protest.

As in her room she pulled off her frock excitement mounted. Of course she would find Mac Cameron and Danny in Luigi's log hut on the bluff. It was the only place in which the boy would feel safe from pursuit. She and Nicols had investigated it the night Maw Budge had seen them together. "You shouldn't have did it, Di. Terrible risky," Asaph had protested. Risky or not, she had been convinced that if she could get inside Luigi's headquarters she would find some evidence that would "railroad him out of town." She had waited for a night when he would take Trudy to a movie and a dance. The packing case marked EXPLOSIVES and the cleverly concealed radio she and Nicols had uncovered, in the back room, would take some explaining.

How would she get there? The station wagon would have the stealthy approach of a brass band. . . . Her wheel. She could keep in the pedestrian paths along the highway. She would wear something dark.

The maddening perversity of inanimate things! . . . Why wouldn't the talon on her blue slacks zip? It was like trying to hurry in a nightmare, with every muscle locked and double-locked. Done at last! She pulled a blue jacket over a red-and-white polka-dot sports shirt. Tied a red kerchief on her head. Thrust an electric torch into a pocket.

The mist was thick as she pedaled along the shrub-shaded path beside the highway. It beaded her lashes, dripped from the handle-bar. Automobiles, moving with ghostly caution, sounded warning horns weirdly muffled. If the drivers noticed her they couldn't identify her. She was lost in the anonymity of fog.

Thick as it was she found the way easily. She stopped at the Swinging Lantern Crossroads. Flashed her light along the trail which ran beside the road to the bluff. This was the path she and Nicols had taken. She hid her wheel in a clump of scrub trees and proceeded warily toward the dark bulk she knew was the cabin. All at once she felt a chilly sense of being followed, as of eyes somewhere in the fog watching her. The world was weirdly still. No sound disturbed it save the *drip, drip, drip* from the leaves above her and the swish of the tide below.

She tiptoed along the rough path, stopping to hold her breath at each crackle of a twig under her cautious feet. The

log hut! Just ahead. Not a splinter of light. Perhaps Danny
was waiting outside for Mac. Better get in herself while the
going was good—then no time would be lost. If the key was
where she and Nicols had found it the other night, tucked
snugly between two logs near the base of the door, the rest
would be easy.

It was. She groped for the lock and cautiously turned the
key . . . Slipped in. The room was lighted.

"Diane!"

Mac's voice. He was staring at her incredulously. Beside
him Danny Stark's terrified eyes bulged in his chalky face.

"Thank goodness I've found you. Mac, Nicols—"

Her heart leaped and cut off her voice. The door to the
back room was opening. Luigi!

His usually swarthy face was dirty white. His eyes burned
under their hooded lids.

"It's you again, Miss Fixit," he sneered. "Buttin' in. This
time ya won't get off so easy."

XXVI

Mac's heart was a lump of ice within his tense body as
he stared at the man leaning against the frame of the door,
smoking a cigarette. Luigi's malicious eyes were on Diane,
who stood between Danny and himself. Drops like little
diamonds on her navy jacket and red kerchief glinted in
the dim light, before they vanished like blown-out sparks.
Her eyes were black with excitement; the color had drained
from her face.

Manchusto tossed the cigarette behind him and broke the
spell of stunned surprise. He grabbed Danny's shoulder and
shook him till his teeth rattled like blind slats in a high wind.

"Hey, dope. Whaddya mean bringing the guy and dame
here? Don't you know this Club's private?"

"I know, Luigi, I know." Danny's voice was a hoarse whisper. "I wanted to tell Mr. Cameron why—why I couldn't
take the job an' I didn't know where else to see him."

"Oh, ya didn't? Well, you can tell him outside. Alone. Get
me? I'm keepin' the dame inside. See?"

Fury swept through Mac in a red-hot tide. Steady, he

warned himself, steady. If only he had that revolver that was now securely locked in his suitcase. Better jockey for time while he planned the next move.

"Hold everything, Manchusto." His voice was lightly mocking. "Let up on Danny. I came here myself. Knew you were away. Seized the chance to hunt for the gun with which you shot Major Lovel."

"Me? Shoot his nibs! Say, where'dya get that screwy idea?" He thumbed toward Diane. "From her? Ya make me laugh. Think I'm that kind of a fool?"

"All right, you're not that kind of a fool. Step aside. Miss Vernon and I are getting out and we're getting out now."

"Sure you are; I'll get even with ya for knockin' me down later; but she stays here! Open the door wide, dope, while I chuck him out. Hold the lantern high out of the dame's reach so I can see how far he goes." His laugh was brutal.

Danny raised the light in a hand that shook. Luigi crouched for a spring. With incredible ease Diane kicked the lantern from the boy's hand. Luigi gaped at her in amazed unbelief and in that instant Mac seized him and flung him down. The lantern rolled over and over across the floor, leaving a trail of broken glass, the still burning wick giving a pale, fitful light.

"Danny! Bring me a rope, quick."

"Danny's gone, Mac. I'll find one. I'm lighting another lantern."

"Get out, Di. Run! Your kick saved . . ." Mac looked up for a second, and in that second, with brute strength, Luigi smashed his head against the floor.

The room spun like a plane propeller before his dazed eyes. Diane spun with it. . . . A bang. A door? Where was Luigi? He had had him down. His hair was wet. Was he outside the hut and that brute inside with—

"Mac! Mac!" Someone calling. Nightmare. He couldn't move. He must get to Diane.

"Mac! Mac!"

Who was shaking him? He forced open his eyes. The log walls were still there. So was Diane, bending over him with a tin pail in one hand. Good God! What was that coming from the back room?

"Diane! Diane! Look!"

Her eyes followed his pointing hand. For an instant she stared in trancelike horror at the wisp of smoke curling from the doorway. Mac caught her arm to steady himself as he struggled to his feet. His head whirled like a merry-go-round.

"Fire! Luigi's cigarette. Let's get out of this, quick. Come!" He shook the front door. "Locked! Where's the key you used?"

"Left it in the lock outside. Luigi may have set that fire when he heard us talking so it wouldn't be discovered."

"His cigarette started it. *What* wouldn't be discovered?"

"The radio. Nicols suspected it was used for illegal broadcasting. We were coming here tonight to make sure. Luigi must have seen the smoke. His grin was fiendish when he gloated 'Guess I'll leave you both here.' There's a box in there marked Explosives. Mac! Mac! We must get out before the fire reaches that."

"Looks like Fifth Column stuff. We'll break it up. We're safe enough for a few minutes. Turn up that lantern you lighted. Pump water. We'll douse the explosives pronto."

He choked as he entered the back room and flashed his pocket light over the floor. The smoke was coming from a pile of stuff near a packing case marked Explosives. He stamped out the fire and scattered the oily rags. . . . Not a minute too soon.

He wrenched the top from a box marked Fishing Tackle. Felt under a layer of rope. A radio. Wires through the side of the box, through the chinking between two logs behind it. The cagey Luigi knew all the tricks of his treacherous trade. The battery of his car supplied the power with which he broadcast.

Diane hurried in with a dripping pail.

"That old pump balked at first. You've put out the fire! That's a break for our side." She leaned against the wall and drew a sobbing sigh of relief.

"The fire may be, but we're not out yet. Dump the water over the rags. Quick. I've found evidence enough to jail Luigi, if he isn't deported. Come on, we'll make our exit some way before he finds his fire isn't burning and comes back."

"Mac! Look! Look!"

His eyes followed her pointing hand. In the main room the broken lantern, with its burning wick, had rolled to a corner. Little flames were licking along the moss chinking between the two logs nearest the floor.

"Beat at it with your jacket, Di, while I get water. Damn this pump! It won't work."

"Mac! Mac! It's running like wildfire. It's leaped up another chink!"

"Steady, soldier! Beat at the flames. Keep on while I try the window."

He wrenched off the black curtain. . . . Glass, thank God! He grabbed a lantern. Smashed out the pane. He heard an ominous crackle behind him. Smoke thickened. The burning moss lighted the room.

"The draft is spreading the fire," Diane called hoarsely.

"Come here." He pulled a box under the window.

"Step up on that. You can wriggle through."

"I won't go and leave you behind."

"You heard me. *Step up*. Give me your hands. I'll steady you. Go feet first. Quick!"

It seemed an eternity that he watched her struggle through the opening. Once she stuck and looked at him with terrified eyes.

"You're all right. Wriggle. Wriggle!" he shouted. Suddenly her head wasn't there. A thud. She was safe.

Now to make it himself. He thrust one arm through the opening. He would try going headfirst even at the risk of breaking his neck. If he could push his shoulders through the rest would be a cinch. The air, foggy as it was, was like a tonic. One shoulder was out. Where was Di? Had she been hurt when she dropped? The tide was rising. The oily lash sounded nearer.

He must get to her if he took the side of the hut with him. Suppose she were lying unconscious somewhere near?

With all his strength he tried to force himself through the opening. If that infernal fire behind him didn't stop crackling the explosives would blow him through. Critical as his situation was the thought brought a chuckle deep in his throat. He couldn't get both shoulders out. He'd have to back down into the room and have another go at the door. . . . Curious if after his breath-taking escapes in a South American jungle he should end up a mass of cinders in a dinky log hut not three miles from his stepfather's home. What was tugging at his legs?

"Mac! Mac!" More nightmare—or was it really Diane's voice coming out of the inferno behind him?

"Back down! Back down! The door is open. Danny stole back and gave me a key. He waited till he was sure Luigi had gone. I shan't leave until you . . ."

It seemed years before he could wrench his shoulder free. Terror for the girl gave him superhuman strength. The casing gave way and hung round his neck. He flung it off. He caught her hand tight in his. They raced to the door. Through the woods.

"The stiffening's gone out of m—my knees," Diane quavered and dropped to the wet ground in a clearing.

"That g—goes double for me," Mac agreed and flopped down beside her.

They huddled in panting silence while the fog thinned to vapor, trees took on familiar shapes, became tipped with pink. Dampness had brought out the spicy scent of balsam and spruce, the acrid smell of decaying logs, the pungency of crushed wintergreen leaves.

"You accused Luigi of shooting the Major. Do you believe he did it?" Diane asked when her heart had stopped thumping.

"No. That was to gain time. Danny said—What a curious light! Hear that? Sounds like the popping of gigantic corks. Jiminy cricket! Explosives! Rockets! For signaling! The hut's a red-hot oven! Come on! My roadster's hidden near the Crossroads!" Mac grabbed Diane's hand.

They missed the trail. . . . Dodged trees; crashed through bushes.

"Can't we do something? The woods will catch fire."

"Too wet, but we'll stop and telephone the firehouse. Don't look back. Hurry! You've been anxious to find a reason for railroading Manchusto out of town. You've found it. That illegal radio is doubtless just one of a chain—"

"It seems unbe—believable that a cr—creature like Luigi c—could be important anywh—where," Diane panted as she ran.

"Often that's the only type which will do the dirty work of treachery. Thank the Lord. The Crossroads! And my roadster."

A figure bobbed up from the bottom of the car.

"Trudy! Where did you come from?"

"O Miss Di, Miss Merry was fit to tie when I got home from Maw's. She said you'd gone to find Danny an' she was worried. I told her I bet you'd think he was at Luigi's log hut an' would go there an' he would make it awful hot for you. A boy I know was comin' this way. I told him Paw was goin' to meet me here an' he left me. I heard Luigi's car speedin' by like fury. I'd know the creaks if I heard 'em—"

"Trudy! Trudy! You didn't frighten Miss Merry?"

"Get in, Di. Don't stop to talk. Hop into the rumble seat, Trudy. We'll be at home before Merry has a chance to worry."

They stopped at the first house they reached for Mac to

phone that he had seen smoke as he passed the Swinging Lantern Crossroads.

"That's that," he said as he returned to the roadster.

"Will you tell me why in thunder you came to that log hut, Di?" he demanded as the car shot forward.

"So help me, I haven't thought until this moment why I went there and it's terribly important."

Breathlessly she told of the arrest of Nicols, of the reward Patty-Lee had offered.

"That reward will set the bloodhounds on the scent. The sheriff told you that she claimed to have found the rifle with which the major was shot in Nicols' room? I asked him to keep it there. So what? How did she know it was the same rifle? She's gone screwy or—" Mac snapped off the sentence. He had been about to add *or she knows who shot her husband.* The Major had made him promise not to investigate the shooting and his wife had called in the sheriff and offered a reward. Why?

His mind was turning over answers to that question as the roadster shot past a row of overnight cabins; by spacious houses, ghostly in the thin mist; by gardens colorless in the pale light; past a stretch of shore; into the drive at Honeywort House. Far behind them the banshee wail of the fire engine rose and died and rose again. Diane was out of the car before it stopped. Mac followed her into her sister's room.

"Di! Di, dearest! You're safe!"

White-faced, Merry pulled herself up from the chaise. Eager hands extended, she came forward with unsteady steps.

"Trudy said you'd gone to Luigi's log hut. I've been wild with . . ."

Diane didn't hear any more. . . . Merry standing! Merry walking! She stared at her for one incredulous second. This time her knees gave no warning. Mac caught her as she went down.

XXVII

MORNING sunshine filtered in through the ivory Venetian blinds at the long windows of the Manor living room, and striped the white-velvet carpet with bars of pale gold. Diane frowned at the tiny clock cunningly inserted between the paws of a crystal lion crouched to spring on a carved plastic table. . . . Eleven o'clock? Why had she allowed herself to be persuaded that her presence was obligatory while Patty-Lee Lovel accused Nicols of having shot the Major? Asaph had protested when she had explained why she couldn't work in the herb garden:—

"Cripes, don't you go, Di. They ain't got no business draggin' you into that mess. That reward M's Lovel's offered'll set every loafer in the village snoopin', hopin' to get some easy money."

She met her own eyes in a mirrored wall. Her face still showed signs of the emotional shock of seeing Merry stand and walk last evening. She drove her teeth deep into her lips to steady them. That, following her frantic terror, when she had thought Mac Cameron was caught in the burning log hut, had drained the blood from her brain. For the first time in her life she had fainted. Someone had caught her before she fell. Someone had said, "It's all right, darling," and then she hadn't known anything more, till she had looked up into Doc Reynolds' face and heard him say:—

"You're a glutton for getting into trouble, aren't you, gal? First you crack your head in the brook; next you dash off to the Island to rescue Trudy. Then you barge into a hut where you've no business to be—the Lord knows why—get caught in a fire and as a grand finale scare the daylights out of Cameron by fainting."

"It—it wasn't the f—fire that did it. It was seeing Merry walk when I—I—thought—"

"Don't talk. I understand, Di. She didn't want you to know that she was taking a few steps every day for fear you would be disappointed if she failed. I didn't believe in surprising you, but I gave in. Next time I'll stick to my guns. Drink this. Freda will tuck you in and you'll be fit as a fiddle in the morning, after a night's sleep."

He had been right. She had awakened refreshed, and with a heart singing to waltz time when she remembered that Merry had *walked* to meet her.

And now, a few hours later, here she was in the Manor living room with a sense of apprehension setting her atingle as she remembered that it was her rifle which had been found beside the Major, that it now lay on the table as Exhibit A. She was still shaky inside, but her exterior was composed and soignée in a smart tailored frock of apricot linen, she congratulated herself, as she appraised the looking-glass girl.

Her eyes traveled to the reflection of the mistress of the Manor, as she sat erect on the edge of a deep-white chair. In her lavender slacks outfit she was lovely as a professional model, frigid as an ice hut in the Antarctic and about as human.

The mirror gave back the great room, all white even to the gladioli and regal lilies in tall, crystal floor vases, the bulky form of the sheriff in his hot-looking brown serge, with a squad of fountain-pen tops deploying across the coat pocket. It reflected chalky-faced Nicols, in gray tweeds, and lean, stern-eyed Mac Cameron, in white cardigan and slacks, beside him.

"Mrs. Richards," Barnes announced at the door.

What had brought the Dominie's wife here? Diane couldn't believe that it was really she till the woman's hard blue eyes, brilliant with hate, met hers.

"Mrs. Richards?" Patty-Lee Lovel's voice was charged with annoyance. "This is an intrusion. We are having—"

"A hearing as to who shot your husband?" The words that issued from between the pursed lips were tinged with malice. "I have risked my life—my heart might have stopped—I have gone to the expense of hiring a car, to come here and tell what I know about Major Lovel's valet, who is the suspect. Diane Vernon has been riding round with him at night—doesn't she try to fascinate every man she meets, even the clergy? Wouldn't it be like her to urge this man Nicols to help her connive to get the Major out of the way, before he had a chance to prove that the land she claims is really his by law?"

For an instant the vicious accusation cast a spell on the room. Mac Cameron's sharply drawn breath broke it.

"You venomous old woman. How dare you—"

"Why shouldn't I dare? I have it on good authority that it was her rifle which was used in the shooting."

"What authority?" The sheriff's question was a growl.

"Luigi Manchusto told me. He couldn't get here himself to testify; he had business out of town; so—"

"I'll bet he couldn't get here," Mac interrupted. "He wouldn't dare—"

"What's all this talk about a rifle?"

Doc Reynolds followed his curt question into the room.

His flaming hair was rampant; his eyes were contracted to steel drills.

"What blamed fool said the Major was shot with a rifle? I extracted the bullet." He dropped an automatic to the table beside the rifle.

"It came from this."

The sheriff's eyes gave every indication of preparing to pop.

"Shucks, Doc. You don't say? Where'd you find it?"

"In the Major's room, under the bed. Get through with me as soon as you can, will you, Sheriff? I'm needed elsewhere."

"Sure, Doc, sure. Know you're all-fired busy." The sheriff's voice was tinged with apology. He shook back his shock of black hair. "All you need do is swear that the bullet you took out of the Major was shot from that pistol you laid on the table."

"The ballistic expert declares that it was."

"Shucks, it's an all-fired mystery to me how he can be sure, but they do say he knows. You found that pistol in the Major's room? Begins to look like an attempt at suicide, don't it? Ever see the gun before, Doc? Ever see him—" he indicated Nicols by a jerk of his thumb—"out, well—practisin' with it?"

John Reynolds laughed.

"Never. Your imagination is running away with you, Sheriff. Can that suicide idea and keep to facts. The Major was shot."

"Speaking of facts—" Mac Cameron's voice had a steel edge—"I will remind you again, Sheriff Martin, that Major Lovel clutched desperately at consciousness long enough to exact a promise from me that no investigation of the shooting would be made. He said that someone had made a mistake. He will get well. He is an influential man. I advise you to forget the matter and go about other business. You'll find plenty to keep you busy in what is left of Manchusto's log hut on the bluff. Mrs. Richards, since you have done your Girl Scout good deed for the day, allow me."

He took her arm and led her, protesting between clamped lips, to the threshold.

"Now that this has become purely a family matter I'm sure you won't care to remain. Barnes, call Mrs. Richards' car that she has hired at such expense and see that she gets into it."

He waited until he heard the front door close with a bang before he reminded:—

"You next, Sheriff. Out you go."

The official's fat face puckered like that of a baby about to cry.

"I'm goin'. I didn't aim to butt in on this, an' shucks, ain't I seen rich summer folks cover up things worse than this shootin' before? But she—" he thumbed toward the woman in the white chair—"she threatened to lose me my job if I didn't arrest that English fella over there."

"I didn't specify that 'fella.' " Patty-Lee Lovel's voice was as icy as a mountain stream. "I said, 'Find the person who shot my husband with the rifle I found in the room of his valet.' Do you intend to take instructions from the Major's wife, Sheriff Martin, or from his stepson who is trying to get his fortune? I insist that you keep on investigating until you find the owner of the automatic which was used when the Major was shot."

"Let me in! I got to get in."

The last word and Danny Stark burst into the living room at the same moment. The boy's face was white. The yellow lock dangled over one of his desperate eyes. The butler, who had halted him on the threshold, sprang for him.

"Let him alone, Barnes. What's the trouble now, Danny?"

"I heard the sheriff was here, checkin' up on the shootin', Mr. Cameron, an' I come to give myself up—before—before —to tell him I shot Major Lovel."

"*You*, Danny Stark?" The sheriff shook his head like an enraged bull. "Look at that pistol. Did you use that?"

The boy's terrified eyes followed the pointing finger. Mac laid his arm across his shoulders. Danny snuggled against him like a lost, bedraggled puppy who has found a friend.

"Let me question him, Sheriff." Mac took command of the situation. "Come clean, Danny. Why did you shoot the Major?"

"He—he said he'd found out that I an'—an'—" the boy's confession was punctuated with gasps of fright—"that I was one of the guys that broke into his house last winter; we rigged up like the sea-captain ghost; an'—he was going to get me put in jail next day."

"So you shot him. Nice work for a boy that's been educated in this village an' has a mother like yourn."

"My mother don't know nothin' about it, Sheriff, I tell

you," Danny denied shrilly. "You leave her out of this. She—she don't—*Ma!*"

All eyes in the room followed his as he stared in horrified disbelief at the gaunt figure on the threshold. Hatless, with a black-lace scarf thrown across her shoulders, face as gray as her dress, left eyelid twitching, Martha Hicks stepped forward like a stiff-jointed toy wound up and set going.

"Martha, wh—what are you do—doing here?" Sheriff Martin's voice sputtered out to a whisper.

"Martha. Martha, dear." Diane caught the woman's arm and pushed her toward a chair. "Sit down. Mr. Cameron will see that Danny gets a square deal. You can trust him."

Martha Hicks gently removed the girl's hand.

"Sure, my Danny'll get a square deal, Miss Diane. Why shouldn't he?" Her eyes traveled from one concerned face to another. "He didn't shoot the Major. It was me."

"Ma! Ma! Why did you tell? I was willin' to take the rap for you." The boy's arms were around her. "Gee, course I would, Ma. Ain't you always been swell to me?"

Mac Cameron furiously blinked his lashes to ease his smarting eyes, cleared his throat.

"Sit down and keep quiet, Danny. Your mother won't be hurt." As the boy dropped into a chair and covered his face with his hands, Mac went on:

"Sheriff, I have told you the Major's wishes in regard to what he called a 'mistake.' Let me handle this, will you?"

"Sure. Sure. I don't want to third-degree a neighbor. Go ahead—that is, if M's Lovel's willin'; she brought me into this."

They all looked at Patty-Lee, who had shrunk back into the chair. She nodded acquiescence and flexed dry lips.

"All I want is justice," she said with the air of a martyr.

Diane saw the startled light which flashed in Mac Cameron's eyes as he frowned at her for a split second. They came back to Martha Hicks. He pushed forward a chair.

"Sit down please. Look at that gun on the table. Have you ever seen it before?"

"Yes. I've seen it. Danny borrowed it from Miss Diane and Asaph licked him 'cause he took it without askin' her."

"I don't mean the rifle. I mean the revolver."

"Yes." Mac had to bend to hear the hoarse whisper. "It was my first husband's pistol."

Diane heard Nicols' deep-drawn breath of relief before Mac's steady, reassuring voice went on:—

"You said you shot Major Lovel with it. Tell us how it happened. Take your time. Don't be frightened. You know that Miss Diane is your friend and I am Danny's. Why did you shoot him?"

The room was so still that the crack of the knobby joints of Martha Hicks's fingers, twisting and untwisting in her gray lap, sounded like the snap of firecrackers.

"It was this way." The muscles of her bony throat contracted and relaxed; her eyelid twitched incessantly. "Someone told me that Major Lovel was goin' to jail my Danny. Asaph had driven me 'bout crazy when he licked him. So I thought I'll go talk to the Major an' I'll take the pistol to scare him. I walked 'long the beach till I come to the boathouse, then I sneaked among the shrubs. I thought he'd be likely to be smokin' on one of them terraces, the night was so fine. I waited, an' sure enough, out he come. He was surprised enough when I 'peared in front of him. I didn't wait fer him to ask why I was there. I said, 'Is it true you're goin' to send my boy to jail?' And he swelled up an' said:—

" 'If your boy is that Luigi Manchusto or Danny Stark, you bet they're going to jail an' damn quick, too.'

" 'Take that back or I'll shoot you,' I said. My brain felt like red-hot needles was stickin' in it.

" 'Come now, come now,' he said. 'I don't want to fight a woman but your boy must go to jail.'

"An' then I pointed the pistol at him to scare him more an' 'fore I knew it, it went off an' an' he fell." She shuddered. "I didn't know 'twas loaded when I took it out of the trunk in the attic; I swear I didn't."

"What did you do then?"

"I dropped the pistol—"

"Dropped it!" Mac's eyes flew to the automatic on the table. "Then what did you do?"

"I was scared. I hid in the shrubs waiting for the Major to move. If he didn't I was goin' into his house an' tell someone to hurry out to help him an' just as I was startin' she came out."

"*She!* Who?"

"M's Lovel!" She nodded toward the woman, who was staring at her as if hypnotized.

Could it be true that Patty-Lee had seen her husband lying there wounded and had left him? Mac regarded her as he would a cobra that had suddenly reared its ugly head in his path. She had been willing that the Major should die? It had all happened before he had come back from his swim. She had been playing cards when he had shouted for help. The realization shook him with fury.

"Go on, Mrs. Hicks." His voice was hoarse.

"M's Lovel picked up the pistol with a fold of her shiny-satin dress an' stole back to the house an'—"

"The woman's lying!" Patty-Lee Lovel was on her feet. "I never touched that—"

"Shut up! Sit down, you!" Danny shook his fist at her. "Don't you dare say my Ma lies. I saw the whole thing, too, Mr. Cameron. I'd gone to the Manor to ask the Major to please go easy on me, to tell him you'd given me a job an' that I'd swear I'd make good. An' while I was waiting in the shrubs watching him smoke an' bracin' up my courage to tackle him I heard Ma's voice."

"Did you have Miss Diane's rifle, Danny?"

"Yeah, Mr. Cameron. I was goin' to take it back to her. I'd been sleepin' in the log hut since the old man licked me for taking it an' I stopped on the way to speak to the Major. When he fell I was so scared I dropped my lantern and beat it."

"You stopped first to wipe off the rifle, didn't you?"

Color stained the boy's white face.

"I guess you've got something on me there, Mr. Cameron. Gee, my first thought was if he dies an' they pin it on Ma, it'll be the chair. I dragged the rifle back and forth through the damp grass an' dropped it so folks would think he'd been shot with that. An' then, an' then I begun to think that 'twas me, not Ma, who shot him, because one day when I was looking at my father's pistol in the attic I loaded it, fixed the silencer—I was going to try it out. I heard someone coming an' dropped it back into the trunk. Ma was telling the truth when she said she didn't know it was loaded. O Mr. Cameron, they won't do nothin' to her for shooting him, will they?"

"Sheriff, I told you of my promise to Major Lovel that we would not investigate the shooting. With your consent we'll call the matter closed."

"Sure. All right with me. Case dismissed." Before the sheriff rolled out of the room he cast a scathing glance at the mistress of the Manor, who was touching up her face from a lavender compact which shook slightly in her hand.

"Come, Martha. Come, Danny. I'll drive you home," Diane offered.

Patty-Lee nonchalantly trailed them to the hall. Mac's eyes followed her till she disappeared. With superb effrontery she had offered no explanation of her reason for picking up the automatic and hiding it. Now that the case was closed no one would ever know why she had done it—unless the Major at some distant day discovered the truth.

"Well, as you Americans say, 'That seems to be that,'" observed Nicols beside him.

"You've said it. There is still time to catch the Clipper if I fly you to New York."

"Thanks, Cameron. It will be my only chance of making the plane. There was a hectic minute when I thought I would be retained in this country for the duration and beyond, that I would not get to England in time to help."

"There's just one loose end. Why should Mrs. Lovel try to plant the crime on you? It doesn't make sense."

Dark color stained Nicols' lean face. His eyes met Mac's squarely.

"It does to me. After I'd been with the Major a while she told me—in her most seductive manner—that I was to drive for her when her husband was away. Not a suggestion of anything more than a flirtation to relieve her boredom, you understand. I declined not too courteously and reminded her that I was a valet, not a chauffeur. She never forgave the rebuff and has taken every opportunity in a sly way to undermine the Major's trust in me. If we intend to make that Clipper—"

Mac slipped an arm through his.

"We do. Come along."

XXVIII

DIANE deliberated for the space of a heartbeat between the green and orange jackets, to wear with the white-silk shirt and flannel skirt.

"Green wins," she said aloud and nodded satisfaction as she slipped on her selection before the mirror. The rubber-soled white-calf shoes were perfect for the deck of Larry's cruiser. A green scarf wound round her head for a turban and she was ready.

She flung a kiss to the looking-glass girl, who promptly returned it.

"Pleased with yourself today, aren't you?" she accused.

Merry's going with us! Merry's going with us! Heart and mind chanted the refrain as she pelted down the stairs. From the hall Freda frowned at her tumultuous descent.

"You shouldt not run down like that, Mees Di. Suppose you catch your toe? You trip. Get hurt badt."

"But I didn't trip, Freda. I'm safe at the bottom; besides nothing can hurt me today. I'm slap-happy."

She caught the woman's broad shoulders and whirled her in waltz time. Dopey circled round them, barking excitedly, his black-and-white ears flapping madly.

"Did you ever see a more shining afternoon? It was made for Miss Merry. That slave driver Asaph kept me picking herbs till the last minute. Did she get off easily?"

"Sure she get off easy." Freda smoothed her straw-colored hair, which had been slightly disarranged by the whirl. "Mr. Brewster coom for her yoost as we planned an' she settled back in his auto like she's didt every day. She helped herself more, mooch more. I have t'ank the day never vouldt coom v'en she go on a boat. It vas goodt idea that she get there before the others coom, ya."

"Now that she knows she is really getting better, she is less sensitive about being helped. What a gorgeous day!"

"Ya. It iss very pooty. You shine lak the day yourself, Mees Di."

"Shine! I'm all twinkle, twinkle inside. Don't you realize, Freda, that for the first time in years I'm faring forth on a party without a smothering regret that my sister can't share the fun? I'll say I shine. My heart is so crammed with happiness that it's liable to burst into little glittering pieces like a shattered electric-light bulb. Freda, I love you!" She tapped a few exuberant steps. "I love everybody."

"Don't you go to vaste lof on me, Mees Di. Geeve eet to vun of those fellas who lof you, ya. Iss vun of them taking you to the boat?"

"No. I'm going solo in the sedan Mr. Nicols left for me—to keep until he comes for it."

The thought of the peril Viscount Darnsford might be facing at this very moment enveloped her like a faint-gray cloud. She resolutely shook it off. He would return sometime, she knew he would.

"Mr. Brewster will drive Miss Merry home in time for her

supper here. I'm coming back to change for a dance at the Newcombs', and will have something to eat brought to my room while I'm dressing. Probably she will be very tired. She'd better have a tray after she gets into bed."

"Now, Mees Di, yoost trust me to take care of Mees Merry. Maybe she not vant to go to bedt; maybe she—"

"Gee, Miss Di, you look swell. You're a snappy dresser!" Trudy approved from the kitchen doorway. Scarlet, purring a greeting, pattered back and forth across Diane's feet.

"Thanks, Trudy. I was just planning with Freda about Miss Merry's supper. I—"

"Forget it. Her—she and I'll take care of that. We've got our orders. Miss Merry told me to set the table for two on the terrace in case Mr. Brewster stayed and had supper. I'll bet he stays. He's nuts about her. I forgot, did you see the two men diggin' on this place this mornin'?"

"Digging! What time? Where?"

"Now don't go haywire, Miss Di. It was just at daybreak— I been wakin' up early. I heard a sound and looked out the window. It was light enough to see two fellas diggin'—"

"By the white birches?"

"Not way off there. They were where you told me the Manor land joins yours."

"But that's the line to which we sold the Lovels. Why dig for the V rock there?"

"Search me. Now that Major Lovel's better perhaps he don't want this place. He isn't going to prosecute the guys who robbed his house. Danny Stark's signed up for a job with Mr. Cameron and he couldn't get Luigi, anyway. He's in jail. G-Men got to askin' questions 'bout how he got into this country an' why he was storing explosives and broadcasting from an unlicensed radio. Came out that he's one of those Fifth Column guys. Sent to the U. S. to snoop." Trudy paused only long enough to refuel her lungs.

"Gee, it gives me the willies to think I went round with him. The afternoon he dumped me out of his auto, when he heard the Major was going to die, he thought Danny'd done the shooting and he'd be mixed up in it. Then he remembered that Danny'd had your rifle and decided to get you in wrong. He told Maw he bet you did it—she's sore because I like living here better than home—so she ran to the old *my-heart-might-have-stopped* Richards woman—she's got a dumb slant that her husband's got a crush on you—and told her she ought to set M's Lovel wise that you were mixed up in the shooting. I guess Maw'll keep her mouth shut for a while. She

was scared purple when Mr. Cameron came to the house an'
told her she was likely to be jailed for talkin'."

"Let's forget it, Trudy," Diane interrupted the breathless
monologue. "Did the clock strike four? I shall be late. I'm
off. No, Dopey. You are not invited. Take care of Miss
Merry."

"Sure, we'll take care of her. Have yourself a time,"
Trudy called.

Diane stepped into the black sedan. As the car shot forward, she turned and waved to the woman and girl watching her from the doorway. Dopey, the very picture of
dejection, whined disappointment. Beside him, Scarlet nonchalantly groomed luxuriant whiskers with a velvet paw,
while she lashed a plumed topaz tail.

"He's nuts about her." Trudy's statement recurred to Diane
an hour later as, from an enticing chair on the deck of the
cruiser, she furtively watched her sister. Merry might be any
gay and attractive girl in a white-flannel frock, turquoise-
felt hat and matching jacket lounging in a deck chair—the
center of attraction.

Larry Crane was there in correct owner's nautical regalia.
The soft, salty breeze ruffled Doc Reynolds' flaming hair as
he talked to Cecily Cole and Sally Arnold, who were in icy
white. Patty-Lee Lovel lounged gracefully in a linen costume—in lavender from the kerchief tied over her golden-
blond hair to the "wedgies" on her slim feet. It was difficult
to believe that she was the same woman who, white-faced,
had cringed in her chair that morning in the Manor living
room. She was illustrating with dainty, crimson-tipped
hands whatever she was telling Mac Cameron who, perched
on the rail beside her, was staring down at a cigarette as
he listened. The Dominie, in clerical collar, and beige
Palm Beach suit of somewhat ancient vintage, beamed in
blissful content as he paced the deck.

How had he managed to escape "Violet, my love," Diane
wondered and was immediately ashamed. Why spoil this perfect afternoon with a spiteful thought about a vicious woman?
Weren't they all trying to forget for a few colorful hours the
deep and bitter tragedy of this anguished world? Air and sky
and sea were doing their glamorous best to help. A satin-soft
breeze spread out the Stars and Stripes floating at the stern.
Curious gulls soared and dipped like white cutouts against an
infinity of clear, bright blue. Indigo water striped with emerald rippled in translucent waves away from the bow, as the
cruiser cut through the glistening sea trailing streamers of

pearls in its wake. Three white sails in the distance were beating up to windward.

Glorious world and Merry was enjoying it to the limit. Her eyes were gay and untroubled as she leaned her head back against the cushion, the better to smile at Jim Brewster, who was bending toward her as he talked. Diane's eyes narrowed as she watched him. Was Trudy right? Was he in love with Merry? If so, how about his fiancée Aurelie Leonard? Was she real or was she a myth conjured to quiet Merry's suspicions?

As if drawn by a magnet she looked quickly at Mac Cameron. In spite of herself her pulses broke into a quick-step as she met his intent eyes; a hot color swept to her hair. In a split second he looked away, as if he had seen something not intended for him to see.

Maddening! He couldn't have appeared more ostentatiously tactful had he suddenly come upon her in a man's arms. Perhaps she *had* been gazing at Jim with her heart in her eyes, but it was because of Merry, not for herself. She hadn't seen Mac for a week, not since the conference in the morning room at the Manor, when his Patty-Lee had been shown up as a liar. Didn't he believe that she had taken that automatic and left her husband lying there wounded, perhaps dying? If he did, how could he bear the woman's hand on his sleeve, as she kept laying it there? It was sickening!

She was spoiling this heavenly day again with poisonous thoughts. She sprang to her feet, steadied herself against the slight roll of the deck as she started aft. Larry Crane caught up with her and slipped his hand under her arm. From behind them came gay voices, the tinkle of silver on china, the chime of glass, as the white-uniformed Filipino served tea and drinks.

"Thought you were asleep, Di. Didn't want to disturb you. Merry told me you'd been working like a slave up to the minute she left. Why do you do it, dearest, when I could make life so easy for you?"

"I don't want life too easy. A certain amount of struggle keeps the muscles of my mind from getting flabby."

"You flabby! Don't be foolish. Come below. I want to show you something."

It was a cabin with pale-yellow walls, and ivory furniture with a band of gold. One small bed with yellow-satin coverlet, and a dressing table laden with amber-topped crystal jars and bottles, and gold boxes and brushes. A slender vase of pink roses was on a bedside table, which held a parchment-shaded reading lamp. A door opened into a room paneled in pine, essentially masculine, but not too severely plain. Crane slipped his arm about her shoulders.

"I had this done over for you, Di. Will you take it?"

For the length of a quickly drawn breath she hesitated. Marrying Larry would settle such a heap of problems. It would mean plenty of money with which to help Merry, an apartment in New York for her; leisure for her own writing which she loved; visits to far-off places for atmosphere—if, or when, the convulsed world settled down again; tenderness and love—

She looked up at the man beside her to answer him, but she didn't see him; she saw Mac Cameron's face as she had seen it only a few moments ago, saw the dark intentness of his eyes as they met hers.

The outlines of the room mellowed into mist. Something happened to her heart. It took her breath; it sent her blood racing through her veins; it blinded her. Like a tornado it uprooted her past life and left her clinging desperately to the tenderness in a man's eyes, to the huskiness in a man's voice, to the warmth of a man's arms as he had said, "Sorry, seems as if I never would get through hurting you, doesn't it?" Strange that after all this time the scene by the brook should come back to her. . . . He had liked her then. Now she knew. Knew why she had been frantic with terror when he had been locked in that burning hut. She loved Mac Cameron.

"What's happened, dearest? You appear stunned. As if never before had I told you I was mad about you, had asked you to marry me."

Crane's voice recalled her to the present. The charming cabin was still there, as it had been before this swift and stupendous thing had happened to her. She still stood on the threshold with Larry's arm across her shoulders. Years hadn't passed, only the fraction of a moment, but a fraction so filled with revelation that she felt as if she had been brought back from a world of blinding splendor. His arm tightened possessively; he bent his head:—

"You will marry me, won't you?" he asked unsteadily.

"No. No, Larry." She held him off with a protesting hand. "I'm sorry. I don't love you."

"But you will. I'll teach you—"

"Now what are you offering to teach Di Vernon, Larry?" Patty-Lee Lovel purred behind them. With a furious exclamation he snatched his arm from Diane's shoulders.

"I'm sorry. I'm terribly sorry." Mrs. Lovel apologized with

exaggerated concern. "Honey boy, we have made a break. Looks like we've interrupted a proposal."

"Then let's back out gracefully and *quick*."

The roughness in Mac Cameron's voice set Diane's heart thumping like an Indian war drum. She stared straight across the yellow-walled cabin at a bit of blue-green sea sliding past the open porthole. She couldn't look at him without betraying the soul-shaking truth so recently discovered, the fact that she loved to distraction the man who still loved and wanted the wife of his stepfather. Wouldn't you know when I went off the deep end I'd go fathoms deep? she asked herself. Why didn't Larry say something? For the first time since she had met him he was at a loss for words.

"You told me you wanted me to see the new decorations, Larry." Patty-Lee's voice betrayed a malicious satisfaction in his annoyed silence. She pouted, slipped her hand within his arm and brushed her golden hair against his sleeve. "You told me you wanted me to pass judgment on them, didn't you? They're adorable, if one likes yellow. If you don't mind, before we sail to Bermuda I'll make a few changes."

Anger melted Diane's frozen embarrassment.

"Why not see your dealer about it tomorrow, Larry?" she wisecracked. "Keep tuned to this station and you'll learn things about interior decoration. I'm leaving." Patty-Lee's eyes unsheathed two slim, shining daggers as Diane passed her.

Mac Cameron was talking with Merry when she reached the deck. When had he slipped out of the companionway in front of the cabin? She perched on the rail beside the Dominie, who was leaning against it, and watched a blue heron sailing overhead, one long leg extended. Was he steering his course with that as a canoeist steers with a paddle?

"Well, Miss Diane, this is a treat, isn't it? Do you think it's safe to sit there, my dear? The wind is strengthening; the boat is beginning to pitch quite a little."

"A little! It's lifting to big swells; I love it. I'm a sailor gal."

"We seem worlds away from conflict and hatred here, with the infinite blue, the vast ocean beneath us. It will do us all good," observed the Dominie dreamily. "I wish that Violet might have come, but her poor heart keeps her out of so many things."

Poor fiddlesticks, Diane thought hotly before she said:—

"Remember the old woman in Mother Goose who brushed the cobwebs out of the sky? This breeze is pinch-hitting for her. My mind and heart feel brushed clear of problems." That was a good line but, after the soul-shaking realization of a few moments ago, it was nothing but an able-bodied lie.

"I'm glad to hear that, Miss Diane. You've carried a heavy burden on your heart. Our prayers for your sister have been answered. She's on the way to normal living. . . . Here comes charming Mrs. Lovel with our host. She looks happier than when I called upon her a few days ago. She had been tortured with anxiety for fear she might lose her husband, she said; they had had such a perfect life together. Marriage is like that; if it is real marriage, it deepens and widens the heart and glorifies human relations."

Diane visualized the Dominie's tight-lipped wife, her hard, brilliant eyes. She must have something that it took if he could still believe that after living years with her.

"You have an abiding faith in human nature."

"Life would be a tragedy if I hadn't."

He smiled at Crane, who passed him with a grim nod. Patty-Lee Lovel stopped beside the rail on which Diane perched.

"Did I hear the word *tragedy*, Dominie? And on a gorgeous day like this? I admit, though, if the cruiser pitches again the day will get foggy for me. Don't you mind the motion, Di?"

"I love it. See that huge blue-green wave coming? I . . ."

It happened in a moment. . . . The lurch. A woman's triumphant eyes. The grab at space. Deep, deep under water. Headfirst. The sky again. Someone clutching her. Her voice sputtering.

"I'm all—right. I—I—can swim."

"Sure you can swim. So—so can I. The best thing I do—is pulling you out of—the water, *Miss* Vernon. Old Faithful—that's me," puffed Mac Cameron.

"Don't fuss, Larry," Diane protested, a few minutes later, when he hovered over her, as wrapped in a yellow blanket she sat in a deep chair on the deck, a tray on a stand beside her.

"I never have enjoyed a cup of hot tea quite so much. Run away and play with your little friends, *please*. I hate to have you sit there staring at me when I know I look like the end of a Channel-swim contest."

"If anything had happened to you, Di . . ." The possibility choked his voice. "Good Lord, if Cameron hadn't seen you go and gone overboard you might have—"

"But I didn't, Larry. I'm here. Safe as the gold at Fort

Knox. Will you put me ashore? I hate to bring this outing to a close, but I hate more being blanketed like an Indian squaw. I would feel a whole lot better decently clothed."

"I'll give orders to land at your pier at once. That will be quickest."

As Larry walked away Mac Cameron loomed over her, his hands thrust hard into a green brocaded lounge coat of his host's. Her heart shook her with its pounding; fire ran along her veins. His face was whitely stern. His eyes burned into hers.

"With this sea running will you tell me why you pulled that fool stunt of perching on a rail?" he demanded savagely. "Did you think you were a gull?"

She knew that a man hit out angrily when he was frightened, but his voice did things to her own temper. Didn't he care that she might have drowned? Rage in her heart, scorn in her eyes, memory stabbing unendurably, she smiled. : "No. I didn't think I was a bird, but—your heartthrob, Patty-Lee, evidently thought I was a fish. She pushed me."

XXIX

DIANE lingered in the terrace doorway. The expanse of sea, dark against a spangled sky, was banded by a misty-pink horizon. Vines swinging in the light breeze cast vague shadows on wall and flagging. The scent of mint stole from the herb garden. Somewhere a cricket chirped incessantly. The tide crooned a lullaby to the blinking stars; the buoy moaned wistfully, and from far away drifted the soft purr of a lonely motorboat. Jim Brewster was a dark figure leaning against a post; the top of his cigarette flared and faded. Merry was in the wheel chaise.

It was the same world, her own world. As it had been before she set sail in Larry's boat, before she had waked to a realization of her love for Mac Cameron. It seemed a long, long time since then. How could I have been so dumb, she asked herself? Why didn't I know, when my heart jumped up and plumped down again each time my eyes met his, that I loved him? Why didn't I know that I adored his smile?

Fine chance I have of writing a novel full of real people when I don't recognize my own symptoms.

"Come back to us, Di. You look as if you were walking in your sleep." Merry's voice was threaded with gaiety. "Jim is waiting to drive you to the Newcombs'."

"Thanks a million, Jim. Larry offered to come for me but I wanted to take my time dressing and he hates to be kept waiting." No use to admit that before she left she intended to be sure that Merry felt no ill effects from the unusual exertion of the afternoon.

"Come nearer, Di. What are you wearing? Oh, the new billowy orange net. It glints as if you had been caught in a star shower. It's perfect. Sets off your dark hair and your eyes. No emeralds this time?"

"No jewels. Just a simple country lass. *My-face-is-my-fortune-kind-sir* motif."

"That's telling 'em, kid," Jim Brewster approved. "The ducking you got this afternoon can't keep you down. I'll confess that my heart went into a tailspin when you plunged backward off that rail."

"Mine did for a minute. Then in a flash Mac dived—he must have been watching her to have been so quick—and I knew she was safe," Merry observed calmly.

She wished she could be as calm when she remembered the plunge, Diane thought. Had she been unfair when she had told Mac that Patty-Lee had pushed her? Had he seen the woman's vindictive eyes he would have believed it. Would a wife who stole away from a wounded husband without calling for help stop at a little thing like pushing overboard a girl of whom she was jealous? She would not.

"Forget it, girls," Brewster advised quickly. "Di is shivering. Let's start. I want to get back. Freda told me I might stay until eleven tonight as a special mark of favor. I'm leaving tomorrow."

"Jim! Why haven't you told me before?" Merry's voice was husky with surprise.

"Didn't like to think of it myself. Let's go, kid."

His black roadster was long and low, silent, powerful.

"Are you really going tomorrow, Jim?" Diane asked.

"Sure. I can't play forever. Got to get back to—"

"Aurelie?"

"You're too intelligent to ask that question. You know there isn't any Aurelie, don't you? You know I invented the fiancée so Merry wouldn't think I still loved her and refuse to see me. Dumb of me not to have thought of it long ago."

"I've suspected that the lady was a myth. Merry will miss you terribly."

"I hope so, but perhaps she won't. Cameron's staying, isn't he? Sometimes I think he's the white-haired boy in her life."

"I believed that once, Jim, that she loved him, I mean, but it isn't true. She likes him tremendously, but not so much as she likes you."

"Thanks for them kind words. Doc Reynolds says that if she improves through the winter as she has during this summer there's no reason why she can't marry in the spring."

"Merry! *Marry!* Marry you, Jim?"

"Sure she'll marry me. You didn't think I was talking about another guy all this time? I shan't tell her that though for weeks—if I can help it. You're coming to New York next winter, she tells me."

"I hope so. I shall hate to leave my work here but there will be plenty I can do there."

"You've said it. You do altogether too much as it is." His voice was affectionately gruff.

"Work has been my salvation. I have crowded my days to the brim so I wouldn't have time to feel my heart breaking for Merry. Now she is better, may marry and won't need me. Mac Cameron was right when he said that blue skies always follow a storm. If one would only remember that when one can't see light ahead."

"You've been through some storm, kid. I told you what the Doc said so that you won't let thought of your sister's need of you hold you back from seizing love and happiness when they come your way."

A close-up of Patty-Lee in Mac Cameron's arms flashed on the screen of Diane's mind.

"Those heavenly twins haven't loomed on my horizon yet. I still have a lot of time to devote to Merry." She regretted the tinge of bitterness in her voice. Jim Brewster looked at her sharply as he stopped the car before an open door, through which drifted the music of violins and flutes.

"You never can tell what ship is sailing toward you," he reminded lightly.

Diane's heart glowed from the surety that happiness was on the way to her sister—she would love Jim, she must—as she sat before the great mirror in the Chinese-red powder room at the Newcombs', which reflected and re-reflected the crystal and silver boxes beneath it.

Cecily Cole settled herself on a neighboring red-satin–topped stool and nodded to Diane's reflection.

"How do you do it, Di?" she asked before she carefully reshaped her lips into a scarlet bow.

"Do what?"

"Manage to steal the show. Sally and I, even the glamorous Patty-Lee, might have been foam on the ocean waves yo ho! for all the notice taken of us after your sensational plunge this afternoon. Seriously though, Di, I hope you weren't hurt. You're one of those few-of-a-kind persons who are—are too precious to lose."

"Why—Cis!" The emotional sincerity of the girl's voice tightened Diane's throat.

"Cecily Cole signing off on sentiment. To flash back to the high-dramatic moment of the afternoon—I believe you are still a little frightened. Your eyes look enormously big and blue-black and—and wistful. . . . Come on, or our hostess will think we've gone into the silence."

They turned for a final look at their frocks in the mirror; Cecily's green net, iridescent as a pigeon's neck, made a perfect foil for Diane's glinting orange.

"Not too bad," Cecily approved. She slipped her arm within Di's. "Did Larry bring you here in his de luxe roadster?"

"No. He offered to come for me but I thought Merry might be a bit upset after my plunge. I wanted to wait around till I was sure she was all right. She was. Jim Brewster drove me over."

"Like that Crane person a lot?"

Diane glanced at her quickly. A note in Cecily's voice set her wondering.

"Of course I like him. I like his let's-go-places spirit; but I'm not one least little bit in love with him, if that's what you're getting at so subtly."

"Then you won't mind if I catch him on the rebound? If I don't, that poisonous Patty-Lee Lovel may get him. Of course everyone knows he's gone off the deep end about you—but I'm not proud. I'm just Little Orphan Annie. Doc Reynolds can't see anyone but Sally Arnold—the smell of ether is the elixir of life to both of them; she has decided to run the clinic he is planning. Jim Brewster has Merry on his mind and Mac Cameron—"

"Who's Mac Cameron's present heartbeat?" Diane flattered

herself that her voice was lightly amused. Cecily giggled.

"Ask him. Here he is. Larry, *honey boy*, I've been waiting for you." She slipped her arm about Crane's neck and winked at Diane over his shoulder. "We were made to dance together," her voice drifted back.

Mac Cameron's surprised eyes followed them and returned to Diane.

"Crane looks as if he could bite nails. Snitched him from under your very nose, didn't she? Well, how about it, shall we dance?"

His arm was around her. His eyes burned into her heart. His smile sank deep into her soul. The amused clearness of his voice set her pulses quickstepping. They danced to the magic music of strings and winds, to the occasional beat of brass and the blare of saxophones. 'Cellos sobbed. Violins sang. Flutes piped softly.

" 'We were made to dance together,' weren't we?"

His imitation was perfect, but Cecily's voice hadn't held the vibrant note which set Diane's heart beating suffocatingly in her throat and made her long with every fiber of her body to hear him say "I love you."

Her gold-sandaled feet kept time with his; the top of her mind returned gay greetings; while deep down she was thinking:—

So this was what Merry meant when she warned: "Never marry, Di, until the touch of a man's shoulder against your cheek catches at your breath, the look in his eyes sets you afire to feel his lips on yours, turns you weak with desire to be in his arms."

"What's the matter?" Mac's hold tightened. "You lost step. Come out. You're tired."

She would much better have remained inside, she told herself, as she leaned against a pillar of the terrace. . . . Too many stars. Too much distant music, insidiously sweet. Too much wistful murmur of tide. A man's lean bronzed face, a man's intent dark eyes, a man's broad shoulders too near for her to force her heart to a measured beat.

"That ducking this afternoon took it out of you, didn't it?"

"Nonsense, it was thrilling." Her laugh was a triumph of pride over emotion. "I didn't lose step because I am tired; I'm never tired."

"Awfully afraid you'll be considered human, aren't you?" The humorous glint in his eyes went out. The lines of his jaw tightened. "I have something to say to you, two things, and this time I say them. Come on."

He caught her hand. Side by side they went down the
terrace steps. Diane's bouffant skirt brushed the roses to fill
the air with fragrance as they followed a path through the
garden. Two more steps and the shimmering sea spread
out illimitably before them.

"I discovered this seat one night when I was playing cards
here." He spread a fine white handkerchief on the granite
bench. "This will save that swell frock. Sit down."

Diane conquered a suffocating desire to run. Suppose he
discovered that she loved him? She kept her eyes on the
breast pocket of his white coat—they were safer there—
as she listened.

"Right off the bat I want you to know that Honeywort
House and your land are safe. The Major's advisers had
their wires crossed. The V rock specified in the deed is on
the line to which you sold. It was buried forty fathoms deep
—or words to that effect—but I found it. I told the Major
today. Weak as he is, he smiled and whispered: 'Glad—I—
don't—fight women.' So, you see, you won't need Crane to
try your case."

He appeared boyishly pleased that it had been he, not
Larry, who had solved her problem.

"Then it was you digging this morning."

"Did you see me?"

"Trudy told me. Is the estate really ours? No more fighting?
No more fear that we may lose our home? I can't believe it.
Mac, Mac, how can I ever thank you?"

"By listening carefully to what I say next. I was engaged
to Patty-Lee." He caught her arm and held her as she sprang
to her feet. "You can't go. You've got to hear this. I haven't
cared for her since she threw me over to marry my stepfather. That night you saw us in the loggia, when she had
flung herself into my arms, I hated and despised her as I
hadn't believed I could hate and despise any human being.
Believe me?" His hoarse voice broke.

In a near-by tree a bird woke and sleepily trilled a serenade to a distant star. The tide laved gently along the
shore in shining-white frills.

"Do you?" His hand on her arm tightened.

"Yes."

"Good as far as it goes." He drew a long breath and released it unsteadily. "I know now that I've loved you since
the day I rescued you from the brook. I've loved the perky
way you lift your eyebrows, the funny little quirk of your
lips before you smile." He caught her hands and pressed his

lips against her fingers. "And above all, I love these. Believe it?"

She tilted back her head the better to meet his eyes. Their unguarded, passionate look of possession sent her lids down. For a terrified instant she had the sense of being whirled along in swift water. His arm went round her shoulders. "Do you?" he persisted.

"Yes. I love you, Mac."

He held her close for the space of a heartbeat. "I've dreamed of you like this. You are so sweet, Di," he whispered before his lips tightened on hers.

From somewhere in the village drifted the mellow voice of a steeple clock. Again the sleepy bird trilled to the distant star. Diane lingeringly freed herself from the encircling arms.

"We've forgotten. There's a dance going on somewhere in that house back of us."

He laughed and drew a handkerchief from his pocket. "Let's repair damages before we return to civilization." He gently touched her lips. "That's better. The color was slightly smooched. I'm a bit out of practice."

"Are you really, Mac? I'm terribly glad. And while we're ripping our dark and devious pasts wide open, I'll confess. I haven't been engaged five times, humiliating as it is; not even once."

"You don't have to tell me. I knew it the first time I kissed you. But it's not because you couldn't have been. There have been moments, soldier, when only super-human restraint has kept me from breaking the devastating Larry's neck."

"I never really loved him."

"Where do you get that *really?*"

"All right, boss, I never loved him—I know now—because —because of the way I love you." She clasped her hands tight about his arm. "Oh, Mac—Mac—will we always love each other?"

He tucked a dark curl behind her ear. The smile she adored flashed in his eyes, widened his lips.

"Something tells me that we will more and more, as we take what life hands out to us through the years—together." He laughed and kissed her tenderly.

"Because, you see, *I* just happen to like *you.*"

THE END